Emily's Run

Emily's Run

· ·

David P Holmes

TO   RUTH

LOVE   RON !

David Holmes

2-6-11

NORTH STAR PRESS OF ST. CLOUD, INC.
· ·
Saint Cloud, Minnesota

Cover design: Jeffrey Holmes

First Edition, September 1, 2010

Printed in the United States of America

Published by
North Star Press of St. Cloud, Inc.
P.O. Box 451
St. Cloud, Minnesota 56302

www.northstarpress.com

"Get help and stop destroying other people's lives.
Seek a psychiatrist, or put a gun to your head; I don't care.
All we want from you is to stop."

– Emily Stearns

CHAPTER 1
ROGER

● ●

June 4, 1950, East St. Louis, Missouri

THE HOSPITAL'S CHARITY MATERNITY ward held twelve beds, with just a metal table between each one. No privacy at all, none. The singular window at the end of the ward offered up the only natural light. Bare bulbs hanging from the ceiling cast an eerie glow on the flotsam of welfare patients who filled the beds.

The police officer at Sylvia Parkhurst's bedside is taking notes, asking, "So, your husband beats the hell out of you and takes off. Where do you think he might be going?"

"He's gone, who cares?" Mrs. Parkhurst's voice was filled with resignation that she almost lost her baby at the hand of the dirty son of a bitch that knocked her up. The baby had managed to live through the thrashing, meaning that he might be strong enough to stay alive for a few more years.

With four more assault cases in this same ward, the officer's real concern was fleeting. He droned on, "You want to press charges?"

Incredulous, the new mother looked up at the officer, and said, "Yeah, I want to piss him off more so he can come back and hammer on me again. Ain't it time for your coffee and doughnut? Leave me alone."

This was the fifth time he had been told to mind his own business in the ward, so he felt he had done his best. "Suits me, lady." Handing her a business card, he mumbled, "Call me if you change your mind."

Sharing the back bedroom of a four-unit hovel six blocks from the hospital, Sylvia Parkhurst took baby Roger and walked home the day after giving birth. Her roommate greeted her with, "Oh, Christ, another brat to scream all night."

Blankly, Sylvia asked, "You got an extra joint until my welfare check comes?"

● ● ● ● ● ● ● ● ● ● ● ● ● ● ● ● ●

1957, East St. Louis, Missouri

AT AGE SEVEN, ROGER PARKHURST SAT alone in the principal's office, being lectured on how dangerous it was to hit other kids with ball bats. His mother didn't show up.

"That poor boy's in the hospital with a concussion, Roger. What do you have to say for yourself?"

Idly letting his eyes wander around the office, Roger slowly responded, "Can I go now?"

● ● ● ● ● ● ● ● ● ● ● ● ● ● ● ● ●

1966, East St. Louis, Missouri

WHEN ROGER TURNED SIXTEEN, HE SAT in the police station as the officer told him what a horrible kid he was for shoving a knife into an old lady just to steal her purse. When he got out of the reformatory six months later, his probation officer told him, "Go back to school, Roger. Get an education and make something of yourself."

Wearing a wry grin on his pimply baby face, Roger queried, "Can you give me some money?"

"Look, Parkhurst, I mean it. You don't give a shit about anything or anyone. You're going to wind up in jail or dead very soon."

Not concerned about a grownup's logic, Roger slid off his chair, "We done here?"

Hoping he could get some cash from his mother, he found his way home. A large black plastic bag filled with his only possessions awaited him on the broken cement stair in front of the door. "What the fuck is this?"

Stan Griffin made the "appointments" for Sylvia Parkhurst. He found the johns, collected the money, and made sure she cleaned herself up for the next one. Right now, Stan leaned against the doorway, blocking Roger's entrance. "She says good-bye, punk. Don't come back." It was the middle of December, and sixteen-year-old Roger Parkhurst was homeless.

Three days later Stan Griffin 's bloody remains were discovered behind an old hotel where Sylvia performed most of her tricks.

After beating up young girls and raping them, robbing stores, and finally slicing the face of his mother's newest pimp, he was back in the system. In handcuffs, he sat listening to the detective in the interrogation room. "You're going to trial as an adult. You happy about that?"

"I'm only seventeen, can they do that?"

"You bet your ass they can. Why? You don't like jail? You've been in and out of it long enough to know that's the only place to put you."

Worried at being so young and confined with perverts, he pleaded, "Can't you pull some strings? I'll fucking die in there."

Smirking, the officer asked, "And who'd care if that happened?"

Sitting forward, for the first time in his violent life, Roger Parkhurst was afraid. "Are you sure? I know I've been bad, and a lot of people are after me, but I can't help it. I just go nuts and then I hurt people. My mom says my old man was the same way, only I never hurt her. Well, not too much. You know she kicked me out a year ago, and I've been on the street ever since."

"This is why prison would be perfect for a misfit like you."

"No way, man." Sitting back, Roger's shackled hands covered his face to hide the fear. "I'm scared."

The officer sat back and watched the tough kid from the slums show fear, fear that was deeply imbedded in his remorseless soul. "As much of a fuck-up as you are Parkhurst, I still hate sending a juvvie into hardcore time. Still, we can't let you just walk around the streets screwing with people."

Looking up, Roger showed genuine concern, "I know what they do to kids in there, man. I'll fucking die, I know it."

Leaning forward, the officer quietly said the magic words, "There might be something."

That very afternoon after Roger signed an affidavit stating that he was eighteen years old, he was on a train to Army boot camp. Six weeks later he was being processed into Camp 346 in South Vietnam.

● ● ● ● ● ● ● ● ● ● ● ● ● ● ● ● ● ● ●

Cambodian jungle, near the Vietnam border, late February 1969

THE AREA AROUND THE HOLE HAD BEEN cleared of undergrowth, with the guardhouse situated at the edge of the clearing. The hole itself is a rectangle, about ten feet deep, and the first ones captured were the ones who had to dig it. A couple of the original diggers are still alive and have priority over which corner they live in. The roof is a door made from bamboo and corrugated metal, and the builders were smart enough to slant it downhill for runoff when it rained. During the rain, when the water collects in their hole, they cautiously pour it out through an opening at the lower edge of the door. The smallest man is delegated to sit on the largest man's shoulders in order to do the dumping.

With no drain in the hole, a five-gallon plastic pail has to double as a bailing bucket and a latrine. The prisoners are watchful about the weather so they don't have a bucket of shit when the water starts to collect. A bamboo lattice work has been laid on the bottom to keep their feet out of the mud, minimizing disease.

Once a day a ladder is lowered so they can climb out to exercise and empty the latrine—or bring up the dead. The process of disposing of the dead man is always a problem. It is their responsibility to dismember the previous tenant and feed him to the pigs that the guards keep as pets, which are being fattened up to butcher. Once, a man tried to steal the machete and was fed alive to the pigs as a lesson to the rest.

The newest member, Roger, has taken over the slaughter job but the others pay a price for it—half of their food allowance. They don't like it but they do it anyway, choosing to go hungry over carving up their friends. Roger is very methodical about what he does, and shows no compunction for the dead he is violating, or the process itself.

The guards aren't concerned about watching them too closely. If the prisoners did have a chance to escape, they would be too weak to get far. Fear of retribution is the only fence necessary. The three North Vietnamese Army guards are free to leisurely wander the camp, knowing their prisoners are controlled. On occasion, if a guard got bored, he would spray the door of the hole with his AK47, raking bullets across the sheet metal cover. The GIs got used to that, considering it no more than an annoyance. When the guards realized the prisoners had adjusted to the noise of the bullets, they amused themselves by lifting the cover and pissing all over the Americans.

On Roger's first day of captivity, last January, the others attempted to glean a little news from the new guy. "Hey, Roger, how'd you wind up here?"

His sullen response, "I was on some candy-ass patrol and wandered off, thinking that I could find the coastline and get a ride someplace else. I didn't give a shit where, just away from the boneheads running the Army. I never was too good with following orders."

"How far did they take you?"

"Beats me. I was dragged behind an oxcart across Nam to this fucking place. I should've stayed where I was."

Roger Parkhurst was different from the others. He didn't care about anybody's well-being but his own, and he isolated himself as much as he could in the cramped quarters. At eighteen years old he was the youngest of the group, and in the best physical condition. Just about six feet tall, his non-descript brown hair still showing signs of a GI cut, he had the impressive physique of a young man just spit out of Army training. With his extra rations he was able to expend energy to keep in better physical shape.

Roger told the others his outlook on this imprisonment, "If I stay here too long, I'm going to look like you fuckers. I gotta get out."

"Don't try it, man. You'll be slop for the hogs." Adding a friendly warning, one told Roger, "When they piss on us, just hunch over and cover your face."

Nobody knew the date, or cared, but on the first day of March 1969, a new prisoner joined the group. The bamboo roof opened and a body was thrown on top of them, thumping lifelessly on the floor. They scuttled to avoid being hit by the new body. Scrutinizing the arrival, they all chattered mundanely back and forth. The group tried to analyze the addition to their little family, the babble inanely passing among them.

"Hey, he's alive; I think he's breathing,"

"Good, now we don't have to lug him up the ladder."

"He's taking up too much room lying like that now with ten guys in here."

"I'll help you roll him over to the side. Hey, he's moving, should we help him?"

"I dunno. Hey, Roger, you wanna help this guy? If he dies, you gotta cut him up."

"He looks too heavy to get up the ladder. Roger?"

Roger squatted in his space, odiously watching their curiosity. "I don't give a shit what's done with him. Let's eat him."

"There's no way to cook him, Roger, and I ain't eating no guy that's raw."

"Hey, you fuckers; we ain't eating nobody. Sit him up and see if he's gonna come around."

"C'mon Roger, you can help us."

Roger's answer was simple, "I told you, I don't care if he's up, down, or in and out. If he bothers you, move him. I don't give a shit."

"You can sure be an asshole, Roger."

Squatting next to Roger they all stared at the new guy. He was wearing a silver Air Force jumpsuit with the name Dawson stenciled on the chest. The jumpsuit was in good shape, and they considered stripping him, but if he fought back they might get hurt. He was barefoot, and would have lost his shoes to Roger, if he had any. Roger leaned over to check the pockets, but the guards already stripped them clean.

Roger, finding the conversation humorous, said, "You guys are a bunch of pussies. You want his duds, take them."

"Fine for you to say, you're the only one strong enough to do it. Why don't you quit taking our food?"

Roger grinned, "Why don't you do the chop-chop job yourself? The way you look, Ernie, I'll be cutting you up next. Maybe we can make hamburger out of you."

Ernie objected, "That ain't nice to talk like that, Roger. Leave me alone."

The absurd banter took too much strength to continue, so they just squatted and watched the new guy. In a short time, he started moaning and moving more, his body twitching at the impulse to regain consciousness.

The body mumbled, "Oh, man, where am I? Oh, God, what?" Gaining his senses, he got to his knees and worked his way up to standing, and looked at the group staring at him. "What's going on here? Who are you guys?" Dawson staggered and braced himself against the dirt wall behind him. Holding his hand to the back of his head, he felt the coagulating blood mixed with grime. Scanning the nine dirty faces lined up in front of him, remnants of tattered clothing hanging from emaciated shoulders, he became focused, and stammered, "Who are you? Where are we?" He glanced at Roger, off to the side, noting his better condition.

They didn't care who they were anymore, but they managed to give him the story of life in the hole. Everyone but Roger, anxious to add something, jabbered at once.

The new guy asked, "What are the ranks here? Who's in charge?"

Mute, they gawked at him, and then looked blankly at each other. A small skeletal man said, "We don't know. We just do what we do. There ain't no one in charge. In charge of what?"

The new guy then barked, "Okay then, I'm a captain, and I'm in command here."

They collectively looked at their new leader, until Roger broke their silence. "Nobody gives a damn who's in charge. We eat, piss and shit. Once a day, we climb up a ladder and enjoy the amenities of the resort. You falling in on us to take charge don't make our miserable life any better or worse. Command all you want, but if you piss anyone off too bad, you're gonna get that honey bucket dumped on you. If you're in charge, then you can be the sponge when those bastards empty their bladders on us."

Captain Frank Dawson talked too much. He tried to motivate the others and wanted to talk about escape plans. He chattered on about survival, motivation, morale, uplifted spirits—and always about escape. They tried to explain they were too weak to go anywhere, and if an attempted escape failed, the guards would punish them. Being fed to the pigs was a constant threat.

In a couple of days, as Roger predicted, Ernie died and was stuffed into a corner until exercise time. Then, Roger went to work earning his food allowance.

Watching Roger dismember his dead companion was exactly what Captain Dawson needed to see. Private Roger Parkhurst just didn't give a damn about anything but himself; he was ruthless, stupid, and could be controlled. During the exercise routine, while away from the others, Captain Dawson took Roger aside, speaking quietly into his ear, "Private Parkhurst, if you work with me, we can get out of here. Are you willing to follow me?"

Impassively looking at his feet, Roger said, "Yeah, I'll go, why not."

"Good. Listen, it has to be soon. I have a plan, and it has to be enacted ASAP. Don't say anything to the others as they may not be willing, or able, to move as fast as we need." The captain looked around to verify their secret.

Amused at the captain's actions, Roger grinned, "Sure, man. I'm with you."

"Good. Good, I'll let you know, but, when I do, be ready to move fast."

"Yeah, fast. By the way, Captain, if you fuck this up you know I'll kill you, don't you?"

Taken aback by his remark, Dawson started to admonish the private, but Roger walked away too soon.

The captain was adamant about implementing their plan as soon as possible. It was already March fifth and, for a reason Roger knew nothing about and didn't care to, they had to get out. That evening, in the depth of the dark hole, Captain Dawson nudged Roger and whispered, "Now. Now or never. Get it done."

And with that command, Roger strangled his fellow prisoners, one by one. A few just sat quietly while their necks were squeezed, and one protested by trying to push Roger's hands away. None of their efforts stopped him. The last man, who ironically was the first one to start digging the hole, made the biggest effort to thwart Roger's human destruction. Held back by the captain, the man tried vainly to stop the slaughter. When his turn came up, there was a brief tussle, but he was not strong enough to make a difference. Roger kicked him in the crotch to disable him, and death could have come easily then–if it weren't for Rogers insatiable need to really do damage to another human being. The man, gasping for life, was dragged to the five-gallon pail of urine and waste where Roger submerged his head until he drowned.

Captain Dawson stood back, his head turned to avoid the reality. The gurgling noises of death made him ill, but he let it happen. Seven human were murdered mercilessly, and all for the sake of one man's plan.

The bamboo roof had deteriorated to a point where it could be moved enough for the two to climb out. Piling up several bodies, they were able to get enough leverage for the final hoist up. Cautiously peering into the darkness, Dawson took a chance that they were alone. The guards were fast asleep, so used to the prisoner's complacency they didn't need to check on them.

Quietly creeping to the nearest guard, Roger methodically clamped his hand over his face and quickly wrenched his head to the side, severing the spinal chord. Captain Dawson raised his arm, pointing to the second guard. Deftly holding the first guard's bayonet, Roger laced it across the second guard's throat, pressing it in deeply. The last guard awoke in time to see Roger crouched before him. The bayonet pierced the fleshy under-jaw and was pushed up into his brain. Sitting back on his haunches, Roger exclaimed, "Aw, man, so cool!"

Captain Dawson waited while Roger did his thing, aghast at his calm precision. Taking a pack of Viceroy cigarettes off the last guard, Roger tossed his body into the pigpen. He leaned on the railing of the sty, rolling the smoke around in his fingers, calmly watching the gore and listening to the snorts and growling, while the captain waited. He experienced pure pleasure from the simple freedom to suck nicotine into his lungs.

Frank Dawson needed to treat Roger with a respectful distance so he wouldn't turn on him. He considered Roger a psychotic misfit, but needed the man. If they met any of the enemy on the way out, Roger would be invaluable for killing–or as bait.

"What's the rush Captain? There's nobody around to fuck with us now."

Ignoring the idiocy of the statement, the captain commanded, "Come on soldier, this way. Grab a weapon and find some boots that fit you. We need to hurry."

Captain Dawson knew exactly where to go now, and the two crept through the jungle like cats. They managed to avoid the few patrols, eating bugs, rodents and raw snake meat, with a balance of green leaves, they kept up their stamina. Water was plentiful in the jungle, so the only problem was being discovered–and the well-hidden booby traps. At one point they came across the bodies of five American soldiers, hanging upside down, their throats and wrists slit to drain them of life.

With a vulgar fascination, Roger inspected them, saying, "You know, Captain, if you can eliminate the mess of blood, this is a nice way to kill someone."

Disgusted and abhorred at the curiosity, Captain Dawson urged him on. "For God's sake Parkhurst, they're Americans. Show some compassion." Turning to leave, the captain added, "Let's go. Jesus, what a mess."

"My fucking compassion's in my pants, you moron." If the captain overheard Roger's last comment, he wisely chose to ignore it.

On March tenth they came to an American outpost on the border of Vietnam. Captain Dawson told the CO where the five bodies were, and then arranged for a helicopter to take Private Parkhurst and him straight to Saigon.

One week later, on March 17, 1969, operation *Menu* went into effect, and American B-52s secretly bombed the country of Cambodia–according to the captain's meticulous directions.

● ● ● ● ● ● ● ● ● ● ● ● ● ● ● ● ● ● ●

IN THE SAIGON OFFICE OF BRIGADIER GENERAL Samuel Swelling, the newly promoted Major Frank Dawson sat with a glass of brandy listening to the general tell him what a good job he did. "When we heard your chopper went down, Frank, we thought the mission had to be scrapped. I didn't want to go to the President saying we had failed again. But, you came through. The locations you gave to Ops were perfect. We all owe you a lot, but this one is going to be a secret for a long time."

"I needed to put a target of my own on the hit list, General. I had a few eggs dropped on the prison camp. I thought it best to hide it in rubble."

Finding a polite pause, the major had something else he needed to cover. "General, I need to speak frankly. Some nasty things took place after I was captured. I'm sure all the tracks have been covered, but a loose shell is still sitting in our laps."

The general asked, "Do you mean Private Parkhurst?"

"Yes sir. I gave him orders to kill some of our own ..."

Interrupting, the general brought his hand up to stop the conversation. "Frank, whatever happened while you were out there is trapped in your own mind, and I hope it never comes out. All of us up on this level have insulated ourselves, and we can't be touched. Save your own ass, Frank."

"I know all that, Sir, I just need Private Parkhurst put away for awhile. General, I don't know how he ever got past the Army psychiatrists at boot camp, but the man is crazy–a homicidal maniac. However, without him, the bombing would have never taken place, and I'd still be in that stinking hole."

"Okay Major, I'll have him put away for as long as I can, and if you're grateful for his efforts, I'll spare him. You know that we can have him eliminated, don't you? Wouldn't that be safer?"

Major Dawson said, "Sure it would, but I have a debt to him I need to pay. Spare his life, but like you said Sir, lock him up for a while."

And with that over, Major Frank Dawson went home to Minneapolis, his military career behind him, and joined the police department as a decorated veteran.

Private Roger Parkhurst was quietly sequestered in the mental ward of an obscure military hospital in Japan and wouldn't see society for five years. Roger didn't care where he was as long as he could give the finger to authority and smoke weed, which was plentiful and free. After a while the psychiatrists lost interest and didn't talk to him anymore. The admission orders, signed by General Swelling, said to keep him confined and under observation. They gave him a bed to sleep in, meals to eat, and then forgot about him.

Frank kept in touch with him as much as he could, sending him money and even went to visit him once. At first nobody knew who Roger was, until after a minimal search, they found him laying on the lawn, stoned.

When he was released into the free world in 1974, Frank invited him to Minneapolis and promised a job as a police officer. Frank had established a network of devious dealings and thought he could use Roger's talents, so he managed to get him spirited through the police academy, and pinned a badge on him.

Roger started on the beat in a seedy section of Northeast Minneapolis. When too many reports came in about abuses by Officer Parkhurst, Frank had enough power to get him transferred to a special unit. Roger was just too erratic to be wearing a police uniform, so he went undercover in the Uptown area, learning which deviates and other social lice he could use for his own gain.

He was allowed to wander the streets of South Minneapolis catching the bad guys, and becoming one of them. Roger was at home in the streets with the scum of the earth, where he was able to establish a hierarchy, with himself at the top. He had developed connections for selling narcotics and seemed to have an unending supply, which made him important, and deadly, if he was crossed. His reputation for being unpredictable and quick to fly off the handle was his personal security fence.

Roger was plagued by infrequent headaches and dark moods, and when he became sullen and withdrawn, his cohorts learned to avoid him. Or, when a decapitated body was found.

CHAPTER 2
EMILY

● ●

St. Cloud, Minnesota, August 1976

E MILY COULD NEVER REMEMBER the date she became an orphan—it just didn't seem to matter. She did a good job of pushing it out of her mind. Her seventeenth birthday had come and gone with little fanfare, except for a nice sweater from her mom. It came from the Goodwill, but that was all right. At least her mother had remembered. The most memorable part of her birthday was her dad giving her a kiss on the top of her head, telling her, "I love you, Pumpkin, happy birthday."

Her relationship with her parents was remote, at best. They endured her outbursts thinking that some day a man would marry her and tame the savage side. Her parents who lived just above the poverty level were okay; they were stable, didn't fight or get drunk. The most admirable thing about Marie and Walter Carter was their ability to tolerate their daughter's feisty temper.

Emily was good at pouting, arguing over nothing, and stomping around just for the sake of doing some good stomping. Her childhood status was ending soon, and knew she would be asked to leave when she turned eighteen. They just couldn't afford to have her around if she didn't help out somehow. To Emily, that meant supporting her parents. She spent her wages from her job at the Cash Wise Supermarket on herself, and her drop-out boy friend who was widely considered to be worthless, a "no-load." Arrested in an armed robbery, he had been sentenced to seven years. Skipping work that day, she visited No-Load in jail, knowing it would be the last time she would ever see him. Sadly, it also marked the end of her youth.

On the day that she later considered to be the first day of her life, just returning from her visit with No-Load, she shuffled up to the old frame house her parents rented. Running various excuses for skipping work through her mind, she felt something odd as she approached her house—maybe it was the strange car out front. A tall, skinny woman standing in the doorway identified herself as Shirley Franklin, a Benton County Family Services representative.

The woman held a feigned look of compassion, announcing, "I'm sorry Emily, but your parents are dead."

Stunned, Emily was rooted to the floor unable to fathom what she had just heard. "Dead? There must be some mistake."

"No, I'm afraid not. They were in an auto accident on Highway 23, just east of town."

Emily's mind was stumbling to make sense of this tragedy, numbly stating, "They didn't even own a car."

Genuinely compassionate now, Ms. Franklin told her, "I guess they had borrowed one to go looking for you. You didn't show up for work, and they were worried."

Reeling with despair, Emily, their wayward daughter who had skipped work, now felt responsible for their deaths. Deeply sad, she whispered only, "Mom, Dad, I'm so sorry."

Stepping toward her, Ms. Franklin said, "Well, Emily, you aren't of legal age yet, so we have to find something to do with you." The woman talked with a pinched voice that made Emily wince.

Slowly, with a deep emptiness, Emily said, "I'll be all right. Just leave me alone, and I'll be fine. You can go now."

With a pasted-on social worker smile, her answer was firm, "I'm sorry, Dear, but you aren't old enough. I have a nice foster home in mind that would be perfect for you. There will be some court hearings to make it all legal, and arrange the funding, but you can stay there for now." Wham bam. It was decided. Emily was to become a ward of the county.

Emily's cheeks were smeared with tears, her voice wrenching for reason, "Don't I have a choice?"

"Of course not, you're a minor." Sprightly stepping toward Emily, the social worker escorted her to the car—and a whole new life. "Come on Emily, it'll all work out."

● ● ● ● ● ● ● ● ● ● ● ● ● ● ● ● ● ● ●

Mrs. Hammond was tall and overweight, finding that a muumuu was the cheapest and best-fitting garment she could get into. Her hair seemed to have sprouted plastic curlers that became as permanent as the folds under her chin. She had a habit of running her hand over the mottled dark and light gray strands in an effort to possibly augment her beauty and charm. The woman who ran the foster home was nice enough, but made it clear that she wasn't going to take any crap from a kid. Emily tolerated the rule-reading session, and vaguely listened as her chores were outlined. Two other teenage girls and two toddlers, around two and three, lived in the foster home. The older girls shared a room, so the only vacant space for Emily was in the attic. It was furnished in an unfurnished way, but it was clean, warm, and private, sort of.

The first night was spent staring at the dark wooden ceiling, crying herself into a depression. About ten minutes into the next day, Emily earned her first grounding for arguing and giving Mrs. Hammond the finger. Confined to her attic, she sat through lunch and supper wondering how No-Load was getting used to confinement.

She knew it was time to go to sleep because it was dark outside. The bed was warm, but crowded, especially when Mr. Hammond, her foster father, short, skinny and balding, crawled in beside her the second night.

With her arms pinned to the bed, Emily's flailing was useless. "You bastard, get away from me. No, stop." Yielding to him while choking on her tears, she muttered, "I'm sorry, Mommy," to her dead parent while she was being raped.

Her protest was met with a dull comment, "Get used to it, Honey. Consider this the rent you pay to stay here."

In the morning, Emily was grounded again when she faced Mrs. Hammond, and accused Mr. Hammond of raping her. The coarse voice of the heavy woman followed Emily back up the stairs to her attic, "Hey tramp, you better learn to appreciate what we're giving you."

Leaving that night was easy, as she owned absolutely nothing. Creeping down the stairs, through the front door, and out into a wet chilly night, she ran towards her home—a dry place to sleep, and a change of clothing. All the doors and windows were sealed, with *condemned* signs stapled everywhere. That idea wasn't going to fly.

Emily sadly realized the truth, moaning, "Shit, I'm the one who's really condemned."

Her choice then was to go back and get raped again, or run. She ran. She ran as fast as she could, escaping the bondage of the Hammonds, the system, and even her dead parents. Her feet pounded and splashed the wet pavement, arms pumping aggressively to keep in time with her legs. The rain was running down her face, into her shirt, and soaking her tennis shoes. Blonde hair was matted to her head, and her ponytail swung wildly as her body jarred with each thud of her feet.

The chill was just a reason to keep running. Running on and on, as fast as she could, away from her life, and towards her fate. Racing along Division Street, across the bridge over the Mississippi, she headed toward the highway.

Stumbling to a stop, her exhausted body hung on its frame, unable to go any farther. Panting and gasping for air, she sank to her knees dangerously close to the busy highway—and wept.

Folding over onto herself, she gave in to all of it. She was abandoned and alone. Only rape and punishment waited for her at the Hammonds. If the police spotted her, she would be returned to that disgusting foster home. Looking up into the rain as she crouched, the wailing rolled from her throat, "*Nooooo. Oh nooooo,*" as she uselessly beat her fists on the wet grass.

The Highway 10 traffic whooshing past was fast and frightening. The oncoming headlights, distorted by her tears and the rain, looked like a thousand locomotives bearing down on her, spinning wildly past her eyes. Forcing her body upright, she staggered blindly into the rush of traffic with the goal of ending her agony. Madly waving her arms, she screamed, "Fuck all of you. Come on, get me."

Horns honked, tires slipped on the shiny wet pavement, frustrated drivers gave out angry shouts, but Emily walked toward the traffic. She was soaked through, and her hair was plastered to her face and back. The rain's intensity increased, mushrooming into bubbles as each drop slammed into the road's hard surface.

She didn't see the Chevrolet pull to the shoulder of the divided highway, and didn't hear the driver call to her. "Hey, you all right?" Nor did she see when he ran to her, or feel him take her arm leading her into the Chevy. When her mind started working she knew where she was.

Turning to the stranger, she said, "Thanks." Her chest was still heaving for air, and the shivers consumed her.

Turning the heater on, he asked, "What's the problem? You could have been killed out there."

Nodding, her response was sullen, "I said thanks. That's all I've got."

He looked at her as long as he could without weaving into another lane. "We're headed into Minneapolis. Can I drop you someplace?"

Staring at the wet jeans glued to her legs, she squeezed them with her fingers, shivered and said, "Just into town. I'll get off there. I'll be okay."

He was concerned, but accepted, saying, "Sure. Whatever you want." He paused before adding, "You know, if I wasn't married, I'd take you home with me."

Emily's sardonic look matched the same feeling that swirled in her head. "Yeah, I bet you would."

Silence engulfed the inside of the Chevy; he being too embarrassed to talk, and Emily being too angry to speak. What he said made sense, though. All she had to do was find some guy to shack up with. If she gave in to it, it wouldn't be rape–maybe. As the driver slowed for a truck at the north end of Minneapolis, Emily threaded her hand through the door handle, felt its release and slid out, slamming it shut behind her. Not looking back, she disappeared into the darkened bowels of North Minneapolis.

Emily spent the rest of the night crouched and shivering in the entry of an apartment building. In the morning her only option was to walk. Walk someplace and try to find a safe place to land. But, there was no such place. Her stomach was screaming for food, but if she did find something to eat, she knew it wouldn't stay down.

The next night, she wandered into the downtown area where she was grabbed by three youths who dragged her off the street. Fighting back didn't help; she was beaten and raped, rough hands squeezing and mauling her, tearing away her last thread of respectability. They left her crumpled and sobbing in the alley behind a bar called *Flo's Place*. When she was certain they had left, she rolled onto her hands and knees, working herself into a standing position, and put her clothing back into place. Using the wall as support, she stumbled onto Hennepin Avenue, near Washington. Staggering to get her bearings, tears streaming down her dirt-laden face, she was immediately confronted by a drunken derelict, with a knife sticking out of his chest. When he collapsed at her feet, she screamed, her fists pressed to her mouth. "Oh, God, no. Oh, shit, what am I doing?" and ran again.

By morning, she had drifted to a district frequented by an amalgamated assortment of people, called The Uptown, with its Bohemian atmosphere frequented by artistic wannabes, and gays and lesbians, providing a facade for a variety of illegal endeavors. The area was inundated with pre-depression-era apartment buildings with open entries and furnace rooms that provided a safe and warm place to sleep–if you kept one eye open.

The Uptown area, just blocks from Lake Calhoun, centers on Hennepin Avenue, and Lake Street. Anything taking place eventually ended up at that intersection. After a couple of weeks, Emily learned how to navigate the area, staying close to the safe spots and avoiding the dangerous ones. The Walker Public Library offered the warmest hiding places, but she quickly learned that being caught by the janitor would lead to another beating. Following the locals, she was able to dig some food out of garbage cans, and panhandle for a little cash. Teaming up with another street person, they could roll a drunk or two, stealing their coins and liquor. Occasionally, she managed to get arrested, spending a warm night in jail, where a breakfast was guaranteed.

Homeless, and with winter setting in, Emily faced another problem. If some-thing good didn't happen soon, she was going to either starve or freeze to death. The answer came to her in the form of brutal violence.

On one colder-than-hell night in early November, two gang bangers at-tacked and dragged her into the back of an old van parked by the railroad tracks along Twenty-Ninth Street, and raped her. Satisfied, they stood in the darkness at the rear of the van to gloat over their conquest and share a joint. However, their euphoria was short lived. Emily came out swinging from the inside of the van, burying a tire wrench into the head of one. Before rapist number two could react, without ruining the joint he was toking, she jammed the blade end of the wrench deep into his throat.

Stepping out of the rear of the van, splattered with blood and her clothing in tatters, Emily pulled her pants up and turned to run. Instead of escape, Emily bumped into a man who held her shoulders and avoided her knee aimed at his crotch.

"Hey, hey, hold on there, Blondie. I'm not going to hurt you."

Looking past her at the carnage outside the old van, he smiled, "Nice job."

"Fuck you, let me go." Squirming to gain freedom was useless. This man had strength she couldn't overcome, and he knew how to fight. Her only option was to lean away and wait to see what he was going to do.

A total shock to her, he did nothing. "C'mon, let's get away from here. You don't want to be around when they're found."

Twisting away, she yelped, "Away to where? I don't need another asshole raping me."

Holding up his hands, he calmly said, "I'm not going to rape you." Smirking, he nodded towards the van, "I don't want to end up like them." He lit two ciga-rettes, handing one to Emily.

Cautiously, she gladly took it, wincing at the sting from a cut on her lip as she sucked in the smoke. Her voice low and slow, she said, "Thanks. Who are you?"

"My name is Roger. I've seen you around. You're on the streets, aren't you?"

Guardedly, she answered, "I guess. Why? Who cares?"

Without answering, Roger took a moment to ponder what he had just rescued. The girl was a shade over five feet, a bit over a hundred pounds, and had long blonde hair that wildly encased her head. The smudges on her face, and bruises and cuts on her neck and arms, were battle scars. Although her clothing was grimy and in shreds, her hands calloused and filthy, she was an amazingly beautiful girl, with a nice little round butt. Her defiant look said she was not a push-over. The smattering of freckles on her baby-sized nose stood out from the dirt.

Holding out his hand, he offered a proposition. "You can stay at my place for a while, get some rest and get cleaned up. I promise I won't do anything you don't want me to do."

Sarcastically, she said, "Yeah, so you say. I'm probably safer with the perverts out here."

"Look at yourself, girl. Safe from what? All you're going to get out here is another beating. These guys would even plug you if you were already dead, and keep doing it until your corpse dried up. I've got an apartment just down the street, and you're welcome if you want."

Emily had planted her feet to react to what he might do to her. Instead, he smiled, shrugged, and walked away. Panic set in because she knew what he had said was true. She was nothing more than a piece of meat out here, and she would be in a another fight before morning.

Flicking the cigarette aside, she called after him, "Wait. Roger, wait."

He stopped and waited while she cautiously walked to him. He asked, "What's your name?"

Hesitating, she spilled out, "Emily. Emily Carter."

"Hi Emily Carter, I'm Roger Parkhurst."

Boring her eyes into his, she gave him one last appraisal, telling him firmly, "I don't do drugs, and I'm not gonna hook for you. I'm not a whore."

"I'm glad you told me. Let's go." He let her follow him down Lagoon Avenue to an old brownstone.

Roger had gained her trust. After cleaning up and accepting some clothing from him, Emily spilled her story. It didn't take long for the inevitable to happen, and Roger's bed became hers. Moving into the safety of his apartment in return for sex was an easy way to pay her share of the rent. She told him firmly that she had never done prostitution or drugs, and if he wanted her to, she would rather go back to life in alleys and under bridges. To Emily, the situation was ideal. With the protection of Roger and his status in the neighborhood, she lived in relative safety. Everything she needed was right here: food and a warm room.

As fierce and gruesome as Roger's personal and professional life was, he became enamored with the beautiful girl. Emily's blonde hair hung down her back when she had some control over it. When it wasn't pulled back into a ponytail, it just sat on top of her head, doing what it wanted. Roger found her carefree attitude that when combined with a fierce level of confrontation, to be both provocative and compelling. Aside from her stunning looks, she was the first girl who had ever challenged him, bringing her appeal to its highest level.

He found himself thinking about her constantly, and there was always the good sex. "Man oh man, can she ever bang." And bang she did. If that's what it took to stay safe and warm, then she would do her best to send him to the moon anytime he wanted.

Emily knew exactly what was going on, and understood that she was prostituting herself, but justified it by taking safety instead of money. It couldn't last forever, nothing does. This situation had to be moved to a different level, and she needed to play her trump card to do it. Waiting for the opportune time, she cornered him, saying, "Roger, I'm thinking it's time I moved on. Maybe I'll go to school or something. I just need to get going again."

Startled into a stomach-wrenching state, Roger pleaded, "Oh, come on, Babe, we're happy here. What more could you want?"

Firmly, and with the flash of fire that she knew turned him on, she spat out, "Roger, we're just shacking up. That's nothing, man. I want a solid life–and this ain't it."

"Yeah, so what do you want?"

Seductively, she slowly said, "Sit down and I'll tell you." Settling on his lap with her arms around his neck, she wriggled him into submission with a lap dance. Convinced that he was on her line and well hooked, she whispered softly into his ear, "If you want me to stay, we have to get married." Her tongue followed the curve of his ear to punctuate what she said.

Shocked, he yelled, "Married?"

Defiance wrapped in coquettish charm, she went back to his ear with her tongue, "Yeah, and a house." To be certain she stayed in control, Emily took her proposition to their bed where Roger became helpless, flopping on the skinning board ready to be gutted and filleted.

With little consideration, Roger relented, and Emily Carter was destined to become Mrs. Roger Parkhurst. She knew her fiancé was less than stellar, but at least with a promise of a home to live in, and only needing to give him sex when he wasn't too stoned, she could overlook his misgivings.

CHAPTER 3
ANNA SWANSON

● ●

Minneapolis, Mid-November 1976

THE TWO MEN DIDN'T TRUST EACH other, but they each needed what the other had to offer, so their relationship, while tenuous, was intact. Frank had the brains and resources; Roger had the street savvy, thus he became the enforcer. Frank was the manipulator and planner so he assumed he was in charge, and for the most part, he was. Frank went to unnecessary extremes to keep his partner at a subservient level. Since the episode in the hole in Cambodia, Frank felt he was safer if he was in control. After all, he was more important.

Frank knew Roger wouldn't think twice about putting a bullet through his head, or slicing his throat. After all, Roger did the dirty work, and his unpredictable nature was a constant danger.

The two men watched each other closely, and so far, it seemed to be working. Both being experienced law enforcement officers, they were entrenched deep enough into the system to be confident they were immune from detection.

Frank had political connections; had dinner with the mayor, and was often invited to the governor's mansion for the kind of receptions that were totally outside of Roger's lifestyle. His smiling face often appeared in the social column, usually hosting a benefit of some kind.

Roger's connections came from a much lower form of society. Dredging up a slimy character to fulfill a contract, or serve a prison term, was his bailiwick. Or, dismembering a victim, and if the entertainment value was high enough, he would do it himself.

Understanding Roger's unstable mental capacity, Frank carefully manipulated him. Aware of Frank's propensity to become unnerved at violence, Roger knew that when push came to shove, he was the one who held the trump card. Once their places on the playing field were established, the next step of their dark side went without a hitch, but unknown to either, put the game into another gear.

● ● ● ● ● ● ● ● ● ● ● ● ● ● ● ● ● ● ●

ON THIS LATE NIGHT, sitting in Frank's car, they casually talked about the Vikings, the Twins, what was going on in the office and anything that would draw a chuckle from the other. Finally, Roger was at least smart enough to know he was being led into something that was troubling Frank–some kind of problem Frank had that Roger would have to take care of for him.

It was three in the morning, the streets were deserted and Roger wanted to go home, so he abruptly asked, "How much, Frank?"

Frank wasn't ready for a confrontation so soon, but was relieved it finally came out. Embarrassed about this one, feigning surprise, he said, "Huh, what do you mean?"

"Cut the shit, Frank. It's late. We're not sitting here because we like each other or give a damn about football or baseball. You've got some more crap to clean up, and I want to know how much you're going to pay me to do it."

Pausing, Frank managed to squirm out, "This one is a little nastier. There's a kid."

"Jesus, Frank, I never waxed a kid. Well, maybe in Nam I did, but that doesn't count. How much?"

"What's it worth? You said you wanted to marry that drifter, what's that going to cost?"

"Emily? Yeah, I asked her to stay with me, but she wants to get married and get a house and shit like that. I'm afraid if I don't, she's going to split. Buy me a house, and I'll do your kid."

"I'm not going to buy you a goddamn house. How about a couple grand for the down payment?"

"A couple? No shit, I'll do it." Just what Roger needed to keep his girlfriend happy.

As far as Frank was concerned, the deal was sealed. "Good, let's get it done."

Surprised at the speed it was arranged, Roger spouted, "Now?"

"Yeah, now." Frank started the car and slowly cruised the streets of Minneapolis, drove across the Lake Street bridge into St. Paul, and finally to a grassy area on the bluffs high above the Mississippi River.

Looking nervously at the surrounding area, Roger asked, "This is a park, man. Can anyone see us?"

"Relax, I scoped out the place earlier. There's nobody anywhere near here. Come on."

Frank put his hand on the door handle, when Roger held his arm, asking, "You've already got the kid, don't you!" Frank's hardened glare bored into Roger's question, making the answer obvious.

Standing by the open trunk, the two men stared at the blanket inside. Casually Frank muttered, "I had to give her a sleeping pill to shut her up. She was yelling, and I was afraid someone was going to come and check on the noise. Maybe I gave her too much."

● ● ● ● ● ● ● ● ● ● ● ● ● ● ● ● ● ●

ROGER LEANED IN, PULLING THE CORNERS of the blanket away, uncovering the stark, frail body of a small girl. Roger whispered in amazement, "Jesus, Frank, she's so little. She's just a kid."

Dressed only in a tee shirt and cotton panties, the child's flimsy little limbs quivered in the chilly night air, as she absently waved her fingers in front of her face to push away the fog that still crowded her drugged mind. Rolling her head back and forth, she started to whimper and moan as the pill lost its potency. Through the narrow, clouded slits of her eyelids, she saw the dark shadow of Roger standing over her. Thinking he was here to help, her one arm slowly rose up in a plea to be rescued. Nausea rolled her stomach over and the contents came seeping out of her mouth, dribbling down her chin. Earlier, when she was unconscious, both her bladder and bowels let go, soaking into the blanket and drying on her legs.

Holding his hand over his face, Roger turned away, complaining, "Jesus Frank, you didn't say she stunk. Look at this shit. How am I gonna get her out now?"

Not wanting to see or touch her again, Frank backed away, letting Roger earn his two thousand dollars.

"Come on Asshole, you can help me." Grabbing the blanket by the corners, he lifted the bundle, grunting under the strain, "Jesus Frank, help me. This is killing my back."

Frank had already moved away to avoid what was going on.

Struggling to his knees so he didn't drop his load, Roger carefully laid the little girl on the grass where he straightened her body and the blanket was taken away.

When Frank came from his hiding place, Roger demanded, "Come on, Prick. Help me."

Reluctantly, Frank knelt at the child's head and held her arms still. Her frail and limp little limbs frightened him. This was not how he wanted this to end—in fact, he had never planned on it ending. Now he was at Roger's mercy.

Still slightly drugged, she lay quietly while Roger straightened her legs. In the darkness of the night over the river, Roger noticed her frailty and the rib cage that made her look so vulnerable. "Jesus Frank, she's so skinny; and so young. You sure you want to do this?"

Frank was struck with a queasy feeling that Roger was going to back out. Using his authority over his partner, Frank barked, "Don't worry about it. Just do it, and hurry up."

The crucial moment was here. Now was time to finish what they came to do. Roger's cold and calculating voice demanded, "Hold her tight, she might start fighting."

Reacting to touching her flesh again, Frank drew her arms over her head pulling firmly, while Roger put his knees on her legs. He wrapped one hand around her little neck, and squeezed the once happy life out of Anna Swanson. Her eyes bulged, and her body arched in protest and quivered, twitching a few times until her final sickening muffled gag signaled her death. Her glassy eyes were still open, staring at nothing. Her mouth was frozen open, her red lips framing the imperfect teeth. The silence was astounding—not even their breath was heard as they stared at the dead body of a child who had been a sacrifice to Frank's sickness.

The silly, giggling child that slept with a special doll and had friends she played with, now lay silent and still on the cold, damp grass. She'd never go home again. She'd never again be warm and loving.

Roger looked to see Frank on his hands and knees, shamefully retching and gagging. Admonishing his partner's weakness, Roger commanded, "Get it together, Frank. We're not done yet. We can't leave her here, grab her arms." With Roger holding Anna's feet, they carried her to the edge of the cliff, high above the dark, dirty waters of the mighty Mississippi. The lonely muted moan that belched from the foghorn of a distant tug boat became Anna's funeral dirge—the only show of respect and remorse she was going to get. *Ole man river who don't say nothin'.*

Swinging the child's lifeless body in and out to gain momentum, Frank counted cadence, "One, two and ... heave." Swing in, swing out, swing and do it.

Anna's body floated in the air, graceful in death, peaceful in heaven; almost in a surrealistic slow motion it floated down, down, and down to a splat on the shallow water-covered sand. The waves that washed over her, rolled the body back and forth. Her body might lay there for several weeks before a hiker found her. By then she would have been fodder for the weather, the ravages of time, and whatever animal or bird was feeding there.

Peering over the edge, they looked with morbid curiosity to make certain the body didn't get caught in tree branches, and actually had landed on the river-bank. Fascinated by the splashing water, Roger exclaimed, "Oh, wow."

Driving Roger back to his car, Frank handed him an envelope. "I'll have the rest in a couple of days. Can you wait?"

Taking the package from Frank, Roger noticed his partner's shaking hand. "If you can't handle this kind of shit Frank, don't get involved in it."

Thumbing through the bills, Roger threatened, "Yeah, I can wait. You realize that if I don't get it, you're going to join the kid."

Surprised and intimidated, Frank said, "You don't have to threaten me. Don't forget I'm the one who got you out of that jungle. I thought we were friends for chrissake."

"Sure, we can be friends. And don't forget, I'm the one who got you out of that fucking hole, or we'd both still be there. Well, maybe you. I could've gotten out without you, you know."

Frank, not willing to give in to Roger's logic, protested, "You'd never have gotten out alone, Parkhurst. No way."

"Fuck you, Frank."

"No way, Roger, not alone."

"Yeah, man. You know I could have done it on my own."

After riding in silence for a while, Roger asked, "Who was she?"

Frank quietly answered, "My wife's niece, Anna; Anna Swanson."

"How'd you get mixed up in that shit? There are hookers all over the place. Hell, I'll even see if Emily will do you. Why the kid?"

Frank glanced at his partner, not knowing how to justify any of it. "I don't know. It just happened. You'll keep your mouth shut, won't you?"

Roger didn't answer, and didn't care anyway.

Disturbed at his silence, Frank pressed him again, "You'll be quiet about it?"

Flicking away the absurdity of Frank's concern, Roger waved his hand and muttered, "Yeah, yeah, who cares?"

As they parked behind Roger's car, Frank finally told him how it happened. "I thought she was pretty. I've seen her at family affairs, and I've always been attracted to the way she laughed and ran around. I thought about her a lot, so one day I met her after school and gave her a ride home. That went on for a few times, and she seemed happy with me, so I rented an apartment near the school and took her there one day. I told her it could be hers–that she could be married there. She could be a grown up if she played the married game with me. It was so easy to talk her into it.

"Today, she started getting moody and mad and said her girlfriends told her that kids don't get married. I blew up at her for telling someone, but she said she never let on what was happening. It was supposed to be our secret."

Sighing, he continued, looking out the window, "Then she was getting wild and she didn't want to do it anymore–that she was going to tell her parents. I calmed her down saying we would both tell her folks. I told her she would feel better if she had a Coke and took a pill, and then we'd go to her house to see her mom. It was a pretty potent sleeping tablet. At first I thought she died from it."

Listening patiently, Roger said, "You mean she's been in the trunk all day? Jesus, Frank that's really stupid." Roger didn't give a thought to the little life he just took, but was upset at Frank's stupidity. "I'll see you in a few days for the rest of the dough. By the way, it's gone up to three thousand now." He got out of Frank's car and calmly went home, anxious to tell his girlfriend she would be able to get her house.

With Roger gone, and the girl gone, Frank felt terribly alone. He took some black and white photos of Anna Swanson out of his pocket and lamented at her image. "I wish you didn't end it. Now what will I do?"

Frank didn't believe he was sick. He knew others that did it; judges, lawyers, politicians, and even Dr. Goodhue was doing it. He couldn't be sick; he was a leading pillar of society, a high-ranking police official and a decorated veteran. He wasn't a slobbering creepy slime ball. He could control it, until it would happen again—until the white hot cord that connected his groin to his mind started getting tighter, demanding release.

● ● ● ● ● ● ● ● ● ● ● ● ● ● ● ● ● ●

February 1977

In a small office in the Hennepin County courthouse, Emily Marie Carter became Mrs. Roger Parkhurst. The only other person there as witness was Roger's boss, Lieutenant Frank Dawson. That was fine with Emily; she was just happy that Roger bothered to show up. She was off the streets, and other than Roger's aggressive and crude sexual manner, it wasn't likely she would be raped anymore.

Her new husband realized he had responsibilities now. In order to afford the house that Emily stipulated as her only wish, Roger Parkhurst escalated his drug business, adding the lucrative line of pornography. He was now a respected member of society, and a stalwart employee of the Minneapolis Police department.

CHAPTER 4
ROSALIE

● ●

At home, 1977

EMILY DIDN'T PLAN FOR IT TO happen, but it did. After they were married by a justice of the peace, she got pregnant; probably on their wedding night. The only explanation Emily could offer was weakly submitted, "Roger, all I can figure out is that at last I was relaxed having sex. That might make a difference."

Livid and searching his confused brain for a way to get out of the marriage, he yelled, "Bullshit. All you wanted was a paycheck and this goddamn house. I'm gonna throw your fucking ass out of here."

Frantic, working all her moves, she slid her logic on him, "Roger, please don't do anything stupid. If I go back on the street I'll die, and the baby will go with me. Honey, I promise it won't affect us at all, and I'll still be here for you, anytime you want it. You can come and go as you want."

Grabbing a beer from the refrigerator, he rolled it across his aching head, mumbling, "Maybe you're right. This might be a perfect front for my operation. That's what Frank said, anyway." Scowling at her, he had to admit that she was beautiful, and he loved their love making. Dolefully, he asked. "You promise not to get in my way?"

Encouraged by his relenting, she eagerly said, "Yes, I told you, you have complete freedom."

"You'll still put out?"

"Have I ever said no?"

Convinced this would work in his favor, he accepted becoming a father. Emily relaxed, thinking she had gotten the better part of the arrangement. "*Thank God, he'll be gone most of the time.*"

So, life at the Parkhurst home resumed amiably, for a few years anyway. Roger had branched out from stolen property and selling drugs, stepping up his pornography dealings with live models and photography. He rented an apartment in a rundown neighborhood, but was inundated by hookers looking for a place to do business. As it turned out, the rental was no guarantee of total privacy. The models he had to hire were expensive, mostly dopers, and controlled by someone else.

One day, a wiry black dude wearing a large purple hat adorned with feathers met him at his apartment door. It would have been comical to Roger if it weren't for the two huge ball-busting enforcers that were with him. The message was clear, "You're stepping on my business, mufuck."

When Roger checked with Frank, he was told, "Hands off. He's working for me." Then, Frank said something to Roger that would change everyone's lives, forever. "Stay away from the sleazy whores and addicts, Roger. They're nothing but trouble."

Over the past few years, Frank had been minimally involved in Roger's home life enough to know that now was the perfect time to plant a few seeds that would be to his own benefit. In a very private conversation, Frank introduced Roger to a whole new arena. "Roger, your answer to making more money than you can imagine is right under your nose."

After digesting Frank's suggestion, Roger realized that his path to success was right in front of him. As his daughter grew older and sprouted, he gave some thought to what Frank Dawson was involved in, thinking that keeping this operation at home was a very good idea. So, just before her tenth birthday, Roger dragged his daughter into the despicable blight of his dark, swirling sickness.

● ● ● ● ● ● ● ● ● ● ● ● ● ● ● ● ●

At home, 1986

AT FIRST IT WAS A SLOW PROCESS TO KEEP Rosalie from being alarmed over where she was being led. When her mind was confused enough, aided by mild drugs from the ever-helpful Dr. Goodhue, one of Roger's porn customers, Rosalie was put on display. It didn't take long for him to control her using intimidation, and of course, severe pain. With his fingers placed on her neck, he pinched a nerve that sent her shrieking across the room. Crying, she rubbed her neck and flinched when he approached her. Kneeling down, he quietly said, "Rosalie, if you ever say *no* to me, or tell anyone, I'll make that pain come back even worse."

Trembling, the child whimpered, "Y-yes, D-Daddy. I'll b-be g-good."

"Good, Honey. Now, there are some things I want you to do. A man is coming to see you, and I want you to be nice to him." Again placing his fingers on her neck he asked, "Do you understand?"

Covering her face with her arms, she jolted at his touch, whimpering, "Yes, yes, I will. Daddy, that hurts."

In a very short time her indoctrination was complete, and he had total control over her mind and body. Roger held the strings, and when he pulled them, his darling puppet daughter danced.

Roger told his wife he was building a spare bedroom in the basement so he could have his own place to sack out when he got sick. He made it clear that the new room was his place, and she wasn't to snoop around there. "You've got your bedroom, so stay out of mine."

The lock secured to the door of his room was her message to stay out. Emily's thinking was that as long as it didn't concern her, he could do what he wanted.

● ● ● ● ● ● ● ● ● ● ● ● ● ● ● ●

THE STRANGER WAS WORRIED ABOUT BEING caught and questioned Roger, nervously asking, "She's only nine, what if there's trouble?"

Roger negated his fears by saying, "She'll be ten in a few days, and my old lady'll never find out. Don't worry about it, the kid's too scared to say anything. We're kind of a team with this, and she's used to it now. She likes it, honest."

"Your wife's at work?"

"I told you it's okay, there's nobody else here. You already paid. You going to do it or not?"

The short fat man was sweating with concern, but his mind was swimming with lust. "Yeah, I want to see her. Is she here?" He stuck his nose out like a ferret waiting for a mouse as a reward, drool running down his lip, his chest heaving with a sick burning desire.

It worked every time. Roger couldn't help but be amused, thinking, "*Play on the sickness of these dumb shits, and they'd sell their goddamn souls to do it.*"

Satisfied that this was a done deal, Roger said, "Yeah, she's here. I'll go get her." Putting the money in his pocket, he went upstairs to the girl's bedroom.

Although it was mid-morning, the child's bedroom was dark. She had purposely drawn the curtains over the window when her dad told her she wouldn't be going to school today. Her mom had already left for work, so this thing was between her and her dad. The darkness surrounding her kept her hidden, an element she could use to crawl away and find a veil of safety in. Darkness like that in her mind; like in her soul.

This was not something she wanted to do, but if she balked, he would hurt her again. Besides, it was her fault. She was the object; the instrument they wanted. It was all about her.

There was no doubt that what was happening was bad, and in her mind, that made her bad.

She is not like other kids, for they are clean. Clean and happy with fathers that loved them the way they were supposed to be loved; a fatherly love.

She knows she is different, and she is dirty. Disgraceful and dirty, and she is too embarrassed to be around other kids. If she said anything about it they would point at her, laugh and run away. Then every kid would scorn her and her dad would hurt her again, he said so.

Hearing her dad stomp up the basement steps, she dreaded each footfall. Waiting, she held her breath, her heart thumping a silent plea hoping he would go into the kitchen, or the living room, or outside. Maybe he wouldn't open her door. Maybe he would do something else, or maybe it won't happen anymore. Maybe he would die. If her own parents were dead, she could run like Mom did, but that idea was too evil to think about. "Mom's not hurting me. I just want Daddy to die. Maybe I will be the one who dies. That would be easiest, and then it wouldn't happen anymore."

Rosalie had big plans–to leave as soon as she was old enough. Her mommy had told her about the way she used to live when her parents died, so if she could do it, why not? There were things hidden under her bed she planned to take with her. A backpack, some clothing, snacks, any money she could hide, and a picture of her mom. When the time is right, she'll go. She's almost ten, maybe then the time would be right.

Rosalie absolutely did not want to turn ten. Her dad had mentioned to a few of his friends that she would be ten soon, and she worried then things would get worse. She wondered if getting older meant she was going to have to do more for them.

Her eyes teared up with her mind begging, *please; I don't want to do it.*

Waiting and hoping for the footsteps to go someplace else, she went into her magic world again. The one she will go to when she leaves, running through the lush green field. She sees herself smelling the sweet flowers, laughing at the birds, watching them fly so high. Her eyes shut, smiling, she lifts her arms and she starts to fly with the happy birds. Up and up soaring to any place she wanted to go; and away from where she didn't want to go. Floating and laughing and …

The door knob twisted and she snapped up; he was coming in. The meadow, the flowers and the birds were gone. She was back in the dark room—and so was he.

"Rosalie, it's time."

Reluctantly, she hung her feet over the edge of the bed and slid to the floor, shuffling out to do what she did.

He watched her move and followed to be certain she obeyed. She looked back at him with a mournful plea, but he motioned her on. She mumbled something, but he wasn't interested.

● ● ● ● ● ● ● ● ● ● ● ● ● ● ●

To Roger, his daughter was a commodity, a piece of equipment that generated income. His business had promise of growing, and if he could keep her intimidated and obedient, there would be no limits. He made plans of expanding, with the lure of marketing the pictures his next goal; a sound business decision.

His protection from exposure was strong and the sickness of his clients was a guarantee they would remain silent.

However, hidden deep in his blighted mind he knew that what he was doing was wrong. Occasionally, as the headaches became more frequent, the recollection of how this all began raced through Roger's head. Thinking back to when a chance meeting with Frank Dawson developed into where he was now. Back to that awful place in 1969 ... and long before, when he was a boy.

● ● ● ● ● ● ● ● ● ● ● ● ● ● ● ● ● ● ●

EMILY HAD A JOB IN A WAREHOUSE, DROVE A forklift and ate lunch at a long table filled with other warehouse workers. Once in awhile, one of the men would slap her on the ass, and she would still stop in for a beer with the guys occasionally. Her co-workers learned just how far to go with Emily. If she was crossed the wrong way, she would get in anyone's face. That gal was not afraid of a confrontation. Emily just did not take shit from anyone–until she got home. To ensure her fanatical need for a house to live in, she became a docile example of domesticity. Besides, she had discovered Roger's dark side, and feared him deeply.

Roger knew her limits and understood what she was willing to accept. As long as he made the mortgage payments, he was able to come and go with total freedom. The happy home life had become an excellent cover for his business. Also, there was always the good sex whenever he wanted it. Roger would often comment, "Man oh man, she can bang like nobody else." When he did bother to come home, and wasn't too stoned to perform, she'd give him a good time in the rack, and then wait for him to leave again. Most of the time he would just pass out.

Emily knew it was the sex that kept Roger making the house payments, and it was a pretend family, but it was what she needed for her daughter and herself. Rosalie was all she needed for a family, and was adamant about making sure the child always had a place to call home.

At the scheduled parent/teacher conference, Ms. Harper asked, "Mrs. Parkhurst, is everything all right at home? Rosalie's behavior has changed. She was doing fine until about a month ago. She won't talk or contribute like she used to, and stopped playing with her friends. She's failing in almost everything."

Emily tried to find an answer, and glumly came up with, "She says she doesn't want to go to school anymore. Nothing at home is any different than it used to be. Her father isn't much of a presence in her life, so I try to stay close to her. Lately, she's been pulling away and getting angry with bouts of crying. I thought it might just be growing-up stuff. She hasn't gotten her period yet, as best as I can tell anyway; its way too soon for that. She stays in her room and won't even talk to me."

At home, all of Emily's efforts to open up her daughter were pushed away. "Daddy's not the best dad in the world, but he loves you, Honey."

Rosalie's cryptic answer startled Emily, but she failed to grasp its meaning. "Yeah, I know he does, *but not like you think!*"

Rosalie's behavior became unbearable. Emily didn't want to tell Roger because he'd only make remarks about her being a bad mother. Not wanting to deal with her husband's caustic attitude and insulting comments, she thought it was better to keep him out of it. Finally, Emily decided something needed to be done and made an appointment at the clinic. On the day of the appointment, she stayed home from work, thinking that some time together with Rosalie would be nice.

Sorting through the laundry in the basement, Emily commented, "Might as well catch up with this while I'm home." Then she noticed stains on Rosalie's underpants. "Hmm, maybe she is having her period, but she's too young. I'll have a talk with her and set her on the right track. Poor girl shouldn't have to go through this without some help and advice. The doctor needs to know about this."

Looking closer, Emily saw the brown streaks were not on the crotch, but up by the waist band and in the back. Leaning against the washing machine to study the marks, she glanced up to notice the door to Roger's secret room was slightly ajar. She had always justified the room as a secret fort, like a kid had, and as long as he was happy with it, let it be. However, curiosity took over.

Emily pushed on the door and peered into the room, staring at his toys. It was furnished with a bed, carpeting, lights mounted to the walls, cameras, and a small table that held large photographs of her daughter with strange men.

Unbelieving at first, she pushed the shock away to search for an excuse for what she saw. Rosalie was pictured in disgusting phases of exhibition, exposed to leering creatures of lust and filth. Breathlessly, she wailed, "Oh, my God, no." Turning them over, shuffling through the pile, she frantically looked for an explanation; some kind of photography trick. Leaning back against the wall, her stomach churning, she screamed, "No Roger, you son of a bitch. I'm going to kill you. You bastard." Pressing the photos to her head, she wheezed, "You fucking bastard."

The world spun around her, turning everything into a screwed-up dizzy pattern. Emily sucked in enough air to restart her lungs before her rage took over. Streams of fire rushed through her veins, and her only thought was to kill her husband as she raced upstairs clutching the pictures. Out of breath and shaking uncontrollably, she collected herself outside of Rosalie's door. Slowly settling her rage, she gently turned the knob and went in to have a most unbelievable conversation with her daughter. As controlled as she could get, Emily calmly told her daughter, "Honey, we need to talk."

Confronted with the pictures, Rosalie crowded herself against the headboard, groping for something to tell her mother that would justify the horrendous photos. Rapidly streaming off her excuses, she cried, "Mommy, I'm sorry. I tried to do my best. Daddy told me it was all right, but I couldn't say anything. He said I'd get into a lot of trouble if I told. Are you going to hurt me like Daddy did?" The tears rolling down her quivering cheeks were reinforced by the terror of being discovered.

Pulling the trembling child into her arms, her mother held her close, stroking her hair. "Honey, a terrible thing has been done to you, and it should not have happened. This is *not* your fault, and don't you ever blame yourself for it. Those men are bad and won't come here any more. I'm going to tell Daddy he has to leave and never come back."

"Will it be all right then, Mom?"

"Not exactly, Babe. After we both get calmed down, and sure that nobody is going to hurt you again, we have to go talk to someone who can help you forget what happened here. We, I mean both of us, are going to see a counselor and make everything good again. Do you understand?"

Forcing a smile of relief, Rosalie said, "Yeah, Mom. I don't want it to happen any more. Do you hate me for it?"

"Oh, dear God, Rosalie; I love you more than ever. I'll sit with you and wait until Daddy comes home. Then, when I've thrown his ugly ass out on the street, we can start getting you some help. I'm going to call the police, too. He needs to be put in jail."

She never knew exactly when Roger would come home, so she had to wait until the next day when he came sauntering in with the short fat man, both laughing. Meeting them at the front door, her greeting to Roger was, "Hi, Asshole."

Surprised, Roger stammered, "Emily, what are you doing here?"

She was quick with, "I live here, you prick, just like you used to." Then, with her voice escalating to an uncontrolled stream of obscenities, "I found the shit, you bonehead. I found out why my daughter is so screwed up." Leveling her attack on the stranger, "You here to get a piece of my under-age daughter, you fat pervert?"

The yelling was followed by a torrent of anger that came out as fire and hatred. "Get the hell out of here, both of you bastards." With balled-up fists she went into the street after them, screaming, "You're done, Asshole, I'm taking this to the police."

Roger turned and sneered, "Look at who's in the pictures, Emily. Anyone you would take them to is involved. You're going nowhere with them."

Emily's rage faded into slobbering tears, her body shaking with a loathing abhorrence, she backed into the front steps and fell onto them.

A new voice was soft and distant, but a very welcomed one," Emily. Emily, Dear." Helen Ellsworth was the only neighbor she ever talked to. The matronly lady was kind, gentle, and always visited about something pleasant. If Emily were to choose someone to have as a mother, she would want Helen to take the job. Emily literally loved the woman, and her husband George, was equally as pleasing.

Wearing her trademark apron, her gray hair pulled messily to the top of her head,

Helen put her arm around Emily, saying, "I knew it would end sooner or later. Thank God you found out."

Astonished, Emily jerked back, loudly exclaiming, "You knew about it?"

Helen replied, "No, not exactly, but we could tell something was going on. That Roger is a strange one, and nothing he did would surprise us."

Frustrated, Emily threw her arms up and tearfully yelled, "Why didn't I see it, I'm her mother, I am supposed to protect her."

Helen answered, "You were too close, and it comes about so slowly. When you were at work he would bring men home with him, but it was anyone's guess what they were up to. At least he stopped bringing those awful women around, but then the men came. We could just assume they were up to no good. I was trying to find a way to talk to you, but you know he's so threatening that we were afraid to say something. George and I are just happy you aren't a part of it."

Holding her head in her hands, Emily slowly said, "I didn't know about the women. Oh, God, it's all so sick. And now, this . . . it's unspeakable."

Standing up, Emily said, "Thank you, Helen, but I better go to Rosalie now."

Helen whispered, "Let us know if we can help."

● ● ● ● ● ● ● ● ● ● ● ● ● ● ● ● ● ● ●

Rosalie dictated a statement to the lawyer. He drew up the divorce papers, got a restraining order, and Emily thought it was over. Roger was in jail with an unofficial charge of child endangerment, but no official charges were filed yet. When her lawyer told her to bring the photographs to him as evidence, they had disappeared. Also, the toys in his secret fortress were gone. When Emily and her lawyer went to talk to Roger in jail, they found him, not locked up but playing ping pong with another cop. Totally upset at seeing him with so much freedom, she turned to her lawyer, "What's going on? He's supposed to be in jail."

Sitting on the edge of the table, Roger smirked, saying, "You should have learned a long time ago to not screw with me, Emily. You're just a stupid bitch and are gonna get hurt." The other cop at the other end of the game table snickered.

Ready to do battle, Emily turned red, seething.

Sensing an outburst, the lawyer dragged her back out to the street, telling her, "Go home, Emily. I'll find out what's going on."

Terrified, she told her lawyer, "He's going to come after me. He's crazy and won't stop."

"Go home. I'll get to the bottom of it." He put her in a cab and waited until it disappeared into the downtown Minneapolis traffic. Looking up to the second floor windows of the courthouse, he traded glances with Roger before walking away.

● ● ● ● ● ● ● ● ● ● ● ● ● ● ● ● ● ● ●

ROSALIE WAS SEEING A THERAPIST AND was making some positive progress. There was a glimmer of hope that a reasonably normal life could be put together, with the two of them sharing the grief that Rosalie had to endure. Emily was getting a divorce, and looked forward to the new life alone with her daughter. She would have to make house payments and all the other things that went with a single mother's life, but what the hell, other women did it.

Rosalie started talking again and became closer to her mom. She talked about some of the things that happened, but never went into detail. She was doing better in school, but stayed away from other kids, believing that now she was different from them. It was difficult and painful for Emily to watch, but it was a start.

One late evening, the two were huddled together watching TV, just having some quiet time, and Emily made the happy suggestion of making popcorn.

Suddenly... the blast was loud and shattering, like an explosion unexpectedly crashing into their quiet evening. Emily's first flash was that there was a gas leak and the house was blowing up, but it was not as simple as fire and explosion. The front door blew open, breaking away from the hinges, Roger storming in behind it. Cramming the shock wave into the back of her mind, Emily flew into action, leaping over the sofa to land on Roger, slamming his face with her fists. Her legs were clamped around his waist as she savagely tore into him, beating as fast and hard as she could. Peeling her off of him, he threw her against the wall, leaving her imprint on the broken sheetrock, with the outline of the two-by-four studs that crunched into her body. He followed with a shuddering blow to her head, sending her limp body to the floor.

Rosalie ran screaming into the kitchen, followed by Roger, with Emily staggering behind. He grabbed the girl and was met at the doorway by Emily, digging into whatever part of him she could reach. He wrapped his fist around her ponytail and flung her across the kitchen floor, to crash into the table, tangled in chair legs. A sugar bowl and flower vase broke on the floor with the table landing on top of her.

The pain searing through her head was the only thing that kept her from passing out. Her vision fogged, she saw Roger heading for the door, dragging a terrified and screaming Rosalie with him. Struggling to her feet, pushing the heavy table away, her anguish came out in a moan, "Oh, God, no. No, you're not taking her."

Emily stumbled out of the kitchen, pulling a chair with her, bumped into the door frame and fell on her back onto the living room floor, still clutching the chair. He looked down at her and scoffed, "Stupid bitch, you can't win."

As he reached the shattered front door, Emily struggled up, getting her wobbly legs under her. She tightened her grip on the chair and lunged, swinging it full force into his head. As the pieces were flying, she grabbed Rosalie's hand and ran outside screeching, "Help us, please. *Help.*"

"Emily, here, come here." George Ellsworth was standing at his front door waving. They ran to him, and she pushed Rosalie ahead of her into the Ellsworth house. Helen had called the police, and minutes later, the lazy red light was blinking in the street.

Two officers, accompanied by a bleeding and panting Roger, came to the door and demanded, "We need to see Mrs. Parkhurst."

Emily appeared, "Yes, I'm here." Blood was running down her face, her shirt was ripped and hanging on her, with sheet rock dust covering her side. She limped to the door.

"Ma'am, did you hit him with a chair?" Emily was then handcuffed and arrested for assault.

Roger, frantic, said, "The kid, Harry. Get the kid."

George spoke up, "There is no one else here. She came in alone." The officer had an idea of what was going on and decided the best thing he could do was to leave without the child. Helen hid in the bedroom with a trembling Rosalie, holding her tightly. Calmly she said, "Shhh, child. Be very still. You're safe now."

The next afternoon, Emily was bailed out. Bewildered, she stood in the lobby of the old courthouse, wondering what to do next. Her clothing was in tatters, and she felt like a chainsaw had gutted her. She heard a loud raspy voice, "Emily, psst. Over here," coming from George hiding behind a large marble column.

"Mr. Ellsworth, what are you doing here? Are you the one who put up my bail?"

"Quickly, this way. I don't want the police or Roger finding us."

Emily knew she owed the Ellsworths far more than she could ever give them. Anxiously she asked, "Where is Rosalie? Is she safe?"

"She's perfectly safe. I'm taking you to her now." He went on to explain, "Helen took her to the farm last night. You know we're Amish transplants, don't you?"

"Yes, Helen told me about you living outside the community when you got married."

"We're still connected to our faith, and they have agreed to look after Rosalie while she is in danger. She will be well cared for and safe, but there might be something you aren't going to like about it."

Emily excitedly asked, "What do you mean?"

"You won't be able to live on the farm with her. They are afraid that as long as Roger is looking for either of you, he may bring harm to them all. You can visit, but you must be careful."

Relieved, she sighed, "I understand. Thank you so much." Again she said softly, "Thank you so much."

Smiling, George told her, "Roger left with the police last night so Helen went into your house and took some of your clothing. Not much, but you can sit in the backseat and get cleaned up. There is a package of wet wipes back there also."

She crawled over the seat to reassemble herself while George discretely turned the rearview mirror away.

The countryside rolled past as they cruised through Wisconsin to the charming village of Bayfield. After a few more miles, they pulled into the farmyard that had become the new home of her incredibly disturbed daughter.

Emily was escorted into a large meetinghouse and told to sit in a lone chair in front of two elders, dressed as common farmers. She broke the uncomfortable silence, "May I see my daughter?"

The larger man spoke through a disheveled gray beard, "In a moment. I understand you have been told of the conditions we have set up for the care of the child."

In a soft voice she confirmed, "Yes, Mr. Ellsworth told me."

"You must contact Brother George before you come here again. Let me ask you just one question. Do you love your daughter with all your heart?"

Mystified, Emily's answer came out shakily, but firm, "Yes, of course."

Smiling, the strange man said, "I believe you. Why don't you say good-bye to your daughter now. Then you must leave."

Holding Rosalie as tight as she could, they exchanged a tearful good-bye. "You'll be safe here, Honey. Nobody is going to hurt you here. Daddy is looking for me so I have to leave so he won't find you. As soon as I can I'm going to take you home. Please understand why I have to leave."

Sobbing, the girl wisely answered, "I know, Mommy. That bad stuff won't happen here."

Outside, Helen came to Emily, "She will be safe and happy here, I promise. Call us to stay in contact until it's safe again." Helen took Emily's hand and gave her an envelope with some cash and the keys to George's car. "Take God with you, Dear."

Standing at the door of the old Impala, Emily watched as her daughter was led into the house. Rosalie turned and waved, then disappeared inside. Helen reached out to blot the wetness on Emily's cheeks, and brushed aside a strand of loose hair.

Looking into the pain filling Emily's eyes, Helen hugged her gently, "Don't worry about her safety, Dear. She has a lot of work to do not only to clear her mind of what has happened, but to contribute here. She'll work into a new life and will be given all the love and understanding she can handle."

Driving out of the farmyard, the pain of leaving Rosalie behind was as harsh as the pain running through her body. Certain she had a broken rib and a concussion, Emily braced herself for a life that held more pain than she could imagine.

CHAPTER 5
MA'S OFFER

EMILY DROVE THE OLD IMPALA OUT of Wisconsin, without the slightest clue as to what she was going to do next. She called her boss at the warehouse, "Hi Bill, Emily here. Listen, I've got a problem, I don't think I'm going to be able to work anymore. My ex is after me, and I gotta hide."

Bill said. "Yeah, he was here trying to get your check, but we blew him off. Meet me at The Pub and I'll give it to you."

"Thanks Billy, I'll see you about seven tonight."

She sat in the parking lot of the favorite beer joint waiting and watching as her friends went in and out having a good time, and she missed it so much. A disturbing thought rolled through her mind that if she hadn't spent time after work in this place, she would have been home with Rosalie.

Finally, Bill's car pulled in so she got out, waving him over. She turned down his invitation for a beer, not wanting to put him in any trouble from Roger. He handed her the check saying, "Shouldn't you go to the cops with this? Running ain't right–you didn't do anything wrong."

"Billy, he *is* the cops. They protect their own, and I don't dare go near one."

Not really understanding, he said, "Well, all right, Em, if you need anything, just call. I can hold your job for a few weeks, but then I gotta fill it. We're gonna miss you, Em."

With a tear tightening her face, she reached out and touched his arm, saying, "Thanks Billy, I really appreciate this."

About to leave the parking lot, she twisted in the seat to have a last look at her ex-boss, and watched in horror as Bill Ormand got his face smashed with a ball bat.

Flying out of the car, she screamed, *"No, Roger, stop."* Standing at the open door of the Impala, watching helplessly, she waved her arms as she pleaded with him.

Roger turned to her and flung the bat, but it glanced off the trunk lid, clattering to the pavement. She jumped back in and commanded the big engine to work, getting her away as fast as possible; tires screeching and smoking, launching her into the street.

Roger spun out with the skill of a hot pursuit, his 1980 Olds 88 easily catching up in just a few minutes, and then staying with her,. The first alarming contact was him ramming the rear of the Chevy.

Hanging on to the steering wheel, she swerved through the streets trying to evade him, yelling, "You asshole Roger, go away."

Pulling alongside, he scraped the big Chevy and pointed a gun at her through the open passenger window and fired, but the bullet went off somewhere else. The crack of the weapon jarred her, letting her know she was going to die if he got the upper hand.

He yelled at her above the wind rushing through the open windows, "Hey, Bitch. We're gonna have fun." Turning his Olds into the Impala, it spun her around in a full circle, stopping, but the engine stayed alive.

Emily was frightened to death, but it was over ridden by her anger as she slunk down in the seat, trying uselessly to hide. He thought the chase was over and went in for the kill, pulling in front of her mockingly calling out, "Not like you to give up so easy, Emily. You're gonna die, you know."

Furious, she looked at him through the spokes of the steering wheel. He started getting out when the big 454 Chevy engine came to life, pushing against his passenger side fender. The Impala was built like a tank and did the job very well, with tires smoking and engine screaming, his Olds was pushed sideways into the ditch, Roger yelling in protest.

She stopped, backed up and drove off, arm out the window to give him the finger. Roger stood in the ditch next to his disabled car, banging his fist on the roof.

That night she slept in the car in a back lot of the warehouse. There was no one she could find shelter with, and couldn't bring Roger's wrath into anyone's life. In the morning she asked one of her co-workers about Bill. "I guess he's going to be all right Emily, but you've got to get out of here."

Understanding, she left, wandering homeless again. She still had a home, but it was made by General Motors back in 1975.

Calling the Ellsworths to check on Rosalie and see if Roger was around, they told her, "Police cars are going by all the time, and once in awhile an officer will go inside. I think Roger is still there."

Dejected, Emily replied, "I better stay away, thank you. Please tell Rosalie I called, and give her my love." Emily marveled at the simple courage of George and Helen Ellsworth. They were extremely devout and prayed to their God, and faced life calmly and without fear. Finding a connection to their faith, she found herself at the church where Rosalie had been baptized. Looking at the ornate windows and trimmings, she mused, "I wonder if there is anything to this. Maybe this is where I need to be." It was a miserable gray and chilly day, and she hoped there would be some heat inside as she tugged at the large front door. Dark and quiet inside, it was not as warm as she hoped. Feeling her way along the aisle, she asked herself, *"What am I supposed to find in here?"* She hadn't been in here since last Easter, with Rosalie, but she still considered it her church. Looking at the trimmings on the altar she said, to no one in particular, "What am I supposed to do now?"

Her absent thoughts were interrupted by a middle-aged man in a black suit. He heard what she had said, so he interjected, "Hello, Emily."

Startled, she yelped and turned, seeing him for the first time. "You know me?"

"We see you on holidays, and I remember when Rosalie was baptized. You stuck in my mind because of the look of love you had then. It was special to me because while it was a look of love, I had never seen such a lonely one. Your love for your daughter was obvious and made a nice impression on me. Of course I know you, I've prayed for you often."

Amazed he would remember all that, she had to admit, "Well, I haven't done such a good job with my daughter."

"Keep believing, Emily, it will come around."

She slunk down into the hard wooden pew, shutting her eyes, sighing "I don't know if I do believe."

"If you didn't, you wouldn't be here."

Sadly, she confessed, "I have nowhere else to go."

He put his hand on her shoulder and softly said, "Wherever you go, take Him with you, and you will never be alone."

About to break into tears, she smiled a silent *Thank you* and stood up. The minister watched her leave before he went to the altar, knelt down, and asked his boss to watch over her.

Going back to the Impala, it started to drizzle, and then the cold turned it to a gentle snow. She thought of the familiar house she couldn't go back to, but knew her daughter was warm and dry, and that was all that mattered. She just now noticed the crease along the window mullion where Roger's bullet glanced off the car. Running her finger along the long dent, she realized just how real the danger was to her and to Rosalie.

Winter was around the corner and she needed to start living a new life. If she went south she would be out of touch with Rosalie, and if she stayed here, she would freeze to death and be too close to her ex-husband. "Oh, shit, why me? Why don't you just leave us alone?"

She headed north to the Duluth area, so she could be closer to the farm, and started her life as a vagrant again. Her last life on the street was painfully embedded in her mind, and she didn't want to do it again. She was running away then, also, but it was about staying alive without being assaulted and welcoming the warm nights in jail.

Some of the money was still in her pocket, but that had to be used for gas, and once in a while some food. The legal system had a sheet on her so she absolutely could not get arrested for anything.

Cruising the back streets of Duluth, she parked in back of a dingy restaurant and went in to think about her next move over a cup of coffee; maybe check out some want ads.

Placing the coffee in front of her, the course, heavy-set woman stayed near to make sure she got paid. Emily scraped a piece of dried food from the rim of the cup before inquiring, "You the owner here?"

Curious yet cautious, the woman ground her cigarette on the floor, coming closer, a voice that rattled from deep within her throat, she said, "Why do you ask?"

"I need a job."

The woman questioned, "Can you cook?"

Emily knew the answer, but asked anyway, "Does it matter?"

"No, not in here it don't. What's your name?"

Hesitating, Emily answered, "Parker. Suzan Parker."

"Okay Suzan, call me Ma. You ain't going to earn much, you know."

With a ray of hope, Emily answered, "It doesn't matter. You pay me in cash?"

"Sounds serious; I don't want no trouble. All I can give you is ten bucks a day and a couple of meals."

Emily made her pitch, "If I can sleep in the kitchen at night, I'll take seven."

"Okay, Honey, seven bucks, a couple meals and the floor. You're on."

"Can I start now? Mind if I keep my car in the back?" Emily had one more thing she needed to establish, adding, "I'll run my ass off for you, but I'm not going out front except to pick up the dirty dishes."

Running her tongue across her lips, Ma looked skeptical, saying, "Whatever you say, Honey." Ma's eyes narrowed, watching Emily, her plan already forming.

So, for the next few weeks, Emily and Ma ran the greasiest spoon along the North Shore. Emily burned hamburgers, spilled soup and swore at the water heater. She scrubbed the floor, cleaned grease off everything, and ran her butt off twice a day when they got busy feeding bums and derelicts. Emily got used to sleeping with the mice and roaches; after all it was warm and dry.

Things were working well, and Emily made plans to take Rosalie from the farm at least by spring time. Every few days she would trudge through the snow to a pay phone to make a collect call to the Ellsworths. She talked to Rosalie once, but it was cut short when she ran out of coins.

Then, it all came crashing down when Ma made her move. Sitting on the kitchen floor after the evening clean up, Emily looked up and saw Ma come to her, saying, "Suzan, talk to me."

Like a small electrical shock, a line of trepidation crawled up her spine. Warily, Emily asked, "What do you mean, talk?"

Ma said, gambling on how close to the truth she was, "You're running from something. You wanted? Ex going to kill you?"

Emily stood up, leaving her stomach on the floor, angrily spouting, "What are you talking about?"

Ma had an evil smile, saying, "You're on the run, I know. Been there myself. Working here, sleeping on a greasy floor for seven bucks has to mean you're running. I got a way you can make a lot more dough, Honey. And get a bed to sleep in."

The alarm went off in Emily's head and she knew what was coming next. "Go ahead, Ma. What's on your mind?" She brushed a strand of stray hair behind her ear.

"It's easy, Honey, and I guess you've done it before. There's a guy out there who thinks he's in love with you. Hell, why not, you're a good lookin' dame. Anyway, you service him and there's twenty bucks in it for you."

Disappointed at Ma's offer to pimp for her, she said, "Sorry, Ma. I appreciate what you've done for me, but I'm not fucking anyone."

Ma studied her cigarette, then slowly said, "Well, that's your decision, but think about this. Would you rather spend your night with a john in a warm bed, or sit in the clink tonight?"

"You'd turn me in?"

Ma's answer sealed the deal. "In a heartbeat, Honey. You put out or I call the cops." The smirk in Ma's hard, heavy face told Emily that this old battle horse was serious.

Dejected and disappointed, Emily said, "I thought we were friends, you old hag."

Smiling, Ma said, "We are friends, Honey. And business partners."

"When is this supposed to happen?"

"He's upstairs waiting, now." She ground out her cigarette on the floor and asked, "You in? Or do I call the cops?"

"You're a real piece of work, Ma."

"Say anything you want, Sweetie, just fuck him."

Grabbing at anything to prevent this from happening, Emily desperately pleaded, "Don't do this to me, Ma. Please. You don't understand..."

Ma stood upright, heaving her heavy frame with her, "I understand plenty. There ain't no room for negotiation here. Get your little ass upstairs."

Dejected, with no other choice, Emily followed, certain she was going to wallow in Ma's dirt, like it or not.

Led upstairs, she met a small man she had seen in the restaurant. He was grinning and wringing his hands, with Emily hoping he would waste his load before she got to him. Trying to talk sense into him, she asked, "What's your name, mister?"

He stammered out, still grinning like an idiot, "Stanley. I know you're Suzan; I've seen you."

"Yeah, Stanley. Don't you have a wife or girlfriend? Are you sure you shouldn't be home with them now?"

Worried, he pathetically whined, "Ma said we were gonna do it. I already paid her."

"You already paid, huh. How much?"

Smiling, he reminded her of a pitiable bobblehead, when he proudly spouted, "A hundred dollars."

She pushed him into the room telling him, "Get naked, Stanley. I'll be right back."

Confronting Ma in the hallway, "You got a hundred for me, I want half."

Ma protested, but handed her the cash, sneering, "I'll give you twenty-five, but you're gonna do me too, Sweetie."

"In your dreams, you fat bitch."

Stanley was as happy as he could ever dream of being. She worked him hard to wear him out, making him do silly things that took more energy than brains. Stanley was impotent, unable to finalize his fantasy. Relieved, Emily told him, "That's all right Stanley, go to sleep and we can try it again in the morning."

Like a child, he curled up against her, and actually kissed her, saying, "Good night, Suzan. I love you."

Stroking his dirty mop of red hair, she softly said, "Go to sleep, Stanley." Late into the night, she bent over the little man sensing his snoring to be a sign of deep sleep. She got dressed, rifled his wallet for another twenty dollars, and quietly made her way out to the waiting Impala. It groaned in protest, but finally coughed itself to life.

Coaxing the big Chevy to rock its way out of the snow bank, she was a vagrant once more. When morning crawled into the gray sky, she bought herself breakfast and got directions to a secondhand clothing shop.

Blowing most of her money on oil and filling up the Impala, she wandered through the sparsely stocked store. The only thing left for winter protection was a tweed overcoat. Bringing it to the counter, she set it in front of a young clerk with black hair, black fingernails, and a black tattoo around her neck. There was a ridiculous amount of hardware and trinkets clinging to her face and tongue, causing Emily to wince. A very disturbing thought raced through her mind, "*Please,, dear God, let me get to Rosalie before she becomes like this.*"

The girl, almost as destitute as Emily, said, "Sorry, but all the warm clothing went as soon as it got cold."

Emily slowly answered, "That's all I can afford anyway."

The girl pushed the coat towards her, saying, "It's free today."

Surprised, and deeply touched, Emily said, "Thank you. I mean it, thank you."

She looked at the girl, retracting her condemnation of the facial decoration. "You're a very nice person."

Back in the Impala, she drove off letting the big Chevy go wherever it wanted.

The wind picked up and the cold air was filled with snowflakes. She couldn't see much through the swirling niveous white-out, and the heater and defroster quit working long ago, along with the radio. The pain in her back had left, letting her assume the rib was just cracked, and her headaches and dizziness were waning. That part of her life was in the past, and she had no idea of what lay ahead. She had a notion that Christmas was close, feeling a terrible void that she could not be with Rosalie. Talking to the frosted windshield, "Please be okay, Honey. I'm so sorry." Using her fingernails, she scraped an opening in the icy formation on the window. She felt hopelessly drained and abandoned, with the thought that she may never see her daughter again.

CHAPTER 6
JIM COOPER

● ● ● ● ● ● ● ● ● ● ● ● ● ● ● ● ● ● ● ●

The North Shore of Lake Superior, Christmas 1987

WINTERS IN MINNESOTA CAN go either way. At times they can be the mother of disaster and hit with a tsunami vengeance. Twelve-foot snow drifts, windchill near a hundred below, power lines down, and people stranded and freezing to death. Then for any number of unknown reasons the winters can be wussie and meek, coming in with no more than a mild boring glacial fart. This year there was a snow drought, but along the North Shore the temperature was down to bone chilling, and deathly dangerous.

● ● ● ● ● ● ● ● ● ● ● ● ● ●

JIM COOPER THOUGHT HE COULD DRINK himself to death, but there just wasn't enough liquor to fill his huge frame to do that. For weeks, he had been talking to the Golden Retriever revealing his plan to her. Tonight, she sat close to him while he rambled, "I can't do it anymore, Bella. I miss her so much; I miss both of them, and I can't see her coming back. Sorry girl, but when I do it, you're going to have to take care of yourself. I'll leave the door open so you can get in and out, but I won't be here. And this time, dammit, you leave me out there." Her tail swept across the floor, tilting her head giving him a low growl; more whine than anything. "Don't look at me like that. Stop it now."

Pulling his body up from the chair, he told her, "Well, let's get this over with. I don't want another Christmas going by. Not anymore. Come on, girl, get in the truck."

About five on Christmas Eve, Jim Cooper had just made it to Johnson's Foods in Grand Marais. He bought two fifty-pound bags of Eukanuba, explaining to the clerk, "Don't want to run out."

"Well you made it just in time, Mr. Cooper, we're closing up now. Merry Christmas to you."

Luck was with him as he pulled in front of the Grand Marais Municipal liquor store, seeing it was still open. "Hi, Kelly, a quart of Wild Turkey today. My Christmas present to myself."

Kelly's warm greeting made him feel good, "Merry Christmas, Jim." She knelt down to play with the retriever, her voice squealing with happiness, "You're such a pretty girl, Bella."

He handed her a hundred dollar bill, saying, "Keep the change, Kelly. Merry Christmas."

Her eyes wide, she stammered, "What? You can't do that."

"What else am I going to do with it? You going home now?"

Her eyes still unbelieving, she said, "Yeah. Shawn Swearingen's coming over tonight to be with me and Connor."

"Connor. How is your son?"

Smiling with pride at the thought of her ten-year-old son, "He's great, and he really likes Shawn. The boy needs a dad, and Shawn likes the idea."

Smiling, Jim nodded and left. As he pulled out of the parking lot, the lights in the Muni went out, and Kelly locked up to go home to her family. "Nice girl, isn't she Bella. I'd bet that some day she and that Swearingen boy are going to get together."

Tonight, being Christmas Eve, his was the only vehicle moving, so if there was a problem he would just have to do it in the truck. Not what he planned, but when you put a suicide plot together there can only be one result, if it goes right. Other than the stray dog, he didn't have anyone at home waiting for him, and nobody cared one way or the other if he got stuck, crapped in his pants or froze to death. The only person he would miss would be Wally, and maybe DeAnna. But, that's the way it goes. Babbling to the retriever, "You'll be okay, girl. You showed up one day, and when I'm gone you can go back to wherever you came from. I'll open all the bags of food, and when that's gone, you're on your own."

Ambling north on Highway 61, past five-mile rock, the scene never changed. There were a few motels, closed for the season, and a couple houses lit up for Christmas. For the most part, Jim considered it all desolate and lonely now.

When he saw the vehicle dead on the shoulder, he hesitated, wondering if anyone was in it. In this weather, it would only take a few minutes to succumb to the cold roaring in off Lake Superior. That would be good for his plan, but not for anybody else trapped in it. Earlier, the road was clear here so simple logic told him it was a recent breakdown. He slowed down to see if he could glimpse inside. It looked empty, and as he was starting to stop and check, he saw something on the road just ahead of him. Pulling closer to train his headlights on it, he could see that it was a person, laying face down on the road,.

Jumping out, with Bella following, he braced against the straight-line wind screaming in hard off the lake. He struggled to stay on his feet as he worked his way. Bella got there first, nuzzling a mop of wild blonde hair. The body's arms were stretched out in front and gave him the idea that person had tried crawling farther. He could see it was a woman, but didn't know if she was alive. Rolling her over into his arms, he lifted her up a bit. Her only protection was a light-weight tweed coat. There was no hat, scarf or mittens. He put his gloved hand under her chin to move her face into the stream of light coming from his truck, and he was certain he heard her moan. It was hard to tell with the wind screaming at him and he decided, dead or alive, he needed to get her out of the weather.

Trying to get a grip under her arms, she rolled her head a little bit. Thank God, she was alive. He tapped her cheek, "Can you hear me?"

The only response was more moaning. He needed her to know she was being helped and, if she could, she needed to assist him in any way possible. "Can you stand up?"

Her voice, shaky and weak, was barely audible in the howling wind. "I don't know. Where am I? Oh, God, I'm cold."

"I'm taking you to my truck. You'll be safe there, and warm." He hoisted her up and carried her in his arms to the passenger side of the GMC. He made sure she was settled in and the heater was on full force before trotting back to her car to see if anyone else was left. The car was empty, but a purse was lying on the seat so he snapped it up and struggled back to his truck.

Inside, he took off his gloves, put his packages in the back of the extended cab, and took a closer look at what he found laying in the road. She was breathing heavily and starting to shake. "Oh, man, what do I do now?" he said aloud, but to himself.

She startled him, although her speech was quiet, "I'll be okay. Just let me warm up."

"Your car isn't going anywhere. It's dead in the road like you almost were. Is there someone we can call to tell them you're safe?"

Her eyes shut, she breathlessly murmured, "No, there's nobody to call. I'll be fine, really." After a few moments of more shaking, she told the truth, "No, I'm not. I'm having trouble. Oh, God I'm so cold."

"My house is about twenty miles from here. We need to get you there soon, warm you up and then figure out the rest. Does that sound all right?"

"I guess so. " Her lips trembled as she wrapped her arms around herself. Her blonde hair was falling over her face. He was tempted to reach out and brush it away, but pulled back, afraid to cross a forbidding line.

Bella, in the back seat, had her paws up on the seat back nuzzling the woman's hair, whining.

Jim was getting more concerned about getting home with her. The wind was pushing the truck across the road, with the ice forming hard on the asphalt. Ice and riveting snowflakes pelting the windshield brought Jim's navigation to dead reckoning. He needed to use the highway signs and land marks as guides. Past the Brule River and then, yes, there it is, the Flute Reed River. Arrowhead Trail is just ahead, and then left. Left again on Tower Road, and when Tom Lake Road comes up, he knows he'll be safe.

The long drive off Tom Lake Road, between the towering pine trees, was easier because they filtered the wind, and was actually pleasant. He pressed the remote to open the garage door and felt secure once he was parked inside.

The cabin was a hundred feet from the garage, and he had his doubts about getting her safely inside without her help. He opened the passenger door, "Can you step out?"

Weakly, she said, "Yeah. I can do it."

As soon as her foot touched the floor she collapsed in his arms. "Oh, shit, this is trouble." So, with no other choice, he cradled her in his arms and staggered to his front door.

Bella ran ahead, turning often to be sure she was being followed. Inside, the warmth hit them suddenly, giving a feeling of safety. He laid her on the sofa and gave instructions to Bella, "Keep an eye on her girl, and stay down." Understanding everything, she obediently took up a guard post at the woman's side. Jim ran out to collect the Eukanuba, liquor, and her purse, and close up the garage. When he got back in, she was laying still on the sofa, face to face with Bella, scratching the dog's head.

"I see you've met. This is Bella, and I'm Jim." He extended his hand to help her sit up. "You need to get out of the wet stuff." He hoisted her to her feet, "Follow me, there should be something in here to put on." Leading her into a spare bedroom and opening the closet door that hid a few odds and ends of clothing, he told her, "I'll get the fire going again, and we can dry your stuff." He offered a very sincere, *it's okay, you're safe now,* type of smile and closed the door behind him, as he left.

Alone in the room, she knew she had no other choice but go along with what the old man was offering her. She couldn't remember anything after the Impala just quit on her, and was so tired of running and at that moment, wished that he had left her to die on the frozen road. Stripping off the cold, wet clothing she stood shaking uncontrollably, looking into the small closet.

Almost a half hour later, she came out dressed in a huge flannel shirt, sweat pants and gray woolen socks. Her hair went in every direction possible, and she looked swamped in that clothing. "I must be a sight." Her voice was small and quiet; she stood still, unsure as what to do next.

He stood up from the fireplace and stared at her for several long moments before he caught himself. "Come over here, closer to the fire." He motioned her to a large over-stuffed chair where she eased herself down into it, curling her feet under. The fire was raging and the warming started right away. He covered her with a soft, fluffy blanket and tucked it in around her. Closing her eyes, she felt herself sinking deeper into the safety and softness, and fell sound asleep, letting the heat from the fire pull her away.

Her purse was sitting on the floor so he picked it up to put it within reach of her, tempted to look in to see who she was. "No, that's not right. Mind your own business, you old fool."

He went into the spare bedroom and picked up her wet clothing. Cotton socks, jeans, a tee shirt with a butterfly on the front, and her bra and panties. He put it all into the dryer in the laundry room off the kitchen. He held the underwear a moment, marveling at the dainty femininity and how small they were, like they belonged to a little girl. The fabric had started tearing away from the elastic waistband, a sad indication of poverty.

The memories crawled back into his head again, and the feelings started all over. He wanted to shake her and force her to tell him who to call to let them know she was alive. The tears started welling up and he blotted them with his sleeve. "Oh, no, not again. Please, not again. Not tonight." He stood at the dryer for a few minutes while he filed away the mess in his head. "That's right, put everything where it belongs."

He had made some coffee and brought it to the rocking chair next to the sleeping girl, sat down and studied her face. She was a pretty blonde girl with a few freckles decorating a small perky nose. Her face had a familiarity to it that frightened him. In a way she reminded him of Mary Beth. However, right now, anyone would.

He momentarily forgot his plan to get drunk and kill himself—something more important had come up.

Christmas music by the Mormon Tabernacle Choir quietly filled the cabin and mingled with the crackling fire and howling wind outside. Bella was curled up at the girl's feet, still on guard duty. Allowing Mary Beth back into his thoughts, he tried to bring back some memories, but they were tired and weak by now. He looked up at the mantle to the small package wrapped in fading paper. The bow fell off years ago, but he took it out every Christmas, just in case. You never know… He stopped putting up a tree long ago, but still hung the wreath in the window. The wreath and the porch light were left on as a beacon to guide her home.

He had just started to accept the idea that she would never return, and then this had to happen. Alone, in the glow of the fire, he spoke to his wife. "Margaret, are you telling me to not give up, and that my own life is worth keeping? Why did this happen, Honey? What am I supposed to do?"

Normally, he would be drunk by now, passed out next to the fire with Bella keeping watch over him. Once, when he fell outside with the stupor encasing his mind, he would have cashed it in then if it weren't for Bella laying on top of him to keep him warm. The dog showed up one day as a stray and just stayed. Just made herself at home as if she was born there. Jim was neither superstitious nor religious, but thought that there was always the possibility the dog had been sent to see that he stayed out of trouble, or, she stuck around for a different reason.

Now, he had this new person here and needed to stay in focus for her. She may need help, could be in trouble, and someone would be worried about her. Someone would be sitting home waiting for her, afraid they would never see her again. Someone who loved her and was frantic about where she was and if she was safe. He knew the feeling so well, having lived with it for fifteen years and was just overcoming, until this new person came along to start the torment all over again.

The coffee was good, the cabin was warm and cozy, and he should have been satisfied, but he had a nagging feeling...

● ● ● ● ● ● ● ● ● ● ● ● ● ● ● ● ● ●

THE COMBINATION OF JIM'S SNORING AND the warmth of the fire woke up her mind first. Her eyes followed, blinking to clear it all up, and settled on the flickering in the fireplace. She glanced over to find Bella and Jim both asleep. The old man was sitting in a rocking chair close by, with an empty cup hanging from his fingers, and thought of a Coca Cola sign she saw once with Santa Claus doing the same thing.

She was sore all over but the shaking had stopped, and she was finally warm. Vaguely remembering being put in the big chair, she felt safe and comfortable and discarded the idea of getting up. The big yellow dog sensed her now and had her nose on her lap. Digging her arm from under the blanket, she reached to stroke the animal's head. Looking around the room, she smiled at the quiet charm of the cabin and stared at the old wreath hanging crooked in the paned window.

Jim snorted and woke himself up, shaking the fuzz out of his head, he looked over to the girl. "Oh, good, you're awake, how about some coffee?" He piled some split oak on the dying fire and looked at her to be sure she heard him.

"Coffee would be nice. Don't go to any trouble."

"Not having coffee would be trouble. I'll make a fresh pot." While it gurgled in the kitchen, he sat back into the rocker, leaning towards her, "You need to call your family. They'll be worried about you. You must have a husband, or parents, or somebody."

"No. There's nobody to call." She frowned, trying to let him know his limits at nagging her. "I'm all right, please believe me."

His face took on a mournful cast with his thoughts caught on a twig from his past. Problems born years ago rose again, and he didn't want that to happen. The coffee signaled it was done, startling his mind back to the present. Grunting himself upright, he went to the kitchen, returning with two steaming cups; the rich aroma circling over it. He left again and came back, setting the bottle of Wild Turkey on the small table between them. He sipped some coffee out of his cup to make room and splashed in a bit of the Turkey.

She asked, "Can I have some of that?"

His attempt to be funny fell short with, "You old enough?"

Tersely she replied, "I'm twenty eight. Is that old enough?" She held out her cup and he slid some into it. "Thanks." The hot coffee laced with the incredible liquor, made a wonderful warm burning sensation down her throat, settling in her stomach before radiating through her limbs.

"My name is Jim Cooper. The watchdog is Bella. She's taken to you pretty good."

"She's nice, I love her. I'm Suzan. Suzan Parker," then hid her face in the cup.

Jim suspected she was lying, but let it go for now. He didn't want to frighten her and thought he should let her know he could be trusted before she opened up to him.

"Were you headed someplace in particular when you got stuck?"

She stared into her cup for a moment, "I wasn't headed anywhere. The car is a piece of crap and just died."

She showed a bit of fire in her attitude, and Jim was smart enough to not push too many buttons. She wanted her privacy—and he would let her have it. "When the wind lets up, we can try to pull it out. Maybe I can get it going."

Showing a mellow side, she said softly, "Thank you for helping me." She wanted to say more but went back to hiding in her cup.

"Well, maybe you'd like to get some sleep tonight. We'll see about tomorrow."

"I'm fine right here in the chair."

He stood up and extended his hand to her. "There's a nice bed in the room you changed in. Your clothes are in the dryer, your coat is hanging up and the shoes are drying out. There's the bathroom, and I'll leave a light on so you don't get lost."

She took his hand and he pulled her up, sensing his touch as gentle, but had the feeling of a chunk of iron. He was a large man, and towered over her, but he made her feel safe and comfortable. Lately, a strange sensation for her, and one she welcomed.

"Yeah, well. I am tired. Thanks."

"Good night Suzan Parker, Merry Christmas."

"Oh, my God, I forgot. It's Christmas." She looked up at him, smiled and gently nodded. She couldn't give him any more now and hoped it was enough. Closing the door behind her, she crawled under a massive down comforter. The mattress was soft and the springs underneath made a quiet squeak. Thinking the last bed she was in was with Stanley, she realized the last time her body actually slept in a real bed was the night before Roger burst into the house. She has been on the run ever since, and couldn't go any farther. When the Impala died, she just gave up. She wasn't trying to find help, she was meeting her fate, ready to die.

She would deal with her problems tomorrow and try to not hurt this nice man. "Good night Rosalie, I love you. Merry Christmas, Honey." She snuggled in and smiled herself to sleep, feeling safe and warm.

Jim had another bump of Turkey and then let Bella out for a potty run. She came in, shook off the snow and curled up in front of the closed bedroom door.

He made sure the outside light was on for Mary Beth—just in case. Looking at the wreath, he tried to straighten it, but it wanted to be crooked, so he let it alone. Stopping at the mantle, he touched the package and the pains of the past washed over him again.

Although he'd said it countless times, he apologized to his wife again. "I'm sorry Margaret. I just didn't know how to handle her like you did." His wife had passed away long ago, and he learned to live without her, but was still in love with her. Talking to both himself and the package, "Maybe she'll show up tonight, Margaret, Maybe tonight. Merry Christmas, old woman."

The nightlight was on in the bathroom and he left his door ajar.

Jim never prayed nor did he go to church. Tonight, being Christmas Eve, was a special night so he silently asked to have his missing daughter kept safe and for Margaret's spirit to be well. Then he added, "If you're paying attention Margaret, send some help for the small person in the next room. I know she needs it."

He fell asleep listening to the wind howling and the snow beating against the window—but there were no footsteps outside. No clumping boots on the porch. Who knows, maybe tomorrow. They both fell asleep in their separate rooms silently saying separate goodnights to each other, thankful the other person was there.

Bella lay on the floor of the hallway outside the closed door where the new person was. She knew what her job was now, a silent sentry sent to keep watch over these two people. Two strangers, desperate in their own ways, brought together by unseen forces for a reason yet to surface.

CHAPTER 7
THE LOCKET

● ●

THE NEXT MORNING WHEN SHE woke up, she snuggled under the big blanket and looked around the room for a long time. The frosted windows were as much as she needed to know that it was just too damn cold. She had slept in the flannel shirt and other clothes because they were nice and warm, and she enjoyed the softness on her. The chill of the room tickled her nose, and made a cloud of her breath, so she snuggled deeper. The room was small, but pleasant. A maple dresser was adorned with a doily and was topped by a pile of old books and a small antique lamp that had been rewired for electric. A few pictures hung on the wooded walls, depicting generic scenes of tranquil life.

She had no idea where she was or what she was going to do next. She didn't have much of a choice and had to rely on, what's his name, oh, yeah, Jim, to see how he could help. She knew she had to leave some time, but had no way to do it. Maybe the old guy can do something with the stupid car. In all fairness to the Ellsworths, she thought some day she would have to give it back to them.

The old man seemed nice enough and wanted to help but she had to be careful. Roger had some deep connections through that Frank guy, and who knows what will blow in. She thought, *"Stay on guard and take it as it comes."* If the old guy came after her, she would do the best she could, but that didn't seem likely.

She remembered her purse was still out there and wondered if he snooped at all. He wouldn't find much. She had been careful to get rid of anything that would lead to more trouble. She had sold and hocked everything else, and even most of Stanley's money was gone.

Sounds of busyness from outside the door told her Jim was up, so maybe she should get up also. She didn't want to, wishing she could lay there forever. A headache was nagging her, and she was nauseous. The last thing her stomach had seen was days ago, and that was just a candy bar she had stolen. Hopefully, he would be able to give her something, anything.

She sat up, stretched her arms above her head and swung her feet over the side where they barely touched the floor. The nip in the air brought the coldness closer. A blanket was folded over the foot board so she wrapped it around herself, having had enough of being cold, and slowly opened the door. Immediately, the aroma of bacon and coffee crawled up her nostrils and sent thumping pangs to her gut. She stepped out to find Jim in the kitchen, working some kind of magic with food that she had forgotten about.

"Good morning Suzan Parker, and Merry Christmas to you. I hope you're hungry." He beamed at her, and Bella demanded some attention, pushing against her legs, and mischievously pulling the blanket from her.

Stumbling from Bella's antics, she couldn't believe what she saw spread all over the kitchen–bacon and sausage, scrambled eggs, hash browns and toast. "Sit down before Bella gets it all." Her eyes wide as a bewildered child's, she stepped slowly to the chair he offered her.

They both sat at the old pine table and he poured coffee. "Would you rather have milk?"

"Oh, this is perfect. Thank you so much." Hesitant at first, she abandoned her shyness and started shoveling everything she could onto her plate. Ravenous, she devoured whatever she could hold in her hand, or pierce with her fork. Emily's frenzied attack on the food made it obvious she was bordering on starvation.

Jim sat awestruck at the incredible eating machine ravaging at his table. Eyes wide in disbelief, a smile slowly crossed his lips.

After devouring all she could hold, she pushed back from the table and burped. "Oh, my God, I'm sorry. I sound like a pig."

"Don't worry, it's a compliment. I used to burp, but that was before I became perfect."

He said it with a smile, and she began to get a warm feeling of trust from him. She looked at him for a moment, taking in his crooked grin and quiet sense of humor. Nothing complicated, just nice. Her gratitude could only be expressed in one way, telling him, "Thank you, Jim. Oh, and Merry Christmas." She said it without thinking, but was glad she did.

He stopped toying with his food and looked at her, feeling incredibly close to this woman he didn't even know. "Thank you Suzan. That means a lot to me."

She thought she should do something to at least help out a little and offered. "You cooked and I get to clean up. Bargain?"

"Fine with me Missy; better give Bella something, or she'll tear you to shreds."

Looking at the passive dog, "Yeah, she looks like a killer." Bella sat at her side, her tail sweeping the floor, head askew and panting.

Everything got cleaned up and put away. Jim sat in the rocker before the fire and lit a pipe. "Do you mind?" He asked.

She vaguely remembered someone in her life smoking a pipe. It might have been her father, but she didn't know for sure. "I love the smell. Can I have a puff?"

He was getting entertained now and handed the smoking pipe to her. She held the warm bowl and watched the curling smoke rise over it and a mellow aroma enter her nose. She did pretty well actually puffing like a seasoned smoker. They passed it back and forth until her tongue started to burn and she had enough.

"Do you smoke, Suzan?"

"No, not really. Just a pipe or cigar for laughs." Thoughts of happy times at the bar after work passed by, giving her a reason to grin.

She had curled herself into the big chair and spent most of her time just staring into the fire with the blanket wrapped around her. She lost herself in trying to think of the last time she laughed, and had to go way back to when Rosalie was a toddler. There wasn't much in her life she could recall as a nice memory, and drew a blank trying to recall something happy.

After a few minutes, he stomped out the pipe and rapped it on the edge of the fireplace. "Suzan, are you okay? You seem so sad. If there's anything you need to unload, I've got a good ear."

She looked at him, her eyes were watering. "I have a few problems, but who doesn't. I can work it out."

"It's none of my business, and I don't want to make you uncomfortable, but if you need help, I'm always open. You're safe here, you know."

"Thanks" She wished she could unload on him, but she didn't even know him, and who knows how much trouble could start. To herself, *shut up girl.*

He got up to look out the window, "The wind has died down and the snow has let up. First thing tomorrow we'll see what we can do with your car. The drifts will be cleared by then, and we want to get it before it's towed."

She never thought of that. "I don't want it towed. It can't get towed." She was getting panicked and agitated. Sitting forward, she anxiously asked, "Can't we just go get it now?"

"Believe me, we'd never get to it. I'll call the sheriff. There should be someone on duty that can get a message to the County garage."

"The sheriff?"

Her panic jingled the familiar little bell in his head, but he left it alone. "Don't worry, Suzan. You have to trust me." He picked up the phone, and it was working. Dialing 911, he inquired, "Hello, who's on duty today? This is Jim Cooper."

The dispatcher was patched into his home phone today. "Hi Jim, it's Wallace, what's up?"

"Hi Wally. There's a snowbird that's disabled out on 61, a few miles south of the Brule. I just wanted to be sure it wasn't towed. I'm going out there tomorrow to pull it out. Is that okay?"

"Yeah, that's fine Jim. I'll let the garage know. I think Rusty Johnson will be out, but that won't be until tonight."

"Jim, are you going out on the ice any time soon?"

"You make sure the car is left alone, and I'll package up a mess of walleye filets for you."

"They're melting in my mouth already. See you later Jim. Merry Christmas."

"Merry Christmas, Wally."

She had been listening and inquired, "That sounded friendly. Is everyone around here related or something?"

"Well, yeah, most people are related one way or the other. Mostly, people are just friendly. We'll go out in the morning and drag your car out. Until then, just relax. You can consider yourself at home here for as long as you want. Let me find you something normal to wear in this weather, and you can help me with some firewood."

She followed him into the laundry room and a large walk-in closet. "Hmm, let's see. Oh, yeah, here we go." Kneeling at the closet door, he took out a large box and opened it very slowly. Holding the flaps, as he stared into it his hands started to shake.

Alarmed, she put her warm hand on his, "Jim, what's wrong?"

They looked into each other's eyes. Two entirely different people, worlds apart in every aspect, who each had their own desperations, were reaching out to be held. Two parallel souls tied for life in a deep, sincere friendship.

In a low, calm voice, he answered, "Just like you, Missy. I'll be okay. Just some old memories creeping through." Turning his attention back to the box, he cleared his throat and said, "Let's see, these should be all right." He pulled out a down-filled jacket and ski pants along with a scarf and knit hat. Mittens were snapped to the jacket sleeves.

In awe, she marveled at the new clothing. "These are beautiful. They shouldn't be put away, someone can use these." She caught a faraway look come across Jim's face. "Who do these belong to, Jim?"

"As of now, they belong to you. They've been put away here for long enough. It's time to let go."

She questioned him, "Let go?"

He heard her but ignored the query and shoved the box back into the closet.

"These ought to work just fine," and handed her an almost-new pair of snow-mobile boots. "That should do it, I guess. Let's bundle up and get some firewood." He finished the proposal with a quick rub on her already-messy hair and a gentle shove out the door. It irritated her, but she took as a friendly nudge and kept her mouth shut.

Everything fit as if it was tailor-made for her. She hugged herself when she was all suited up–and she felt new, a good feeling she had long forgotten about. She had memories of some new clothing when she was at home with her parents, but hadn't had anything new for years. Her birthday sweater came to mind, but that was left at the foster home. The things from the Salvation Army or the thrift store didn't count because they were worn out by the time she got them. On the street she could steal a few things, but someone would just steal them away later.

Jim, Suzan and Bella went out into the fifteen-below-zero air and played like little kids. Suzan and Bella chased each other in circles and rolled in the white drifts that ran across the yard. Jim watched them and felt an old glow start in his heart. Enough wood was put up to last a few days, and he let them play as long as they wanted to.

Inside the cabin, the fireplace, the antique trappings, and the warmth of the three of them together made for a charm that was both peaceful and happy. Jim and Suzan nursed a cup of coffee laced with Wild Turkey as he put together what he claimed to be his world-famous Christmas meatloaf. Carols poured from the stereo, and even the crooked wreath was happy. Suzan helped with chopping onions and mixing the mess in a bowl, with Jim putting on a bogus show of complaining about a woman in the kitchen.

After dinner, they sat before the fire sharing Jim's pipe and incredibly good cups of coffee, listening to solemn sounds of the season coming from the stereo. She broke the silence, "Is it always this happy and peaceful here?"

The answer, hard to get into his throat, took a few moments. "Suzan, until I found you on the road nearly frozen to death, my life was a pile of shit. I haven't enjoyed the company of anyone like this for a lot of years. I usually just get drunk every night and well, do things I shouldn't. I've been alone for a long time–and I don't like to be alone. At least while you're here, I'm not."

This was Christmas, and in the absence of Mary Beth, it was just the right thing to do. Jim went to the mantle and picked up the dusty and faded small package. He held it for a moment before handing it to her. "Merry Christmas, Suzan Parker."

Suzan protested, "No, you can't. This isn't mine. I have nothing for you. No," and tried to push it away.

He set it in her lap and placed himself on the arm of the chair, next to her. "My dear little girl, you have come into my life at a time when I didn't have anything left to live for. I'd given up on everything, and then you showed up. There weren't any other cars on the road, and you would have died if I hadn't come by. I didn't save you–you saved me. You've given me the most precious gift of all . . . a reason to live."

He sighed and went on, "Fifteen years ago my daughter, Mary Beth, walked out and never came back. She left on Christmas Eve, and the last thing she said to me was *"I hope you die, Asshole."* She was only seventeen. It was winter, and cold, so I couldn't just let her go. I chased after her, but evidently she had it all planned and had someone waiting for her. Almost daily I'd think about walking into the woods and letting fate do what it wanted with me. I didn't care and had nothing left. If I didn't have Bella to take care of, I would be dead now. Mary Beth was angry because she didn't want to live here in the woods. She wanted the city and all the lights and stuff. I couldn't move because my wife died here, and I needed to be close to her memory."

Settling back into the rocker, "I've blamed myself for driving her out, and not seeing what was important to her. She was, is, my daughter–and its my fault she left. I wrapped this Christmas gift the day she left, but she won't ever be back. Please, you'll be making me very happy if you accept it."

A horrible memory came wafting through her mind, recalling the social worker telling her she didn't have parents anymore, and her home was gone. She turned the fragile package over in her hands, and pleaded, "Jim, I can't."

Quietly, he said, "Please."

The paper fell off easily after so much time in waiting. She took the cover off the box and stared at a silver locket topped by a small opal on a tiny chain. As she picked it up, the chain flowed slowly through her fingers and hung loosely. Putting it to her lips she sensed the fragility of not only the chain, but of her life, and started to cry. "Oh, God, I don't deserve this." As the tears started a trickle down her cheeks, she put her feet up on the chair and buried her face in her knees and shook from the sobs.

She got up and ran to her room, closed the door and sat on the bed with the precious gift pressed to her lips, tears streaming from her eyes. The crying had nothing to do with the locket. She was racked in agony over the life her daughter is being forced to live. She is Rosalie's mother and can't be with her for Christmas, her birthday or any other day. She always tried to make Christmas and birthdays happy for her daughter because she knew how much it hurt to have it missed by people who are supposed to love you. The only gift she ever got from Roger was flat on her back in bed.

Calling out loud to her daughter, tears flowing down her cheeks, she wailed, "Oh, Rosie, it's not supposed to be like this. Please be strong Honey, I'm coming. You're safe, and I love you."

Her back against the old headboard, she thought about what brought her here, and of what Rosalie has had to endure. Emily's mind labored at the thought of strange men tearing at the child's mind, body and heart. She thought of the long journey she's had staying ahead of trouble, and the long journey yet to come.

"I'm going to bring it together, Honey. Mommy loves you, and we're going to be safe and happy."

She swallowed hard, wiped the mess from her face and slid to the floor, heading to the bedroom door. She had only one thing to give him in return, and she needed to consider that very carefully.

●　●　●　●　●　●　●　●　●　●　●　●　●　●　●

IT WAS CHRISTMAS EVENING AT THE AMISH farm. The chores were done, the group had eaten together, and the prayer session was over. A lady who was assigned to watch over Rosalie was concerned for the child, being away from her mother this Christmas. She approached the child, asking her, "How are you, Rosalie?"

With a smile, Rosalie told her, "My mom says she loves me and we're going to be safe and happy."

Concerned, Sister Alysia sat on the edge of Rosalie's bed, softly asking, "You heard from your mother?"

The smile on Rosalie's face was deep, happy, and sincere as she explained, "Yes, my mommy and I can talk to each other–no matter where we are. They aren't words, but feelings we get."

Satisfied, Sister Alysia stood up and said, "That's nice, Rosalie. Goodnight, Dear." She left the bedside and returned to her own room, confident that Rosalie had a special guardian angel.

CHAPTER 8
A GIFT IN RETURN

● ●

COMPOSING HERSELF AT THE DOOR, Emily came out to find Jim sitting on the floor, leaning against the big chair, scratching Bella's head. The almost-empty bottle of Wild Turkey was on the floor next to him. The fire had been built up, sending a glowing warmth throughout the small cabin. It was dusk outside and the only light inside was from the fireplace and the dull glow of the tiny bulb in the crooked wreath.

She settled herself on the floor next to him and put the bottle to her lips, draining it. It was warm in her throat and blended with the flames at her feet. "I drank all the booze," her voice small and soft.

"It was my Christmas present to myself. I usually drink whatever swill is on sale. You being here makes it special."

"I'm sorry I ran off," and that was the only explanation he was going to get for now. She leaned against him and put her head on his shoulder. "Thank you, Jim. I love the locket, and I'll keep it forever."

"It was my wife's. She got it from her grandmother and wore it all the time. It became a part of her and now it's yours, and I'm happy you have it. I wrapped it to give to Mary Beth all those years ago, but she wouldn't have taken it anyway. She hated me too much to take a present from me."

Caressing the locket with her fingers, she looked up at him, "Will you tell me about your wife?"

He smiled a little and played with Bella's fur while the right words came to him. "Margaret was one of those people who could make anyone feel important. She had a way of listening, and then finding answers before you were done talking. She was soft-spoken and as gentle as a breeze. She never had a reason to get angry, and always had a happy thought to give you. I called her Angel because she was one. She was misplaced here on earth, and I think she just handled time until it was her turn to leave."

Staring into the flames, he continued, "Cancer took her way before I was done loving her. Mary Beth was one of those people who just had to have conflict in their life, and Margaret was the only one who could make her happy. I think Mary Beth got that trait from me. The kind of work I did makes a man aggressive, and I didn't always leave that in the office before I came home. Margaret would calm me down when I got home, but Mary Beth wanted to be the center of attention, so she acted the same way I did. In a way, I suppose that was how the girl thought she could reach me. Instead, it drove us apart.

"According to Mary Beth, it was my fault her mother got sick, and she never missed a chance to grind it into me. I'm not going into the dirt of the relationship between my daughter and me, but I loved her very much, and her leaving was as difficult as Angel dying."

Jim pulled Emily tight to him with his big arm, and hugging her, he bent over and kissed the top of her head. Bella lay next to her and put a paw and her head on her lap. They sat in front of the fire for a long time, silently watching the flickering flames dance and crackle on the wood, keeping the warmth of a new friendship where it belonged. Finally, it was time for Bella to make a potty run outside, and Suzan was up first to let her out.

Stepping outside with the dog, inhaling the cold fresh air, arms stretched over her head, she marveled at the black sky dotted with millions of tiny brilliant lights. She thought back to what the minister said to her in the church, wondering if there was a God up there–and how could this incredible sight happen without one. She wished her daughter could be here now and share this treasured moment.

Bella came back from her romp in the woods and got a thorough scratching, as Emily dug deep into her fur and hugged the happy animal. "Oh, Bella, you're a good girl. I know Rosalie would love you."

Back inside she put another piece of oak on the fire and sat on the hearth warming her backside. Jim groaned himself upright, stretched his bones back into place and decided that his day was over, finishing it with a goodnight salutation, "Well, Missy, I'm turning in now. Shut everything down when you're done. See you tomorrow."

"You leave the porch light on, don't you?"

Jim paused pensively, quietly answering, "No, I don't think that's necessary any more. Good night, Suzan."

"Good night, Jim." She settled back on the floor with Bella, watching the flame while fingering the locket. A lot of thoughts rolled around her mind before she went to bed. She did indeed have something to give this old man, but should she? Where would it lead to, and how would it muck up what she started to do in the first place? Bella followed her into her room and jumped up on the bed.

It took her a long time to get up the nerve before deciding it was time. She was sure Jim was asleep, and that was good. She slid out of her clothing and crept into the chilly hallway with the only light coming from the dwindling fireplace. His door was ajar, just like last night, and she slowly peeked around it into his dark bedroom. Listening to his heavy breathing, she walked towards it, bumping against his bed, and felt for the edge of the covers. Pulling them down, she slid between the sheets and covered up. Reaching over to touch him, his body was warm and huge.

Jim awoke with a start, sitting up, blinking in the darkness, "Huh. Suzan? What are you doing?"

Her voice hushed, "Jim, lay down. I need to tell you something." She reached up and pulled on his bare shoulder, keeping her hand on him.

He laid down and put his hand out, touching her side, and pulled back at the feeling of her nakedness. "Suzan?" She put her fingers on his lips to quiet him.

Whispering, "Please, listen to me. What I'm doing has nothing to do with anything other than sharing. I owe you so much, and this is the only thing I have to share."

His curiosity rampant with confusion, he muttered, "Uh, yeah. What's going on?"

"Today when you gave me the locket, you said it would make you happy if I accepted it. And I really thought you were sincere, so I took it. It was the most beautiful and wonderful gift I ever got because I know it came from your heart. Remember the story of the Little Drummer Boy who had nothing to give except the playing of his drum?"

"Yes. Of course I do. What's that … ?" And she shushed him again.

"I have only two things to give you, Jim. One, my friendship, and the other is myself. I want you to receive me as I received the locket. Don't give me moral objections, please. Just accept it as I did the locket, from my heart. Tomorrow you'll learn all about me and what I'm doing here. But, for tonight, please accept me. Accept what I can give you." She leaned over kissing him lightly, and then slid on top of him.

With a heavy sigh of surprise and pleasure, "Oh, my," came from deep within him.

● ● ● ● ● ● ● ● ● ● ● ● ● ● ● ●

THEY LAY IN BED LATE INTO THE MORNING just holding each other. After a long spell, she sat up, pulling the sheet with her, and spoke the first words of the day. "I hope I didn't do the wrong thing last night. I thought about it a lot, and I wanted to. If you think I'm bad, I'll go. But I'd like to tell you my story, if you want to hear it."

"Suzan, you don't have to explain anything. I'm really happy, and after last night I feel great. Who wouldn't?"

She smiled and scratched the top of his head as a wave of relief come over her. "I was really nervous about doing it. I don't think we'll be lovers or anything, but at least I can be useful." Tossing the covers aside, she scampered out of bed, telling him, "Wait here," and went to the bathroom, not bothering to close the door tightly. His eyes followed her out the room, marveling at the motions her little round butt made, with tiny dimples just above it. A small ladybug was tattooed above her left cheek.

Coming back she had her hands over her head, trying to smooth out her wild blonde hair, with the flushing noise from the toilet trailing behind her. As she climbed back into the bed, he noticed she had another tattoo of a butterfly on her shoulder blade. The locket was draped around her neck, seeking the gentle cleavage.

"Suzan," he began, "I'm an old horny dog of a man. If we're to ever do this again, it has to be you that initiates it. I don't want to do anything that's going to be wrong or make you mad. I don't want anything more than to be your friend and, if I can, I want to help you." She lay in the crook of his shoulder as he gently pulled her in to him.

"Fair enough. Maybe once in a while we can get it on, we'll see. Thanks for being so nice."

He smiled "It's me who owes the thanks."

Sitting with her knees pulled up to her chest, she began her story, "Here we go, and I promise to be truthful. My name isn't Suzan Parker, it's Emily Parkhurst. I was married to Roger Parkhurst. He's an undercover cop down in the Cities, and he commits more crimes than the guys he arrests. I'm here because I'm hiding from him. I have a daughter, Rosalie, who's almost eleven. I found out he'd been selling her to men for sex since she was almost ten."

What he just heard sent Jim through the ceiling. "Wait a minute—he did *WHAT*?"

"Let me finish, Jim. There's more." She went on, "Rosie was scared to death and starting to act out and cry all night. She wouldn't go to school or eat, or talk to anyone.

One day I found pictures he had of her, with men. I divorced him and kicked him out of the house. He gave the police a story that I was the ring leader of a pornography business and he didn't do anything. It was to cover himself and the other cops involved in it."

Jim's stomach was twisting into a knot, sending acid reflux on a rampage through his chest.

"I got questioned more than that asshole Roger did. Finally, I got Rosie to understand what was happening. There was a real chance that they were going to send me to jail and give him custody."

She had her hands to the sides of her head trying to press out a headache. "Jim, do you have any aspirin?"

"Yeah, hang on." He lumbered into the bathroom and came back with a bottle of Bayer and a glass of water.

"Thanks. Do you think we could finish this over a cup of coffee?"

"Suzan, Emily or whoever, that really sounds good."

"My real name is Emily. I'm sorry to have lied, but I was scared. Call me anything you want."

"I've already hung the name Missy on you." His jaw rigid with anger, his voice low and firm, "What you're telling me is some very bad stuff, you know, and I want to hear it all." He hung his head a moment, and then mumbled, "Son of a bitch! I'll kill the guy."

While Jim assembled the morning offering, she dug one of his old sweatshirts out of the closet. Its enormous size hung below her knees, and allowed her fingertips to peek from the sleeves. Sitting on the sofa with the coffee, she launched into her story again.

"Rosalie told a counselor some things, but I know there was a lot she had pushed too deep into her mind to talk about. We told the lawyer what the asshole was doing, but it seems that about then everything started to back up on us. The evidence disappeared, along with all the crap he used to take the pictures. Roger was put in jail, but no formal charges were filed; something about the lack of physical evidence. Rosalie's testimony could be regarded as the prattling of a child guided by a distraught mother.

"She's really screwed up and needs a lot of counseling. She'll probably never be the same, ever. I can't be with her while I'm running, and that's making it even harder for her to deal with it all. I've got her hidden with some people, but I can't contact her directly. I call some friends who pass messages to her. I try sending her a card or letter, but I can't let on where I am. Just too dangerous, to me and the people she's with.

"After I divorced Roger, I thought he was out of our lives, but then a problem came up."

She got up and refilled both cups. Replacing the pot, she paused and leaned against the kitchen sink, covering her face with her hands. Shaking, she slid down to the floor. Jim bent down next to her, holding her tight with his cheek against the top of her head. She wiped the sniffles with the sleeve of the old sweatshirt. "Sorry, I'll wash it."

In an attempt to lighten her mood, he told her, "That's all right; I like snot on my clothes."

She smiled at his response and punched his arm.

She continued, "A technicality came up, and for a reason I'll never understand, he was let out of jail with all charges dropped. I was never told he was out, and he came to the house one night and beat me up, but good."

"Aw, Jesus, no." Jim winced at the sound of that, but pushed his rage out of the way.

"He was after Rosalie. I pulled myself off the floor and saw him dragging her out of the house. I picked up a kitchen chair and broke it over his head. He went down, and I grabbed Rosie and ran outside screaming for someone to help me. A neighbor saw me, took us in and called the police. A squad car came and Roger told them I attacked him, and he wanted to press assault charges."

Emily brought her knees up and laid her head on them. Jim struggled to his feet and held his hand out to pull her up. "Honey, I'm too old to be on the floor this long. Let's go sit on something my bones can handle."

Back on the sofa with her legs drawn up under her, "And now for the best part. The frigging police came and put me in handcuffs. I went to jail. Roger said he wanted Rosalie but, the only people who were thinking clear then, my neighbors, said she wasn't there, that I never brought her in with me. I had a feeling the cop knew what was going on, but he did what he had to do with me—and let my neighbors do the right thing."

Jim was on the edge of the sofa staring at her in disbelief "That's the biggest pile of crap I've ever heard, but it really doesn't surprise me."

Emily continued, "Anyway, I spent the night in jail, and the neighbor bailed me out the next morning. They were aware of everything that led up to then, and knew Rosalie needed to be protected. They hid her for me and came up with the idea to get her away for good. Through them, she's safe, but I'm on the run. Roger is trying to find me, and I'm a wanted criminal with kidnapping and child pornography charges on me, as well as unlawful flight. My daughter was sexually abused and the police want to give her to him. What's wrong with the world, Jim? Why do things like this happen?"

Jim got up, shaking his head "Wait a minute. I want to show you something." He came back with a shoebox and sat down. Lifting off the cover he showed her a Smith and Wesson .38 Special revolver, and a leather pouch. Opening the pouch, he held up a tarnished badge with the words *COOK COUNTY SHERRIF* written on it.

"I'm a retired law enforcement officer, Missy. I've spent my life trying to correct the wrongs of society and pretty much failed at it. I know bad things happen that shouldn't happen.

People like you get the shaft and your ex uses the law to turn the screws the way he wants. He's a dirty cop and needs to be brought down."

Her forehead wrinkled in disbelief, and she blurted, "You're a cop? Oh, man, you should have told me. I've gone too far to get this close to the law, and I'm not going to let my daughter get hurt. I can't get caught, Jim. I can't." By now, she had bounced off the sofa and was pacing about waving her arms, chattering about getting screwed again by the law. A startled Bella scampered into the bedroom seeking safety.

With the strength of an ox, Jim pinned her arms to her sides and lifted her entirely off the floor. "Now hold on and put the fire out. Nobody is going to hurt you or your daughter. If anyone can help you, I can. I've still got connections and a little know-how, so sit your little ass down and tell me the rest, if there is any more."

Bella stuck her head around the corner to be sure it was safe to come back. She pleaded, "Jim. Please, if this is going to backfire, just let me go."

"I promise I will never do anything to harm or jeopardize you or your daughter. I will do everything I can to help. Honest. And at this point, you really don't have much of a choice. If you want to help Rosalie, you need to stay in control, act smart and trust me."

After settling down, she started again. "The car I got stranded in belongs to my neighbors, Helen and George Ellsworth. I'm going to have to tell you what's been done with Rosalie, but I make a vow here. If you do anything to let anyone know about it, I'll spend the rest of my life planning your death. That's how serious I am, Jim."

"Missy, I understand the pain you're going through. The confusion and fear you feel must be awful. I'll do everything I can, Honey. You said your daughter is safe, and now you're safe. We'll do something to work this out and get you two where you belong."

Taking her hand in his, he was compelled to share her grief. "Missy, you've been honest with me, so I at least owe you an explanation on how I happened to come along on Christmas Eve. I really think it was ordained that I was to find you. On the fifteenth anniversary of Mary Beth leaving, you come into my life, and keep me from ending my own. I've never been very religious, or believed in fate too much. However, when I found you, I had to wonder if there was an underlying something I don't understand. I've given up on Mary Beth coming home, and couldn't find any reason to sit and wait for her any longer. When I saw you in the road, I was on my way home to give my life to nature and become compost in the forest. Now, fifteen years after she walked out, you come in. Maybe my purpose in life now is to do one final good act, if I can."

Stunned, Emily looked at him, "My God, Jim, you can't do that. I believe a lot of people would miss you. You're a good man. Don't talk like that. Promise?"

Smiling, he said, "Well, at least I've got you now. Is there any more to the story?"

Bella jumped up on the sofa to be closer to her. Scratching the dog's ears, she went on, "The Ellsworths are transplants from an Amish community. They got married and decided to live in the outside world, but are still close to the rest of their family on the farm. Rosalie is there, hiding with an Amish family in Wisconsin. She's adopted the family's name, and as long as she fears being taken by her father, if you could call him that, she will stay there. She has a lot of problems, and the last I heard, she was still waking up screaming. They're trying to soothe her with prayer and stuff, and if it works I might even become Amish."

Jim sighed, "Let's get that car pulled out and think about what we can do. He shooed Bella off the sofa and pulled Emily to her feet. "Get suited up, Ma'am. It's mighty cold out there."

The three of them got the GMC truck out to the highway where the Impala was still marooned. The snowplow driver had taken special care to avoid swamping it, and Jim thought he should fillet a few walleye for him also. He had to crawl underneath to find a place to hook up the chains without damaging anything. Emily crawled into the cold Chevy and took Bella with her.

Shaking his head, Jim mumbled, "Damn, I think she's stolen my dog."

It took a while and some clever maneuvering, but the old car finally crawled out onto the frozen roadway. It was out of gas, and having done this many times before, Jim knew enough to bring jumper cables and a can of gas with him. However, the car had been sitting too long and wouldn't even turn over, so he'd have to tow it home dead. It took a couple of hours but eventually the parade pulled into his driveway where he parked the heap in front of his garage.

He had an old Case tractor in the shed that he used to plow his driveway. Emily sat in the Impala while Jim used the blade on the tractor to push her car into the garage. In this cold it would be impossible to fix it, but at least it was safe and off the highway.

In awe of the huge machine, Emily jumped up on the Case with him, "This is so neat. It even runs."

"Of course it runs, but like a woman, you have to treat it right." Jim showed her how to work the hydraulics and how to control the plow, and since she wasn't ready to come in yet, he told her to clear the drifts out of the long driveway. Calling to her perched high up on the seat, he yelled, "See if you can clear out the mailbox without running over it."

"Oh, cool. Awesome man, totally awesome." And away she went with Bella sitting beside her. The tractor bucked a few times, and she had to grind it back into life, but she caught on quickly. She lowered the blade, and when the throttle was cranked open, it punched diesel smoke and fumes into the cold air.

Jim, muttered to himself, "What an amazing girl." The big rumbling engine on the Case told him where they were, and as long as he heard it, he was satisfied they were safe.

● ● ● ● ● ● ● ● ● ● ● ● ● ● ● ●

WHEN EMILY AND BELLA CAME IN FROM the cold, he had a pot roast in the oven. The scent pulled them into the kitchen to snoop at the meal, and opening the oven they both had their tongues out. They sat and had a beer while the roast and potatoes cooked, and Jim unfolded his plan, hoping she'd buy it.

"When Mary Beth left, I had a trace put out to find her. I wouldn't force her to come home if she didn't want to–I just wanted to know she was safe. A social worker from town got involved and made noises about my being unfit and forcing the girl out. Well, that went away pretty soon, and believe it or not, she and I started dating. Her name is DeAnna Wishoult. Polish name I think. I haven't seen her for awhile, and she made it clear I wasn't going to be her soul mate. She didn't want to get involved with a cop, and it might interfere with her career. No trace of Mary Beth ever came up, so I just fell back into my own life, waiting and hoping she'd show up some day."

"Yeah, that's cool, Jim, but where's the frigging plan?"

"My idea is to get DeAnna to look into your ex's ability to get your daughter. With his background, somebody has to see the fish in there."

Based on her experience, her rejection was blunt, "No, keep the social workers out of it. All they want is a good placement record. There has to be something better."

"Well, I have another thought. I'd like to put a trace on what's his name."

"Roger Parkhurst."

"Yeah. We can do that without arousing anyone. At least we'll see where he is."

"That's a start. Do you want to meet Rosalie?"

"I'd love to. Are you sure you want me to?"

"Yes. I want her to get to know you. Isn't that roast done yet?"

They wallowed in the pleasures of the roast, potatoes, gravy, and vegetables. Emily nagged him all the way through dinner for dousing the luscious meat with steak sauce.

"Damnation, woman, who's eating this, you or me?"

Against his strict orders, Emily fed Bella table scraps that almost equaled how much they ate. "Damn dog is as spoiled as you are, Missy."

With gravy oozing down her chin and waving a spoonful of mashed potatoes, she confirmed his comment with a muffled, "Yeah."

They sat by the fire after dinner was all cleaned up and just casually talked before Jim announced he was tired and went to bed. She followed him into his room, asking, "I hope you're not too tired? Merry Christmas, old man."

The next morning Jim leaped out of bed with a smile so wide it wouldn't fit through the doorway.

Poking her head from under the covers, her eyes were welded shut. In a raspy voice she asked, "What's making you so happy?" She knew but couldn't understand all the fuss over getting laid. A fleeting thought had her wondering if Stanley got his money back; probably not. She had to chuckle at the sight of Ma servicing him to pay him back.

With a spring to his step, Jim gleefully said, "I'm just so glad to find out that after all this time, it still works."

He put together sausage, pancakes with homemade blueberry syrup, and raisin toast. "The syrup came from an old guy who lives across the lake. In the springtime the blueberries are so thick it looks like a Smurf attack. You always have to watch for bears because they love the berries."

"Bears?"

"Oh, sure. When you find a pile of bear poop near the blueberries, you stick your finger into it to see if it's soft or hard. If it's hard, go ahead and start picking berries. If it's soft, it's new, and you get the hell out. You have to watch for moose also. They are, without a doubt, the nastiest, smelliest and meanest critters alive."

Teasing, she said, "Worse than you?"

"Yes, worse than me." Jim loved the banter; it put a bright light into everything, like Margaret used to do.

● ● ● ● ● ● ● ● ● ● ● ● ● ● ●

L ATER, THEY LOADED UP A SLED BEHIND THE Artic Cat snowmobile, and made their way out onto the frozen stretches of Tom Lake. Emily hung on behind, with Bella sitting on the tow-sled.

It took all of twenty minutes to catch ten good-sized walleye. Jim pulled in the first one and showed Emily what to do with the rest. She dragged them in as fast as he could get the minnow on her hook again. Listening to her squeal with excitement and watching her eyes dance in her head made him as happy as she was.

Back in the warm cabin, laced with some good coffee, he taught her how to fillet the fish. She was a natural at it and, possibly, better than he was. Next came the art of frying them to a golden brown. With his homemade tartar sauce, she compared the taste as satisfying as making love.

He looked at her with a wide grin, with her backing away. "Oh, no, Old Man, I'm not going to be responsible for your heart attack. You've had enough for awhile, and so have I. Don't you ever get tired?"

Evidently not.

The next day they drove into town to deliver the promised fillets to Sheriff Wally Stearns at the sheriff's station. Introducing Emily, "Wally, this is Emily, a very good friend of mine."

His eyes glued on Jim's new friend, Wally forgot to breathe for a moment. His mind spun into space, and he just stood still, looking incredibly stupid. Amused, Emily extended her hand to break his trance, "Hi, Wally, nice to meet you."

When Wally's brain found his mouth, he stuttered, "Hi, yeah, nice to um, meet you. Um, I'm Wally."

Suppressing an urge to laugh, Emily answered, "Yes, I gather that." Looking at Jim, Emily did her best to salvage Wally's pride, "Jim, why don't you give Wally the damn fish and get this over with."

Jim was having too much fun at Wally's expense to stop it, but did the decent thing. Handing the now smelly and dripping packages over, he said, "Give one package to Rusty also. They should get put in the freezer before all the cats show up."

Pointing to a chair for Emily, Jim took the other one. "Wally, we've got a situation here that needs some discretion. We can't have the authorities involved yet."

Wally had collected himself, and became a law enforcement officer again, saying, "I hate to break the news to you, Jim, but we *are* the authorities."

"Now don't go mucking this up with logic, Wally. Emily has a daughter that is in danger of being abducted by a sex pervert, and maybe even killed. Her ex-husband is a dirty cop in Minneapolis and has pulled some strings to cover his tracks, pointing to Emily as the perp. There's a sheet on her, and I need to keep her out of sight until this can be cleared up. You'll help us, won't you?"

"Jim, if she's wanted, why not let the system take care of it?"

Emily exploded, almost leaping across the desk to wring Wally's neck. Yelling, she blasted him with, "Because it's the goddamn *system* that screwed this up. Open your ears and listen to what you're being told. I can't get arrested because they'll give my daughter to the prick that wants to kill her. *Understand?*"

Reaching over to keep Emily from dismantling the sheriff, he said, "Hold on, Missy, don't stick your ass in the fan. We're here to help you, and nobody is going to turn you over to the authorities." To diffuse Emily's outburst, he turned to Wally, "Buddy, do you have any coffee made? Why don't you get us some?"

When he came back with three cups, Emily buttered up her outburst, saying, "I'm sorry. I've been on the run so long, I'm wound up kind of tight." Looking directly at Wally, she tilted her head slightly, saying, "Sorry, Wally."

Taken in by the girl's upsetting story, his compassion took over, and he said, "Don't worry about it. I guess you've earned a right to be upset."

Sipping the incredibly bad coffee, they chatted about possible avenues they could take without jeopardizing Emily and Rosalie. Finally, Emily stood up, announcing, "I can't drink this puke; it tastes like an enema." Without asking, she stepped to the coffee pot and threw out Wally's weak concoction.

Wally looked wide-eyed at Jim, who just grinned.

Bringing them each a new cup of coffee, Wally sipped and smiled. Looking at Emily, he said, "If you want a job as coffee maker here, I'm sure I could fit you in."

Emily's response, "Let's hope you catch bad guys better than you make coffee." Wally and Emily exchanged a soft glance that lasted a bit longer than necessary.

Getting back to business, Wally strode over to his computer screen and set up a surveillance site on Roger Parkhurst. "Now, if he uses a credit card or his social security number, or does anything with his name attached to it, we'll get a download. Also, his records and any files attached to his name will come through. Someone may notice the transfer, but they won't be able to tell where it came from." Pushing back, satisfied, he turned to them, proud of his work.

Impressed, Emily asked, "Can't anyone just go into your website and see what's there?"

Still grinning, Wally answered, "Only if they know the password."

Emily moved her chair closer to him, asking, "What's the password?"

Getting nervous at the closeness, he managed to answer, "Kumquat." His grin showed more fear than pleasure.

In unison, Jim and Emily said, "Kumquat?"

"Yeah, you know, those little orange football-shaped things. Clever, huh?"

Then in a move that paralyzed the hapless sheriff, Emily put her hand on his leg, and said, "It certainly is sheriff. Clever is the word." Turning to Jim, "Are we done here?"

To Wally's disappointment, he answered, "Yeah, I guess so." Then, quickly adding, he asked, "Have you seen DeAnna Wishoult, Wally?"

"Hell, Jim, she's been in the Twin Cities for almost a year now. Some kind of family services thing down there. You've been stuck in the woods too long."

Surprised and feeling sorry for the mess he left her with, Jim felt bad she was gone. "Too bad, but anyway, we'll be checking with you on any information that comes back on Parkhurst."

"Jim, you've got to level with me at all points. I don't want to get my tit squeezed by being dumber than I really am. Tell you what though, to keep this thing on the up and up so there's no fallout, I'm going to make you a deputy and assign a 'Senior Officer Eyes Only' status to it."

Jim questioned, "What the hell is 'Senior Officer Eyes Only'"?

"I don't know, but it will keep all our efforts in bounds and authorized. I just made it up. Get your old badge out of mothballs. And for God's sake, keep me informed."

Before he got up to leave, Jim shot back his last comment, "You just want to be my boss, and when are you going to learn how to make coffee?"

Back in the cabin, Jim and Emily made pepperoni pizza. While it did its rising and baking, they drank beer and Emily won three dollars from him playing rummy with cards that were bent, torn and wrinkled. "If there were fifty two cards here, you might win once in awhile, Old Man."

That night Jim got another Christmas present. In the morning, before getting out of bed he had a suggestion for her. "Why don't you just sleep here every night, Honey?"

Afraid of getting too involved, she said, "I don't think you can handle me every night. Besides, I already said we'd never be lovers, like that, anyway. I don't want it to become commonplace. It has to be special."

"You are special, in a lot of ways. You sleeping in the same bed with me doesn't mean there's always a boink attached to it. I just like you being here. Besides, it's cold outside, and you're nice and warm."

Rather than answer what he was asking, she had something else she needed to know. "Tell me about Wally. Is he married?"

"No, Honey, he's not. You sure played a game on him in his office. Are you trying to brand him or maybe just confuse him?"

Quiet for a moment, she slid out of bed, saying, "I don't know. I don't think I need another man in my life right now." Before getting dressed, she leaned over him to kiss him lightly, "Except for you; you're special. I don't ever want to be without you, Jim. I think I love you, you old goat. You're my friend, and I've never had a friend I could say that to."

CHAPTER 9
THE FARM, THE SHERIFF AND THE LAWYER

● ● ● ● ● ● ● ● ● ● ● ● ● ● ● ● ● ●

FTER A CALL TO THE ELLSWORTHS, Jim, Emily, and Bella drove to the Amish farm in Wisconsin. Through Hovland, Grand Marais, Duluth, and Superior, and along the northern border of Wisconsin, they approached the charming town of Bayfield. The farm was located in the rolling hills of fertile land, and even covered with snow, it had a quaint and peaceful feeling. At first, they were greeted with curiosity and mild respect, until it became known that the mother of the new disturbed girl was here. At that point, the warmth of the Amish greeting was overwhelming. Bella jumped out and made the rounds getting pets and scratches from most of the kids. They were shown to a large dining hall with long tables covered with sparkling white cloths, all ready for lunch.

A pleasant woman kept them busy with small talk while someone went to get Rosalie. The Amish woman told them," You realize that if she doesn't want to see you, she won't be forced to. She's had a very hard time escaping her past and adapting to the new life we've offered her. Rosalie is a warm and gracious child, and we think there has been some progress. Also, I want to emphasize that when she reaches the point where she is able to be a dependent adult, if she chooses to stay with us, we will support her. You must understand that may be a conflict with you."

Jim spoke, "You seem to know what needs to be done with her fears. Is that all from a religious teaching?" He was familiar with the Amish and knew they could be difficult to deal with if backed into a corner.

"If you mean faith, yes, partly. I've been working closely with her myself. Let me assure you we don't use voodoo or unorthodox methods. I was educated at the Harvard School of Medicine and hold a doctorate in psychology. She is in good hands."

"I'm thoroughly impressed," he replied.

The woman, who gave her name as Sister Alysia, nodded to a young skinny boy standing at the door. He poked his head out, mumbled something, and stood aside.

A young girl dressed in a black gown with a white bonnet tied under her chin, slowly walked into the dining hall. She hesitated, and step by step, advanced to where the group was standing. At first, the child just stared, a concerned knit to her brow. She stumbled one step forward, then shouted, "Mommy," and ran to jump on Emily, wrapping herself around her mom.

"Rosalie, my baby. Oh, Rosalie," kneeling down to her daughter's level, Rosalie buried her face in Emily's neck and cried for joy.

They stayed coupled for a long time, until Emily took her child's hand and led her away to a bench at a dining table.

"Honey, I've missed you so much. I've been hiding so you're father wouldn't find me and know where you were. That man I came with is Jim. He's a policeman who is helping us. We still have to hide, but some day we'll be able to be together and not be afraid."

"I know, Mommy. I know what the evil is and why I'm here. It's really nice and the people are friendly. We always have food and are warm. Every night when I go to bed, I look at the cards you sent. Sister Alysia told me everything. I know I have to stay here longer to be safe. I don't want that happening to me anymore."

Holding her daughter close, she spoke softly into her ear. "I'm going to see you more often, Honey. See Jim, over there. He's a very good and honest man. Don't ever be afraid to go to him. I trust him, and you need to also."

Rosalie gave Jim a long look and smiled at him. Jim returned her smile with a simple nod of his head.

Sister Alysia stepped up to them, "I'm afraid she has to go now. All the children have chores, and Rosalie is needed in the kitchen for serving duties. It's all part of our life that we adhere to firmly."

Emily gave her a giant hug and smothered her with a kiss. "Bye Mommy. Please be safe. I love you." The youngster went up to Jim and held her hand out. "Please take care of my mommy, and thank you, Jim. She told me I could always trust you."

"You bet, Rosalie. I'm your friend, and I'll help keep you safe."

Sister Alysia stepped up to Jim and Emily, "We don't get visitors very often, but we'd like to invite you to dine with us. It will give you a few more moments with Rosalie. In this case, we'll allow her to sit with the grown-ups."

As a guest, Jim was prompted to give the blessing. Totally at a loss for any phrase that would be fitting, he announced, "I'm honored to be allowed to dine with you, and to be asked to bless the meal. If I try to put a proper prayer together it will be immediately obvious that I don't know one. Instead, I would like to ask the Lord to bless all of you wonderful people and especially Sister Alysia. I would ask Him to give Rosalie strength, and to guide her mother in her quest for safety and justice."

The crowd at the table murmured, "Amen." Brother Samuel, at the head of the table nodded his approval, "Very well done, Mr. Cooper."

The meal was simple, but plentiful. At the end, Rosalie was to help clear the table and assist in the kitchen again. She hugged her mom and even gave Jim a squeeze. Smiling, she turned and waved to her mom, then disappeared through large swinging doors.

Bella was outside playing with some kids who evidently didn't have kitchen duties. "Say bye, Bella. Let's go." The large dog leaped into the back seat of the truck and spread slobber on the window.

The trip back home was quiet, and Jim drove slower than normal. Coming to the outskirts of Grand Marais, he surprised her, "Lets go on a date. I want to treat you to a fine dinner."

Being practical, she said, "We can eat at home."

"I want to treat you, okay?"

"Dinner out sounds good, Mr. Cooper, you got a favorite place?"

In the middle of town he turned left onto the Gunflint Trail. Fifty-five miles up a lonely deserted road was a first-class restaurant, The Trails End, that sports a fudge factory next to it. In the middle of desolation, pine trees and moose poop, the parking lot was full. They had to sit at the bar for a half hour waiting for a table.

"Jim, this is awesome. Where'd all these people come from? This is the wilderness."

"Locals with a taste for good food served on a paper plate. Try the prime rib. It's like you say, *awesome, man.* Au gratin spuds to kill for."

They followed the waitress to a small table in a back corner. "Janice, could you bring us another Windsor Coke?"

"Sure Jim. Good to see you again."

Emily's eyes followed the waitress as she walked away, then goading Jim into a conflict, "Good to see you again? One of your conquests?"

Raising his eyebrows, "Conquest? I should be so lucky. Janice lives in a cabin a few miles from here. No electric or running water. Her grandpa left her the place, and she snowshoes here everyday. She's got a degree in journalism, and is working on a book about woodsy stuff or something. Nice gal. Nice butt too."

Janice brought the drinks and left a friendly smile for Emily. Sneering behind the waitress' back, she launched her rocket again. "Well, Mr. Cooper. Let's settle something."

Jim braced himself for one of her serious forays. "What's to settle?

"What's going on with us? What are we? Lovers, shack-uppers, where do I fit in here?"

"Whatever happened to being friends?"

The glint in her eye came back betraying her serious look. "Yeah, well, we can be friends." After toying with her swizzle stick a moment, the glint got brighter, "Is there such a thing as boinking friends?"

"Dad gummit Missy, you're doing everything you can to pull my chain tonight. I'm not going to let you provoke me. I'm in a good mood, and you aren't going to spoil it. I've been around long enough to know when a game is being played, and you, my horny little friend, are playing a game."

Feigning a deep hurt, she chided, "What do you mean horny, you old goat?"

Smiling at her, he understood her dilemma. He changed the encounter with a soft tone, "Missy, if you want to get involved with Sheriff Wally, just do it." In a turnaround again, he smirked, "Hell's bells, you might as well screw up his life, too."

She folded her napkin over her hand so the other diners couldn't see her lift her middle finger. With a sneering giggle, he said, "Missy, if I was younger, I'd be married to you by now. Let's be realistic. I'm sixty-eight years old. I could be your grandfather. Besides, you're moving things around in your heart for our sheriff. You're free to do what you want. You know all this already, and I suspect you need to hear it once in a while. Honey, my home, my life and anything else I have is yours. Ours is a strange relationship, you know. It's confusing, but you've wormed your way into my heart, and I'll never be without you. Hell, you've already won over my dog."

"You're pretty smart for an old man. I have a real thing about having a place to call my own. I need roots, Jim, and I've found them here."

She had ordered the prime rib and gave him a boatload of grief when he had the hamburger steak. "Damn it all to hell woman, I'm the one eating the damn thing." But she was so busy gorging, she tuned him out.

She was careful to save a nice piece of beef for her new dog, and kept reaching over to pick at Jim's French fries. On the way out they got a big box of fudge to munch on the way home.

The next morning Bella wouldn't get up for her usual potty run. She was listless and moaned a lot. "Hey, Girl; what's with you? This isn't like her, Missy. She's not doing good. Maybe something she found in the woods." The dog quivered and barfed on the floor.

Emily was on the floor holding the dog's head, "All I gave her was the meat and fudge. She shoul ..."

"Oh, shit, you gave her fudge? Missy, don't ever give a dog chocolate, it poisons them." He made an effort to control his voice so he didn't scare the girl. His temper reeling, Jim calmly told her, "I'm sorry. I shouldn't have busted on you like that. She'll be all right. We have to go to Duluth to talk with a lawyer about the charges against you. We'll get Wally to watch her while we're gone."

Devastated by what she had done, Emily tearfully asked, "Jim? I didn't know about the chocolate." On her knees, she buried her nose in Bella's neck fur, "I'm sorry, Baby. Please get well."

Softly, Jim reassured her, "She'll be just fine, Missy. Don't worry about it."

Looking up, she said, "I'm such a bonehead."

Trying to assure her everything would be all right, he said, "She's got a strong constitution. Bella will be fine, Honey. Stay with her and talk to her. She'll come around."

Emily slept on the floor that night, cradling the large dog in her arms. If she slept at all, it was minimal, as she spent most of the time stroking and whispering to Bella. In the morning, the trip to Grand Marais was quiet and morose. Emily sat cross-legged on the truck seat with Bella's head on her lap.

Her soul was hanging as low as it could get when she looked at Jim, she said, "I'm such a fuck up, Jim. I can't do anything right. If Bella dies because of me, I don't want to be reminded of it every day. This was her home, and she was fine until I came along."

He had been expecting her feelings to come out lower than ancient dirt, and tried to bolster her with, "We all live and die. You, me, Bella and even Rosalie and Sister Alysia. The purpose of life is to make a circle, then we get off and someone else gets on. I made you a promise I would do all I could to help you and your daughter. I'll make another one that I'm just as sincere about."

He reached for her hand and vowed, "I promise you, from my heart, if Bella doesn't make it I will never, ever blame you in any way. Deal?"

"I know, Jim. I know you're right, but how do I keep from blaming myself?"

"By accepting fate as your master. If it's Bella's time to go, it's quite simply, her time."

Behind her pathetic smile, she asked, "How do I get smart like you?"

He smiled and felt the little pieces of his world come together again. "Live a long time, and put your love in the right places."

Engrossed in his concern for how she was feeling, his attention had been in a different place today. Just now he took another look at her, doing a double take. Puckering, he slowly whistled, chiming, "My oh my, what has my little friend done to herself? Missy, my dear, you are beautiful."

Turning a shade of light pink, she smiled and said, "Shut up, you old goat." Glancing at him, the pink turned red, and the grin became a smile, "All right, so I took a shower and got clean, so what?"

Emily had finally combed her hair straight back into a ponytail that showed off her face and the Nordic glow it sported. Her dark blue eyes and the little ski-jump nose that held a few freckles gave her a sensuous, yet happy look. "So I'm clean. Let's drop it."

Grinning as she slid down into the seat, she mumbled, "Stupid old fart."

Not done with his taunting, he ground on her some more, "If I had known this was hidden under that blonde mop I would have locked you up for myself. Is this for our sheriff?"

The grin turned into a smile and then a laugh that rocked through the cab of the truck, giving Bella cause to perk up and lick the fresh new face. Emily was alive and radiant, and best of all she was happy. "What sheriff? I just combed my hair, you idiot. Leave me alone."

Almost to Grand Marais, she broke the silence, "Am I good enough for him, Jim? He seems like such a nice guy. Why would he want someone who's been knocked around so much? Besides, I absolutely cannot get involved until Rosalie is safe and well."

Slowing down so he didn't get to the sheriff's station too soon, he told her, "Yes, he is a nice guy. And if you ever wanted a good husband and a father for your daughter, you couldn't find a better man. Don't worry about your past. If love grows into this thing, that's all either of you need."

His next comment earned him a punch in his arm. "He might as well suffer like the rest of us."

As they entered the sheriff's station, Emily was walking behind Jim so Wally didn't see her at first. Happy to see his old friend, Wally started his greeting, "Hi, Jim, good to ..., oh, my. Hi Emily."

Wally's tongue had filled his mouth, making it impossible to speak fluently. Stammering at the sight of her, all he could get out was, "Umb, oh, ah, mmm."

Bingo, she knew her clean-up effort had worked. Now to twist him up a little bit, she chirped, "Nice to see you too, Sheriff. Have you learned to make coffee yet?" Not waiting for an answer, or invitation, she marched to the counter and did the job herself.

Wanting to get down to business, Jim sat at the computer trying to access the site. "What's wrong with this thing? I can't get in."

Wally, assuming his important stature, told him, "It's called security, Jim. Not like the old days. I set up a secure site for SOEO.com. You remember, Senior Officer Eyes Only?"

Amused as well as confused, Jim said, "You're for real, aren't you!"

"You bet boss. Let me show you how to access it." Wally sat down and flew over the key pad. "The password is *kumquat*, and we three are the only people that know it. This is a secured site that can't be infiltrated from the outside without the password."

Scratching his head, Jim asked, "Does it have to be *kumquat*?"

"Don't fight progress, Jim."

Emily brought them coffee, making a slight effort to let her fingers brush Wally's as she handed it to him. "Careful, it's hot," she warned.

Wally's tongue got hard again, and he was afraid to look at her. But, he did anyway.

The screen jumped to the website, and Jim casually mumbled, "Okay Chief. You're in charge. Let's see if we've got any bites." And indeed they did.

Emily stood behind them, her elbows resting on both chairs. Feeling her breath on the back of his neck made Wally extremely nervous. As she pointed to different items on the screen, she brushed against him, and at one point rested her hand on his shoulder. All seemingly innocent, but deep in Emily's head, her thought was, *Gotcha!*

The sheriff forced his attention back to what Jim was reading from the computer screen. "Roger Parkhurst was arrested and charges were dropped when he agreed to lead the police to a pornography ring leader. The warrant against Emily Parkhurst is for flight on the assault charge, still pending, plus parental kidnapping. It also says that Emily Parkhurst is wanted for questioning in the pornography case. You're standing in a pile of shit, Missy."

The three sat in Wally's office for a long stretch of uncomfortable silence. Emily spoke first. "Maybe I should just go and face it. As long as Rosalie's safe, I can take whatever they give me."

Wally was absorbing all he could to put a complete story together. "There would be some jail time Emily, and the kidnapping charges would bury you."

She shot him a lost and longing look, wondering why she was sitting here talking to strangers about her problems. When she thought of Rosalie living with strangers, she broke down crying.

Embarrassed, she got up to leave. "I'm sorry. I don't belong here."

Jim, louder than he intended, yelled, "Shut up and put your little ass back in that chair. I told you before, we're going to help you, and if you help us, it'll be a damn sight easier. Now, my little squirrel, instead of running away all the time, accept what we're trying to do."

Wally, wide-eyed at the whole thing, as well as Emily's good looks, asked, "And what is it that we're trying to do, Jim?"

"Don't go mucking this up with logic, Wally. We need to come up with a plan."

They sat again in silence, sipping the rest of the coffee until Jim spoke, "I'm going to Minneapolis and get into the middle of this thing. I need to be reinstated as a full deputy so I can move in official channels, and Missy, we're going to Duluth to get you a lawyer."

Wally smiled, "Sounds like a good start, Deputy Cooper. Any questions Emily?"

"Yes. When are you going to learn how to make coffee?"

Wallace Stearns was surrounded. "Why don't the two of you just leave me alone?" He agreed to take care of Bella while Jim and Emily were in Duluth. He'd rather take care of Emily and send Jim and Bella to town, but he kept his mouth shut.

Just then the dispatcher opened the door, "Wally…, sorry, I didn't know you had anyone in here."

Jim got up and extended his hand to the rookie. "Jim Cooper. I used to be the big poop around here, Son."

"Oh, sure; I've heard a lot about you. Glad to have you around, Sir."

While acknowledging Jim, the dispatcher's eyes were stuck on Emily. Wally, trying to establish a level of professional behavior, said, "Ted Marks, this is Emily. She'll be around here once in awhile, so do your best to make her comfortable."

Mumbling, "Oh, yeah," with his attention totally on Emily.

"Ted, are you busy out there?" Wally reminded the dispatcher what he was here for today, so Ted gathered his pride and backed out, shutting the door behind him, taking a last peek at Emily.

In Duluth, Jim and Emily checked into an EconoLodge motel and called Leonard Walburn, his friend and lawyer. Then Jim announced, "Missy, if you're going to start messing around with men, we're going to Walmart to get you some decent clothing. We can't see Len until tomorrow anyway. By the way, do you like Chinese food?"

"If you'd been paying attention you'd figure out I like anything that's food. And I don't want to go to Walmart."

"Yes, you do want to go to Walmart. You've been wearing the same stuff for over a month. What's wrong with you?"

"I don't want you spending all your money on me. I feel guilty."

Jim pulled her into his arms in a good old bear hug. "What else have I got to do? What I'm doing for you isn't free, you know."

Her face buried in his chest, he picked up her muffled response, "Aha, I knew there were strings attached."

"You bet your cute little ass there are strings attached. In return you have learn to live with me as long as you want, love my dog because she's yours now, get out of trouble and be with your daughter, and understand how happy I am you're here."

She quit struggling to get loose and put her arms around his big body, "Chinese?"

Emily changed into some of the Walmart loot before the two walked the few blocks to an obscure, but excellent chop suey joint. She ordered plum wine over his protest on not being able to drink beer, telling him, "Sooner or later you have to become civilized, old man. Now, shut up and enjoy it." He embarrassed her to tears by making a fuss over ensuring there were no mushrooms in his chow mien. The two bickered, squabbled, argued, and laughed themselves silly throughout the whole meal.

Everyone at nearby tables was smiling at the folly of their relationship. Most people took them for a very close father/daughter team, and some thought she was much too young to be having such a good time with such an old man.

The waiter finally caught on that they weren't going to get into a fight and joined in the enjoyment of two very happy people. When the bill and the fortune cookies came, Jim told her, "You have to take the one closest to you so you don't screw up fate."

"How much more screwed up can it get?" She cracked hers open and hid it, along with her smile.

"It's not supposed to be sad. What's it say, Missy?"

Ignoring him she responded, "What's yours say?"

He pretended to read, "You will get very lucky tonight."

"Bullshit." She grabbed it from him and read, "There are many stars, but the brightest one is close." Smirking, she added, "Who comes up with these things?"

As they left, he picked hers off her plate and put it in his pocket. Back at the motel she went into the bathroom, so he took out the little piece of paper and read, "Hold tightly to what you cherish, and let loose of what you fear."

Pondering this counsel, he thought: That's not a real happy fortune, but not so bad. Seems like good advice.

Coming out of the bathroom, she saw the fortune in his hand.

He worried about her reaction to the saying and asked, "Are you superstitious? This doesn't seem so bad."

She took the small piece of paper from him, looked at it again and threw it away. "I've been trying to lose what I fear and just got buried deeper. I'm tired of running, Jim. I'm tired of waiting to go to jail and fearing for my daughter's safety. I'm tired of making other people worry about me and my problems. I'm just tired."

He held her gently and tried to comfort her. "You're not alone anymore, Honey. You've got friends now."

● ● ● ● ● ● ● ● ● ● ● ● ● ● ● ● ● ● ●

THE NEXT MORNING THEY SAT IN Leonard Walburn's office talking to a very angry lawyer. "Dammit to hell, Jim, this girl is a fugitive—and you want me to help her? Let the law straighten it out."

"Len, it's the law that got it all screwed up. Pay attention to what we told you. She's a victim of the system and needs our help. Her daughter is in real danger."

Calming down, the lawyer sat back, "I know, I know. Okay, I am officially your lawyer. Don't talk to anyone or do anything stupid without talking to me first. That's the only way I'll work, and if you break that rule, you're on your own. No questions or ifs ands or buts. Agree?"

Emily, in a fit, got red. "Aren't you supposed to be working for us? How do we know you can help, and I don't like being controlled and told what to do. I've been framed, and it shouldn't be that hard for a lawyer to untangle it. I didn't do anything wrong, and I'll go to jail before I turn my daughter over to a child molester."

The lawyer let Emily know exactly where he stood. "Maybe you're right and maybe you're lying. I don't care. My job is to see that these charges are dropped. That's all."

Jim, trying to calm her down and let Len know they would work with him, admonished her, "Jesus St. Jenny, you little squirrel. Learn to trust the people who are trying to help you. Start thinking about Rosalie–and keep your mouth shut."

Setting back into the chair, she knew she was wrong, and to appease them, she admitted it. "Sorry. The lawyer I hired to help me with the case against Roger was a crook, so I'm drawn to think that all you guys are alike. I promise I won't cause any problems. Well, not too many."

Len spoke to Jim as if Emily wasn't even there, "Jim, I'm taking this as a favor to you. Keep her under control, or I'll take your money and close the door. I know where this is going, and it's going to get messy."

Turning to Emily, "Stay out of sight and do what you're told. Yes, the system is screwy and good people get hurt, but smart people are working for you."

Jim nodded and put his hand on Emily's shoulder. "We'll do anything you say, Len." Sternly he added, "Won't we."

Shrugging, with a serious attempt to look submissive, she said, "Yeah, yeah. Don't worry, I'll be a good girl." However, she couldn't hold back her sneer for the lawyer. She forced a polite smile and thought about hitting him with one of his silly desk ornaments.

It was time for the lawyer to get to work, "Give me a thousand bucks, go home, and I'll call you when I get something."

On their way out of the office, Carla, Len's secretary, held out her hand to stop Emily. The gravel in her voice contradicted the sincerity of her advice, "He's a good lawyer, Honey. He'll take care of you."

Surprised, yet pleased, Emily smiled and said, "Thanks. I have a problem with trust lately."

Outside, on the way to the parking lot, she screamed through her teeth and waved both fists in the air. "A thousand dollars?" She put her hand in his pocket and had to double step to stay up with him.

Mostly they were silent on the way home, except for a brief moment. She had been staring at passing telephone poles and the bleakness of the cold day until she said, "Jim?"

"What's on your mind, little one?"

She looked at him with a tremendous amount of love and respect, saying, "Thanks."

In an inexplicable moment, their hands met on the seat between them, entwined in a common bond.

CHAPTER 10
THE FINAL BOND

EMILY AND JIM KNEW ROSALIE was safe on the farm. Sister Alysia, as well as the guardianship of the rest of the Amish family, had her under their wing. She was counseling her, and some days could see the glimmer of hope that Rosalie could become a somewhat well-adjusted child. Jim and Emily made frequent trips to see her, and occasionally, Emily would be allowed to spend an overnight with her. On these trips Emily went alone, but made certain to never set a pattern that could be followed by anyone else. Jim gave her some schooling on how to detect if she was being tailed—and how to lose one.

Like the wussie winter, except for the temperature, March went out like a lamb. April Fool's day was warm and sunny, and Jim thought he had put off fixing the old Impala long enough. He charged up the battery, did some cursory checking on things he could reach, and called the Cobblestone Garage in Grand Marais. It finally started and spit a black cloud of smoke all over the yard.

Waving his arms through the murk, he wailed, "Good grief, Missy why don't we just leave it sitting there for mosquito control?"

Ignoring his being engulfed in the smoke, she was ecstatic over the car actually starting after all this time. Raising her arms in joyful triumph, she wailed, "*Waa-hooooo.*"

Watching her delight at seeing the Impala come to life again, a thought clouded the back of Jim's mind, and he was afraid to ask a very simple question. Cornering her, he solemnly asked, "Emily, if we can get this car to run again, what are your plans?"

Her answer was disturbingly somber. "I don't know, Jim. What should I do?"

He slowly lowered himself onto an old wooden chair that had graced the yard for years, and replied, "You know you are free to do what you want, and go wherever your heart takes you. If you decide to leave, I'll give you everything I can to help you. If that's what you choose, I'll send my love and blessings along. But, I want you to know that you not being here will be the one of the worst things that's ever happened to me."

"You've had people leave you before, Jim. You survived."

"My wife was sick for a long time, and I had a chance to get ready for it. Mary Beth left me with a hole I could drive the tractor through, but she left with hate and anger. That's a different hurt. You gave me life, Emily. You kept me from dying in the woods. You make me happy just knowing you are here. No, you aren't tied here, but I will never love anyone like I love you, and there is no bandage for that. Please don't leave. Not yet."

She straddled his lap with her arms around his thick neck, "I'm not going anywhere, you old poop. I love you too, Jim, and I wouldn't know what to do without you."

The weight of both strained the old weather-worn chair. They held each other for a long time. The two people, so different in life, and so similar in heart, became one in love and friendship, joined forever, even after death, in the final bond.

She followed in the truck as he nursed the Impala thirty miles to the garage.

Speaking to the head mechanic, "Yes, Clovis I know it's a piece of shit, but I want it cherry when you're done with it. Tires, get the radio to work, alignment, and hell, even wash it. Okay?"

"Your money, Jim. I'll screw the tail pipe if you'll pay for it."

"If you need it that bad, go for it. Keep in mind, it's a boy car."

Disgusted with the conversation so far, Clovis finished it, "You even ruin my fantasies, Sheriff. Come back in a week. Bring a lot of money with you. It's about time I got even with you for that DWI."

Jim put his hand on Clovis' shoulder, "You still clean, Buddy? How's Doreen?"

"Thanks to you, Sheriff, I'm cool, and that's all Doreen needs. We're gonna have a baby."

Feeling satisfied that at one time he actually did some good for the community, Jim left and Emily drove them home. "I'm going to Minneapolis, Squirt.

I need to see if I can dig into Roger's doings and find out what's going on. Maybe see if an old friend of mine can help."

"Cool, when do we leave?"

"The only thing you've got wrong is the *we* part. I'm going alone. You need to stay here and watch Bella and hold down the fort. See if you can get Rosalie out for an overnight at your house for a change."

She smiled and reached over to squeeze Jim's huge hand. "Thanks, I'd like that."

The Impala was finished so Jim took it to Minneapolis and left the truck for Emily. He knew the GMC wouldn't give her any trouble and wanted to see how good of a job Clovis did on the big Chevy. It cost him $1,752 but it purred like a sleeping lion, the big 454 engine swallowing gas with an unquenchable thirst. Clovis replaced the old AM/FM radio with a spare stereo with a cassette player he took out of his own car.

Jim didn't realize it but Clovis was less than generous with the radio switch. He claimed someone stole it, and let the insurance buy him a new one.

His first stop was to the northern Minneapolis suburb of Brooklyn Park to pay a call on Helen and George Ellsworth. Mrs. Ellsworth made coffee for them, and they sat on the patio talking for about an hour. He explained he was a deputy for the Cook County Sheriff's office, and a little bit about what he was doing in town. He didn't want to implicate them so he kept a distance with the information.

"Emily visits Rosalie as often as she can and hopes to have her back as soon as we clear up the mess she's in. She'll probably be going there this weekend, and if Sister Alysia says it's okay, she'll try to bring her home for a few days."

George Ellsworth sat up on the edge of his chair, "Well, Sheriff, that sounds good, except it may not be too awfully safe at the farm."

Frowning, Jim set his cup on the glass-topped table. "Explain that."

"Well, you know that Emily's house is just a few doors away, and Roger has been staying there. He came over a while ago and asked if we knew where his wife was. Of course we denied any knowledge of where anybody was, but he made us nervous by his even asking. He's a nasty one, he is. We've got no time for him."

"Why would that mean trouble at the farm?"

"He brought up our having been living there and asked where it was. He asked where our old car was, also. We told him we sold it to a stranger."

Helen Ellsworth broke in, "We didn't tell him where the farm was, or anything. We were really afraid he would do something to us, but he left then. George called the farm, and they said they would keep an eye out for trouble. Some of the children will be posted along the road as lookouts."

"Well, this is important. Thank you for bringing it up, and be sure to let them know that this Roger character can be dangerous." Getting up to leave, Jim asked, "Do you really want to sell the car?"

Jim gave them $500 for the beater, and then finished his business with, "If he mentions seeing the car out here, tell him the buyer came by with a question on the title. And here's my cell phone number. I won't tell you where I live because the less you know the better for you. If he, or anyone, ever asks about Emily or Rosalie, it's important that you call me."

Jim thanked them for the hospitality and went towards the door. "You may see me again around here. I'm going to keep an eye on the house to see if I can find out what that jerk is up to."

George added, "We certainly don't want any trouble, but we aren't going to let Emily or Rosalie get hurt. If there is anything we can do, just ask."

Jim smiled, "Just keep my number handy. Thank you."

Jim Cooper had been in law enforcement for a long time. He had a good reputation and is respected among his peers, and now Jim had a few favors to ask of an old friend. He took

Highway 169 south to St. Louis Park, a predominately Jewish community, and a clean and safe one. Turning off of Minnetonka Boulevard to Hampshire Avenue, he pulled up in front of a house that looked like every other one on the block. A simple bungalow in a row of other simple bungalows. Jim got out and shuddered at the closeness of the buildings.

Before he got to the front door, Art Peterson came out to greet him. Jim stuck his hand out to welcome his old partner, "Hi Buzz. What's shakin'?"

"Jim, Jim, Jim you old fart. I thought you'd be dead or locked in a whorehouse by now."

"Not a chance, Buddy. They kicked me out for eating up all the profits."

"Come on in before the neighbors see you and call a real cop."

"See me. Shit for shit, Buzzer, we're sitting on their laps. Don't you ever get claustrophobic living here?"

Waving off the remark, Art Peterson held the door open for his friend and former partner. At the kitchen table over a bottle of Grain Belt beer, "This can't be a social call, Jim. Our only contact since you started living with the squirrels is a corny Christmas card. And I didn't even get one of those this year."

"I wasn't sure I'd be alive by the time Christmas got here this year. I've been bumming about Mary Beth and just about gave it all up."

"Still no word, huh?"

"Nope. She's been swallowed up or something. I don't know. Something happened to me at Christmas, and I decided to quit looking. If she's alive, or at least curious, she'll come around, maybe."

"What's on your mind Jim? I've known you almost my whole life, and I know when there's something cooking in that old skull."

"Yeah, it's been a really long time since we graduated from West High School together. It's not even there anymore. Did you know my dad went there? Jesus, that was in the early twenties."

Art replenished the beer. "I think they tore it down in 1984, or near then. We almost never made the cut. We were both so drunk at the commencement, old lady Westby nearly kicked us out." They toasted Ms. Westby and a few other memories.

Jim explained what came into his life when he found Emily on the road. He confided to him about Rosalie at the Amish farm and the possible danger with Roger Parkhurst.

"I need to get a lock on this guy, Buzz. I need to find out what he's up to, and if he's looking for them. According to Emily, he's dirty and working underground. He could pop up anywhere. I also need to see what the scoop is behind the charges on Emily, and it has to be done without raising any flags."

"I don't know how effective I am anymore, but maybe we can pull a few strings. Tomorrow we can start turning some wheels. But for tonight, old buddy,

I've got a surprise for you. I know a couple of gals just itching for some action. They can pick up a pizza on their way over."

"Come on Buzz. I'm getting all the slider I need back home. Pizza's fine but we're too old to be doing that with strangers."

Buzz was already on the phone, and the deal was closed. They would have company tonight, like it or not. "They're not strangers, Jim. You remember Vivian Mackstrom? She was undercover vice for a few years until she got shot, then quit the force."

"Vivian Mackstrom? We went to school with her."

"Exactly. She's bringing her friend along."

"She's an old lady, Buzz. What's wrong with you?"

"Oh, that's funny, Jim. Take a look at yourself in case you forgot your weenie may be in a wheelchair tonight."

The two women came over, and they all laughed at old stories, reminiscing times gone by. The four horny geriatrics drank all of Buzz's beer and went out for more, plus a second pizza from Beeks on Minnetonka Boulevard. The women went home just after midnight when the two party boys both fell asleep on the living room floor. In the morning they would both have backaches, and the room would stink from old man farts.

● ● ● ● ● ● ● ● ● ● ● ● ● ● ● ● ● ●

South Minneapolis, the Uptown area

ROGER PARKHURST LEFT THE HOOKER'S apartment and stepped into a bright April sunshine. It was mid morning, and the traffic on Hennepin Avenue and Lake Street was in full congestion. The area, known as Uptown, was filled with trendy shops and coffee houses. Just a few blocks from fashionable Lake Calhoun, it attracted just about everyone.

Young women dressed in designer garments, and gay couples, strolled the avenue trying to make connections. The slime of society was hidden behind the facades of restored buildings, selling drugs, sex, and stolen electronic gadgets. The politicians showed off the redevelopment, and took pride in putting tax dollars to good use. When an attractive white girl got raped or murdered, there was an outcry and most always a speedy arrest. The unfortunate minorities were considered the crust and were cut away.

Roger forgot where he had left his car because he was stoned last night, so he walked three blocks to the pavilion at Lake Calhoun. He knew he could usually make a connection there and talk his way into a ride from somebody.

People knew him here, and he threw enough cash around to make the punks think he was important. But now, he had given the whore too much money on extra services and was short. Later, he'd invent a tip for the cop that came by and get some snitch money. It was also time to get another payoff from Frank. For now, he'd have to play on his reputation.

After the lucrative business of selling his daughter dried up, Frank forced him into working the underground. Roger Parkhurst became a ghost, an unknown entity floating among the evil and corrupt. His undercover status, however loosely held, was known only to Frank. To the cop on the beat, and the local population, Roger was just another slime ball.

He called to a skinny boy on a bicycle he thought would be anxious to do him a favor, "Hey, Donny, come here, punk."

Donny rode over but kept some space between them. "Hi Rog. Whatcha want?"

"You're my man, kid. I need a favor."

"I ain't doing no favors, man. I got busted last time, and you said you'd take care of any shit I caught. Now, all the fuzz in Uptown know me. I can't go no place without being watched."

"Come on Donny, I need you to find my car for me. You can even drive it back here, I'll give you twenty bucks."

"Screw you, man. I told you I ain't doin' nothing for you." Donny pushed off on his bike before Roger could grab him, and disappeared up Lake Street.

Muttering to himself, "Screw *you*, you little moron." He walked out to the dock where the rental canoes were kept, lit a cigarette, and sat on a bench. He had to get some money and find his car, he was flat broke, and had one cigarette left. "Shit."

Detective Gary O'Meara had been watching Roger since he left the hooker's apartment. He discovered Roger's car late last night and had it towed to the impound lot. It was time to put more squeeze on the would-be crook, and Detective O'Meara needed to get something done to satisfy the Lieutenant. The sting on Parkhurst had been going on too long, and the operation was going to be scuttled if something didn't surface.

Walking out to the boat launch dock, he sat next to Roger, "Good morning, Roger. Nice day."

"Hey, O'Meara. I've been looking for you. I got a tip."

"What you've got, Parkhurst, is shit in your pants if you think I'm paying for more fairy tales."

"Whoa, Man. I've always given you straight stuff. Come on O'Meara, I need some money."

"What you need, you two-bit fuck, is a wake-up call. C'mon, walk with me; I've got something to tell you."

They both walked slowly up Lake Street towards Hennepin Avenue where most of the shops were, to a small parking spot behind the Uptown Theater. "Hey, what the fuck is going on? This is where I left my car."

O'Meara had parked his car in the spot where Roger's was towed from. The detective told him, "Get the picture now? What I'm trying to tell you is that I'm the one pulling the strings, Roger. I had your car pulled into the impound lot after you went up to see Mandy. You can't afford her anyway. The money from me has dried up so you have to be your own whore."

Roger lit his last cigarette and leaned against the detective's car, saying, "I thought we were going to work together on that porno stuff. Then, I need to find Emily so I can get the reward."

O'Meara motioned to him, "Get in, I'll take you to the impound lot. Something's come up."

Moving slowly with the traffic, Gary handed Roger a half-full pack of Marlboro, then told him, "You were given immunity in exchange for leading us to the center of the pornography ring. You said you could prove your wife was running it, but so far we haven't got shit from you. If something doesn't come up soon, they're going to remove the immunity and bust you to put a finish on it."

"Hey, I can't help it she took a run. She's got the kid—and can't be that hard to find."

O'Meara pulled into the parking lot where Roger's car was held. There were a lot of loose ends connected to this pornography deal, but unaware of his undercover status, Gary was confused how Roger fit into it. Detective O'Meara had been handling cases for twelve years, and had never been so far out of the loop as he was with this one. Something was different now, and his gut reaction was to find out what. But, his gut also told him to be careful.

Shutting the engine off, he said, "Personally, I don't think your wife has any connection to any pornography dealings. Getting her involved was someone else's idea. Nobody tells me anything, just go out and catch a crook or two. Tell me Roger, just what is the connection between you and the Lieutenant?"

A light went on in Roger's head telling him there might be a problem with Detective O'Meara. Covering his concern, he answered lyrically, "He just loves me, Gary."

Gary responded, "Yeah, I suppose you love him too. I'll get a release on your car. There's been an inquiry on you from some hick-town sheriff. The closest our computer analyst can get is it came from up north—Duluth or maybe Grand Marais. He can't hack into the source, but is certain it came from there. If you want the reward money, you have to go find out if your wife is there."

When Roger got home he went straight to the telephone and punched a set of numbers. The ringing stopped. Only silence on the other end.

Quickly Roger spit out the message, "We have to meet."

After a short pause, the call was disconnected. Now, he just had to sit and wait until it was time for his one a.m. meeting with his boss, Lieutenant Frank Dawson.

Outside, a block away, Detective Gary O'Meara slouched in his car, sucking on a foam coffee cup from McDonalds. Playing with the last of his French fries, his gaze was glued to the front of Roger's house.

CHAPTER 11
A MAJOR PLAYER

● ● ● ● ● ● ● ● ● ● ● ● ● ● ● ● ● ● ● ●

WAKING UP ON BUZZ PETERSON'S living room floor, Jim had to roll over on his side to get up, which woke his sleeping headache. He was lying on top of the pizza box with crust pieces stuck to him, and his morning pee was screaming to get out.

"Jesus H. What else can go wrong?" Stepping over Buzz's snoring body, he raced to the bathroom.

Bracing himself in front of the toilet, he found the zipper but the fly in his shorts had disappeared. Desperation taking hold now, he dropped his trousers and shorts and let it go, splashing the seat cover. Looking at the clothing collected around his ankles, he saw his shorts were on backwards; fallout from last night. At Jim's advanced age, urination was not a steady forceful stream anymore. Patiently, after waiting for the final drip, drip, drip, he bent over and straightened out his wardrobe.

Arthur Buzz Peterson didn't cook and had no intention of starting now. Today, he managed to brew a pot of coffee to give them something to help wash the aspirin down. Jim came into the kitchen cinching his belt buckle and grabbed the cup of coffee that Buzz was holding.

Later, sitting in Denny's restaurant in front of a generic plate of breakfast, Jim asked, "Is this how you live? You keep this up, and I'll be at your funeral."

"At least I'd get a visit out of you." Pushing his sarcasm aside, "It just felt right, Jim. I don't get out much, and I was glad to see you. Like a celebration."

Jim sighed, "It's good to see you too, Buzz. It was good to see Vivian again. By the way, how did you happen run across her?"

Wiping egg smear from his face, Buzz answered, "Well, Jim, you know we dated in school, don't you?"

"Yeah, I know that, but how come you ... , oh no; you two aren't, you know, dating again are you?"

Smiling, Buzz said, "No, we've been ... well you know."

"No, I don't. If you two were seeing each other, why would she go home last night?"

Slow with his answer, Buzz told him, "Her husband isn't that understanding."

Frowning, Jim said, "You're going to get the shit kicked out of you, Buddy."

Pushing his plate away, Jim got down to business. "Well, if you can keep your zipper pulled up for awhile, I'd like to know if you have any connections left in the department. I need to get a handle on this Parkhurst guy, but I don't know anyone."

Scratching his chin, Buzz thought, "They don't take too kindly to us has-beens wandering around the station, but I think I remember which door to go in. Let's just go down there and see what we can dig up.

"That's not too encouraging, Buzz, but it's a start. Let's go downtown to see if you still have any friends that will talk to you, and won't shoot you for screwing their wives."

● ● ● ● ● ● ● ● ● ● ● ● ● ● ● ● ●

WHILE LAST NIGHT'S PARTY AT BUZZ'S HOUSE was in progress, Roger Parkhurst sat in his Olds 88 waiting for the meeting with Lieutenant Frank Dawson to take place. He always got there early to be sure there were no problems—or unwelcome guests. This time he was aware of an intruder watching, but wasn't sure if it was back-up for Frank or a spy working on his own. He knew who it was—and let it be for now.

The Glock semi-automatic was tucked under his leg on the seat, cocked and ready. He watched the dark shadow cruise by and disappear, coming back a few minutes later. Roger didn't like this part because he couldn't see if there was anyone else in the other car. Holding the Glock lightly in his right hand, he switched on the recorder.

The Buick pulled along side, close enough so he could hear the whine caused by the window gliding down. He sat face to face with Frank, neither man willing to fully trust the other. Dawson also had his pistol ready.

Frank Dawson spoke first. "What do you want?"

"O'Meara said you were going to pull the plug. What's going on?"

Frank answered, "We need to close the porno case with your wife and kid. Somebody from the *Star Tribune* is going through cold cases trying to get some headlines. The mayor is going to run again on a law-and-order issue and wants some cases solved. I need this one to disappear quietly. My involvement can't be found out. You're in it too, you know."

Roger said, "Yeah, but I'm not important, am I? My wife and kid are gone, and I live like a bum so you can stay respectable. I need some more cash."

"That's the way it works sometimes. People like you work for the benefit of people like me. Here." Dawson reached through the open window and passed an envelope to Roger, telling him, "Make that last awhile."

Roger felt the heaviness of the package and knew it was larger this time. "What's the deal with an inquiry from up north?"

"It looks like someone is trying to find you. That's all we can figure out. Also, Child Services said a lawyer in Duluth asked for some files on the runaways. O'Meara raised some questions, and I want it kept quiet. Go up there and see what's happening. I put as much information as I could in the package. I knew that sooner or later something would surface. Make sure it all goes away. And don't forget what they do to child molesters in prison."

Roger let his boss know the vulnerability went both ways. "Almost as bad as a child molester who happens to be a cop. When is this going to end?"

"Never mind. You're undercover for good now. As far as the police department knows, you're through as a cop–that you went too deep to come out. When this is over, you have to get a job someplace else. It'll end when your wife and the kid are dead."

Roger sat in the Olds for a long time after the Buick left. The spy, off in the distance, was still watching him while he played the recording back–his insurance policy that he would file away with the others.

Roger knew what he had to do now, and to him, it was just another job. He was supposed to murder his daughter and wife so Frank Dawson wouldn't go to jail. Roger and Frank each had their own evidence linking the other to child pornography and molestation, and murder. It was what kept them working together. If one were exposed, the other would be also.

Frank's obsession with children, and in particular, Roger's own daughter, continued because it was profitable. To Frank it was an adrenalin rush he couldn't control. To Roger it was nothing more than an envelope full of money. Now, it was a matter of getting rid of the only witnesses that could put Frank in prison. Roger's lack of remorse or consciousness had left a void, and had turned him into a monster, and the headaches have been coming back, now worse than ever.

Roger couldn't afford to have a conscience. Misgivings about what he did would paralyze him. He didn't know if the headaches came from remorse, or a brain tumor, and he tried to ignore either excuse. They started keeping him awake at night so he knew the feeling was changing. There was no doubt that he was going to murder his own wife and daughter, but was bothered by his memory of Rosalie, and what he allowed others to do to her. Compunction— feeling of shame and regret—was strange to Roger, and he didn't know how to deal with it.

Roger turned off the recorder and drove home, careful not to lose the car tailing him, thinking he needed to see the doctor again. Roger pulled into his driveway, used the remote to open the door, and slowly drove inside. After closing it, he took a very quick glance down the block at Gary O'Meara's car parked a couple houses away.

Gary had witnessed the meeting and knew it was the Lieutenant Dawson's Buick. He could only guess it had something to do with the recent inquiry about Roger. This was getting strange, and the man he used to think of as a dipshit, was becoming a major player. He lit another cigarette, shading the glow to keep his surveillance intact.

It was late and his wife would be waiting for him, so it was time to call it a day. Gary put all his thoughts together as a puzzle for tomorrow and reached to start his car, when the tapping on the window startled him. Looking into Roger's smiling face, he lowered his window, groping for an excuse as to why he was here. If he did manage to say something, nobody heard it as the blade quickly slashed across his throat, almost to the spinal cord, nearly decapitating him. Roger waited a moment for the spurting blood to subside before jamming the knife into Gary's gurgling mouth, leaving it for the crime scene investigators to figure out. Stepping to the passenger door, Roger reached in and grabbed the camera off the seat next to the dying detective. Glancing at Gary, Roger was amused to see his eyelid quiver. Satisfied after checking the dark, deserted street for intruders, he went home to get some sleep before driving up north tomorrow. Opening his prescription, he made a mental note to reorder more, and then popped a few painkillers to smooth out the throbbing in his head. In spite of the medication, Roger had a fitful sleep. The dream seemed so real, with the vision of a pig eating him alive while the guards watched, laughing. It ended differently tonight. He finally found the relief of undisturbed sleep, with him tucking Rosalie into bed and kissing her goodnight, but before he closed the door, he saw the room filled with men inching their way to her. Before he could stop them, he was asleep.

The next morning he heard the screams from the housewives when they escorted their children to the bus stop. School was cancelled for the neighborhood kids, and a few of them wouldn't leave the house for days after viewing the grotesque scene left on their quiet suburban street.

The neighborhood was crawling with police. Squad cars were parked askew up and down the street, and the forensics van sat in the middle, not caring how much room it took. Besides, nobody except Roger was going anywhere for awhile. Yellow plastic ribbons stretched around Gary's car, investigators were on their knees taking pictures, and a dozen confused detectives stood around, dumbfounded. Uniformed officers milled through the crowd, going door to door, taking names and interviews.

They questioned everybody, including Roger. Of course he was shocked and asked the officer, "Are you sure it's safe outside? I'd like to know when there's going to be an end to the violence. No, Officer, I was asleep last night and didn't hear any gun shot."

Disgusted with the routine, the officer responded, "We'll have patrols in the area for a while. You'll be safe now. Thank you, Sir."

A few minutes later, a familiar figure stood in his doorway, and said, "Hi Parkhurst, I see you fixed the door."

Roger looked up to see the same officer that came to the house when Emily was arrested. "Harry, what are you doing here? Step inside before you draw too much attention."

"That's a stupid thing to say, Roger. What do you know about the mess outside?"

"Don't push me, man. If you blow my cover, you're going to answer to Dawson. I don't know anything. I heard it was a cop, though. Is that true?"

"Yeah, his name was O'Meara. Didn't you know him?"

"I've only heard his name once in awhile. No, I didn't know him. Who did this?"

"They think it was the work of one of the new Asian gangs running drugs out here. The way he was left points to something strange like they'd do."

Roger showed his compassion long enough to be convincing. "Look Harry, I've got to get to a meeting with some sleazy people, and if I'm late I'll screw up a lot of work. You were undercover before you got reassigned here, so you know what it's like."

Harry said, "Yeah, I remember. I'm glad I got out before I wound up like him." He threw his thumb in the direction of the mess in the street. "I'm leaving. I was on call for this one so I thought I'd see how it's going. How are the wife and kid?"

Pushing Harry to the door before he got too inquisitive, Roger answered, "She took off with Rosalie. Nobody knows where they are."

"Well, too bad it got so messy. Goodbye Parkhurst."

When he was alone again, Roger leaned against the door, pinching his throbbing forehead. That was just too close; he had to wind this up for good, thinking that Emily and the kid need to get put away as soon as possible.

Outside, Officer Harry Slocum stood for a minute trying to unwind something from his mind that bothered him. It was one of those things that puts an edge to your thoughts without knowing what it was. He walked away, thinking he would dig into it later—but he would have been better off forgetting it.

● ● ● ● ● ● ● ● ● ● ● ● ● ● ● ● ●

THE IMPALA SAT IN A PARKING LOT NEAR THE Minneapolis Courthouse with Jim staring at the cell phone in his hand, his mind trying to find a place to land.

He thought of Emily and knew he had to get hold of her, but needed to be sure she didn't react the wrong way and run off with Rosalie.

Buzz, sitting next to him, asked, "What's going on, Jim? You've got that look that means trouble. I'm your partner, Pal. Talk to me." He rolled down the window and spit.

"Roll it up, Buzz. I need to make a call, and I can't hear with all the noise out there. I need make sure that Emily's all right."

Curious and obedient, Buzz cranked up the window, and the car became relatively quiet.

Jim held the little phone hoping he could quit shaking long enough for his over-sized fingers to hit the right buttons. "Damn things. What's wrong with a normal-size phone?"

The ring tone quit and was replaced by the Grand Marais dispatcher's voice, "Sheriff's office, Deputy Marks here."

"Ted, this is Jim Cooper. Is Wally there?"

"No Sir, not at the moment. He took your dog out in the patrol car to check on a disturbance near the American Legion. Should be back soon."

Without trying to sound frantic, which he was, he told Ted, "Have him call my cell number as soon as he gets in. And give him a message too." Jim's mind was spinning, trying to remember Wally's clever password, but drew a blank. In desperation, he said, "Tell him, little orange football. Got it, Ted? Be sure to tell him that as soon as he comes in."

Ted sat at the dispatcher's desk with his twenty-five-year-old head in total confusion. "Yeah, whatever. I'll tell him, but he's gonna think I'm playing games on the phone again."

"Don't worry Ted. He'll know what it means."

Jim palmed the tiny phone and tried to rest his forehead on the steering wheel, but his stomach got in the way, so he just sat upright and sighed.

Buzz looked at him, "Well, now that I know everything, we can start looking for the little orange football. Goddamn it Cooper, what the hell are we doing here?"

"Sorry, Buddy. I was hoping the sheriff in Grand Marais would be in. I think Roger Parkhurst is headed up there, and he needs to get Emily out of the way."

Just then, Jim's cell phone chirped, startling him to the point of almost chucking it up on the dashboard. Curtly answering, he snarled, "Yeah?"

"Mr. Cooper, George Ellsworth here. I thought you should know there was a killing out on our street last night. A man got his throat slit. Can you imagine that?"

Jim sat up, asking, "Who was it?"

"From what I gathered by the gossip out there, it was an officer. I overheard a policeman say his name was Gary O'Meara. I'm pretty sure that's what he said."

"Well, thanks for the news, Mr. Ellsworth. If you hear of anything else, get back to me right away." Fumbling with the off button, Jim asked, "Buzz, did you know a cop, Gary O'Meara?"

"Not real well. We had a beer at choir practice a couple times, but I retired before I spent any time with him. What's he got to do with this?"

"He was found in his car in front of Parkhurst's house with his throat slit."

Confused, Buzz rhetorically asked, "What has he got to do with this?" Looking at Jim, he said, "Right in front of the Parkhurst house has to mean some kind of connection."

"That's what we have to …" As Jim glanced out the window, his jaw dropped. "Oh, my God, look at that."

Stopping mid-sentence, Jim had the door of the Impala open with one leg out, struggling to get from under the steering wheel. Completely confused, Buzz yelled, "What? What're we looking at? For Chris' sake Jim, what are you doing?"

"That woman there." Jim pointed to a tall woman in a gray power suit with a briefcase in one hand and a pile of folders clutched to her chest. She was walking double time towards the courthouse, bent over slightly, making herself look busy.

"Yeah, so what. She looks like a lawyer. Do you know her, and why do we care?"

Jim was hauling his frame out of the car, "Come on, Buzz. We need to talk to her."

Buzz had lived in the city long enough to know you always remember to close the door, and you never leave a car unlocked. He stayed behind to take care of the details and salvage the keys from the ignition, before catching up to Jim and the important woman. Mumbling to himself, "Just like the old days, you run off and I get to do clean-up. Some things never change."

Jim, dodging traffic and huffing his way towards her, called, "DeAnna. Wait up."

DeAnna Wishoult turned at the sound of her name and almost dropped her papers at the sight of Jim lumbering towards her. "Jim Cooper. My God, you look like a barrel with legs. What are you doing here?"

"DeAnna, I need to talk to you. Wait a minute." Panting, Jim took a few breaths and continued as Buzz caught up to them. "Honey, this is my old partner, Art Peterson. Buzz, this is DeAnna Wishoult."

Buzz nodded his head and responded, "Glad to meet you," although he had no idea why.

Cordially, she answered, "Mr. Peterson." Then, less than polite, she turned to Jim. "First of all Mr. Cooper, I am not *Honey*. I'm really busy now and have to be in court in a few minutes, and why in the world would I want to talk to you?"

To the point of begging, he said, "Please, it's important. Can we get together later? It's concerning someone who's in a lot of trouble."

"Well, connected to you there would have to be trouble, wouldn't there. All right, meet me at The Loon about five o'clock. And you better have a good story to tell." She nodded to Buzz, turned on her heel and hurried off.

With a triumphant smile, Jim said, "I think she can help us Buzz. By the way, where's The Loon, and what is it?"

The Loon is an upscale, trendy bar where most people meet to have an after-work cocktail and a good meal. Located close to the courthouse, most of the clientele are lawyers and judges. More pre-trial agreements are made at The Loon than in court. It's quiet and reserved, with an air of a common tavern and very comfortable. The two old guys nursed their beer and incredible hamburgers for three hours, waiting for Ms. Wishoult to show up. Jim explained to Buzz that he and DeAnna had dated in Grand Marais, and of her involvement in his efforts to find his daughter.

Being realistic, he added, "Also, it's entirely possible she'll blow us off and not show up." That worried Jim because he didn't know what else to do.

They had been in The Loon for about twenty minutes when Wally Stearns returned his call. Fortunately it was early and the crowd was small, so it was quiet enough for him to hear.

"Thanks for calling Wally. There's going to be some trouble up there. Roger Parkhurst may be coming your way to look for Emily. A Minneapolis detective was murdered in front of Parkhurst's house last night, but he never got tagged for it."

"I'll run out to check on her. How much do you want her to know?"

"Just make it look social for now. If she knows Parkhurst is getting close, she may take off again. Don't take the squad car out there. It's too noticeable, and you could pick up a tail. Hell, Wally, take her to a movie or out to your place. Just stay close to her."

"Jim, she's going to think I'm a pervert or something. I just can't take her home."

"Wally, do something smart."

"Dang it all, you're squeezing my tit again, Jim. I'll think of something."

"Wally, call me back and tell me what's going on. Please."

"Sure Jim, as soon as I get something."

While waiting for DeAnna, Jim told Buzz everything he could think of. They sat reminiscing for a while and toyed with a few more beers. Finally, she came and sat down with them.

She ordered a white zinfandel before confronting Jim. "If you promise not to call me Honey, I'll spend a few minutes with you because I sense it's urgent. Does it involve Mary Beth?"

"No, but you're right about it being urgent. If this goes wrong, a little girl is going to be hurt, and possibly killed, along with her mother. I'm going to tell you something but I need you to promise you won't make a judgment until you hear it all. By the way, what are you doing in Minneapolis?"

"I was offered a job in Family Services here. I moved almost two years ago, but of course, you would never notice."

"I'm sorry, DeAnna. I've been really screwed up. I've got too many problems for a decent person like you."

She looked at Buzz, wondering why he was even here. He sensed her question and just shrugged. The best thing he could do now was to listen.

Jim started, "A Minneapolis detective, Gary O'Meara, was murdered outside Roger Parkhurst's house this morning. Roger Parkhurst is chasing his wife and his daughter and will probably kill them both if he finds them. There was a pornography scheme a few months ago, and Emily Parkhurst was fingered as the leader. She has her daughter hidden, and is on the run from her ex-husband. He showed up one night to take the girl, but Emily hit him with a chair and got the girl away from him. He was a cop and had her arrested for assault, and now she has a kidnapping charge on her head. The child made a statement that the father sexually abused her, but for some reason the charges were dropped. I believe Parkhurst is getting close to finding them. I already told you what would happen if he does."

Jim pensively waited for her response.

"I'm familiar with the Parkhurst case, and after we met on the street today, I had a suspicion you were involved. Leonard Walburn, as I remember, was your good friend and also your attorney. He made an inquiry about Emily and Rosalie, asking for the files, saying he was now representing them. I was glad to see that because I've always felt something was fishy with the whole case. Especially after Rosalie gave a statement on the abuse."

Jim gave a happy sigh, "Does that mean you'll help us?"

"There isn't much I can do. The charges are filed, and Emily is still a fugitive. All I can suggest is that you have Len file a motion for his clients. The law is screwy at times, Jim, but I am obligated to uphold it. I will deny we ever had this conversation."

Now, Buzz interrupted. "Don't you also have a bigger obligation to protect the child?"

DeAnna paused and marveled at the wisdom that came from the grizzled old retired cop. Smiling, "Yes, Mr. Peterson, my first responsibility is for the child's safety. Backed into a corner, I would tell you to bring her in for protective custody, however, at the risk of getting my ass in a jam, all I can say is I will do what I think is best for the girl."

Jim added, "We have to keep the mother and her daughter out of sight and away from Parkhurst. I don't care what the law is DeAnna, my only concern is their safety, and Parkhurst is going to have to crawl over me before he touches them."

"Jim, is this more personal than it seems?"

"Yes. I have Emily hidden and I know where the daughter is. They are both going to die if that asshole gets to them."

Staring at the table for a moment, she said, "There's a police lieutenant, Frank Dawson, who tried to get the file from my office. I had it on my desk and just decided to be the bitch everyone thinks I am, and kept it away from him. I didn't like his involvement or his attitude."

Buzz, being wise again, asked, "Where is the file now?"

"On the floor between my feet." She tapped her briefcase with her toe and slid it toward Jim. "I have to go to the ladies room for ten minutes. Please watch my things while I'm gone." Then she stood up and walked away.

They hauled the briefcase up on the table where Jim took part of it, and Buzz had the rest, both making notes, particularly the names and any addresses or phone numbers. By coincidence, DeAnna came back just as they slid the briefcase back to her chair. She sat down and drained her glass. "I should leave now. I'll fax the file to Len when I get home."

"Thank you, DeAnna. It's good to see you again."

Concerned, she asked, "Did you ever find Mary Beth?"

"No. Not a trace."

"I'm sorry I didn't do more for you back then, Jim. I was too tense and started getting involved with you. It wouldn't have worked."

"She wanted something I couldn't give her. Not knowing is the worst part."

"I know you too well Jim. Don't let yourself get so deep in the Parkhurst woman's problem that it buries you."

"It's the kid, Dee. It's all about the little girl."

DeAnna nodded and commented to Jim, "I'm sorry about Mary Beth. I can imagine the grief you must still be feeling."

Jim's mind went into oblivion, and he quietly said, "Thanks, I just began to accept it, and …" Deciding to keep his plan of suicide to himself, he finished with, "Well, I just figured there was nothing else I could do. She might come back; I don't know."

Nodding to Buzz, she looked at Jim for a long moment, and then got up and left them.

Buzz, just a bystander, said, "She doesn't like you very much, does she."

Sadly, Jim said, "No. I think it went bad when I got drunk and barfed on her."

CHAPTER 12
UP NORTH

● ●

WALLACE STEARNS, DRESSED IN his nicest shirt, drove his Jeep Cherokee up Highway 61 to Hovland, and then turned left to Tom Lake.
He drove slowly to give himself time to come up with a convincing story about his visit that Emily would believe. She had stopped by earlier to
pick up Bella, so maybe that could be his connection. It was a weak one, but he
was ready to grab at anything. Besides, he was nervous as a tick whenever he was
remotely close to the woman, and this time it was even worse.

Wally knew how to use evidence as a guide, but he wasn't good at telling
stories or making up things that sounded convincing. He knows he should have
called first, but was certain he would blow anything he thought of. Besides, he
would probably freeze up when talking to her anyway. He was just too shy, and
the gorgeous woman intimidated him.

Jim's GMC was in front of the garage, and a light came from the cabin. Wally
was disappointed that he couldn't turn around and use the not-at-home excuse,
but, regardless of his feelings for her, he was here and this needed to be done, so
he'd better get on with it. Running away was not an option.

After a tenuous couple of knocks, the door was opened by a child. Assuming
her to be Emily's daughter, he would place her to be around ten or twelve. She
had an aura of maturity that let Wally know that she was sizing him up, but was
undecided what to do with him.

Her one outstanding feature disturbed him terribly. She had a mature appeal
well beyond her young age. Knowing what her circumstances were, he felt guilty
for even looking at her. This little girl who stood squarely before him had already
endured a lifetime of warfare, and it sickened him to think that he was here to tell
her it wasn't over yet.

Dressed in jeans and a baggy top that hung almost to the knees, he noticed the long blond hair tied into a ponytail. However, the most riveting feature were the deep, piercing dark brown eyes that were challenging him. She didn't have to say anything; her presence alone asked *what the hell do you want?*

Bella came from behind her and was jumping and running in circles around Wally's feet, knocking him off balance.

Emily's concerned voice dripped with a bit of sarcasm, "Hello Sheriff, what brings you out here?"

Wally put on his best grin and tried to hide from the embarrassment of being so awkward. The thought flashed through his mind that his fly could be open, but there was no way to check on it.

"Uh, hi Emily. I talked to Jim and he asked me to keep an eye on you. So, I just thought I'd drop in. See how you're doing. You know." Wally felt like crawling under the floor boards. He was just no good at this.

Emily peered past him and queried, "You alone?"

"Yeah, just me. Checking up, you know."

"Well, close the damn door and come in, Wally." It sounded as if she was mocking him, and he felt a touch of ire surfacing. He didn't like cold calls—and didn't like being made fun of. Wally took responsibility seriously, and knew why Jim asked him to come out here. He was trying to help, and decided to be the sheriff again.

With a hint of firmness, he told her, "Look, Emily, I'm here because I need to be sure you're safe. Jim is in Minneapolis, and I'm going to help you, like it or not."

Quick to stem off any reference to trouble in front of her daughter, she interjected, "Wally, this is Rosalie. Rosie this is Wallace Stearns. He's a friend of Jim's and is the sheriff."

"Glad to meet you, Sir." The precocious little girl held her hand out for Wally to shake.

"Hello Rosalie. Yup, I'm the sheriff in town. I came here to see if you and your mom are all right."

Rosalie looked at her mother for confirmation. "Yes, honey. Wally is one of the good guys like Jim. You can always trust him, and I want you to remember him. Baby, I think it's time for Bella to go out. Would you please take her for me?"

"Grown-up talk? I'll take her. C'mon girl."

Waiting until Rosalie was outside, Emily's hard glare slammed into turned to Wally. Direct and to the point, Emily wanted the truth, "Sit down, Wally, and tell me what you're really doing here."

With a polite nod towards the door, Wally said, "Nice girl, Emily. You should be proud of her."

Emily's voice was firm and commanding, "Cut the shit, Wally. If you can't tell me the truth, why should I trust you? Get to the point and give it all to me. *Now!*"

Stunned by her directness, he said, "Oh, wow, I don't get cornered like that too often. Yes, there's a problem, and I need to dance around it to be sure you don't react in the wrong way. Roger Parkhurst is coming this way."

Rosalie, at the door, startled both of them. "Mommy, he's coming here?" She stepped inside and started shaking, tears crawling down her cheeks. With her arms out stretched, she stumbled toward Emily, wailing, "Mommy?"

Witness to Rosalie's reaction to the news, Wally now understood the trauma that lived within this small child.

Pulling the child into her arms, "Honey, Wally and Jim are making it safe for us. They're going to make sure we're okay." Fiercely, her eyes bored into Wally, and demanded, "Tell her Wally. Tell her what your plan is so we know we won't be hurt." Emily had an edge to her voice that told Wally he was going to die if he didn't have a good plan to make them safe.

"I have a house outside of town that nobody will find. It's got alarms and can be guarded from all around. I think it would be safer than the Amish farm now. This place is safe, but it's just too far away from the police. Rosalie, you're going to be all right, and we're going to see that this trouble goes away so you'll never be afraid again."

Emily's need for answers came out now. "If this place is safe, why do we need to be someplace else? What are the police going to do, no matter how close they are?"

Now Wally was the sheriff again and had his logic in place. "I have a direct line connected to the office. I can put a safe switch on it so all you need to do is hit it and an alarm will sound not only in the office, but in my patrol car."

Her eyebrows rose in admiration, but with a touch of derision, Emily asked, "Where did a hick-town sheriff learn to do all that?"

Embarrassed once more, she made him feel like a clown. "I went to college hoping to be an engineer."

Rosalie, nestled in her mom's lap, asked "Why'd you give that up?"

"That's a long story, Rosalie. You sure you want to hear it all?" Wally thought he was gaining their confidence now, and the closer he could reel them in, the easier it would be to handle them. Here is where the trust started.

Emily confirmed Rosalie's curiosity, but she seemed to be mocking him. "Yes, Wally, tell us."

Wally didn't know if she was confronting him, challenging him or really was curious. He went on. "I was a junior at UMD, you know, in Duluth. My dad was shot while he was hunting. Jim was the sheriff, and also my dad's best friend. We went through the funeral stuff and all that, but Jim was uneasy about something. He said there was a funny smell to how Dad was shot. Jim is like that. He can smell something wrong. Anyway, I went back to college and about a month later, Jim came to tell me that he arrested somebody for shooting my dad. The guy confessed and is in prison. Anyway, I knew then that I wanted to go into law enforcement. I switched my major, worked for Jim a few years, and when he retired I became sheriff. The electronics thing is still embedded in my head, so I like to play with computers and gadgets and stuff. The remote connection to the office and patrol car are my own idea. It seems to work, but never really put it to a good test."

Firmly, Emily asked, "Wally, I know you wouldn't have come out here unless you thought it was important. Do you really think there's a problem?"

Looking deeply into her eyes, he quietly said, "Yes, I think so."

Emily sighed, looked at her daughter, and then said, "When should we go? We might as well be guinea pigs and test out your alarm gadget."

"Pack up some stuff and we'll go now. You can follow me in the truck."

Giving Rosalie a quick kiss on the cheek, she told her, "Come on, you little shit, pack your evening gown, we're gonna go visiting."

A few minutes of shuffling around and crunching things into a plastic trash bag they were ready–almost. "Wait," Emily said, and rushed back into the bedroom, coming out with a flannel shirt rolled into a bundle. Wally reached for it to help, but was pushed away.

"Let's go Sheriff Stearns."

Emily, with the flannel package sitting on her lap, followed the sheriff.

● ● ● ● ● ● ● ● ● ● ● ● ● ● ● ● ● ● ● ●

Roger's house, Brooklyn Park, Minnesota

TRAVELING LIGHT, ALL ROGER TOOK WITH him was what he could easily grab from a dresser drawer. He made certain the information from Frank was packed, and most important, a small stash of pot. Backing out of the garage, he took note of a couple police cruisers and a small phalanx of detectives and crime lab workers. Slowly milling around Gary's car, one looked up and took a disinterested look at Roger leaving his driveway. Roger's leaving was an innocuous move to the cop, but of greater interest to George Ellsworth, peeking from behind his living room drapes.

Leaving the Minneapolis suburb and the bloody scene on the street behind, Roger drove the Olds up north. Instead of the faster and more direct route of Highway 35, he stayed off the freeway and took Highway 23 east through Milaca and Mora, then running parallel to Highway 35, north and out of sight from the Minnesota Highway Patrol, to the run-down section of South Duluth. Checking into a nondescript motel on Commonwealth Avenue, he paid cash and signed the guest book as Elmer Fudd. The only thing he took into the room was a manila envelope and his stash of pot. Lying on the bed for the rest of the day getting seriously stoned, he tried to figure out what came next. Emily and the kid were up here someplace, and he reminded himself that his objective was to find and kill them.

Lying back with the joint, he lamented over the memory of his ex-wife, "Emily. Oh, what a girl Emily was. I never met anyone who could bang like she did." Roger was still in love with Emily, and whether he would admit it or not, he missed her.

When Roger told Frank about Emily finding the photos, there was no doubt that he did something incredibly stupid. However, Frank was able to make the pictures and everything else that was incriminating disappear, and it looked like smooth sailing. Yes indeed, everything looked good, and it would have been if it weren't for Roger's little box of blackmail that he thought was hidden.

The pile of papers on the bed had the names of the people he needed to deal with. The lawyer, Leonard Walburn, was in Duluth and had some papers about Emily and his daughter. "What the hell am I going to do about a bunch of papers? Let's see, it says here there should be case files about what happened back home when she hit me with the chair." And then, a word jumped out that scared him. "What the ... , Child Services?"

He flopped back down on the bed and held his head. "All I want to do is get to the broad and the kid. I don't know what I'm supposed to look for." If he took any more painkillers he wouldn't wake up on time, so he laid still and counted the beats on the inside of his skull. Confused and too stoned to think anymore, he fell into a light sleep.

About one that morning, the rain woke him up. He was greeted by a pounding headache and the stench of pot filling his nostrils. Heading for downtown Duluth, the open window let in a rush of fresh air to clean out his head, and a Stevie Nicks tape to fill it up again.

Cruising slowly through alleys and deserted back streets, Roger found a curbside parking spot behind the building that housed the Walburn law office. The delivery door was padlocked so he got a giant bolt cutter out of his trunk, and snap, free access. Up on the second floor, he gave Leonard's office a quick scan from the hallway. From what Roger could see there was no alarm system. If there was, he would just have to work faster. He poked and prodded at the door jamb with a sharpened screwdriver, and soon the door swung free.

"Open, Sesame. No alarm yet, so take my time. It should be a law that people get alarm systems that work." Roger smiled at the irony. "No bells and whistles yet, so just look for something. I don't know what I'm looking for anyway. This guy can't have anything too important if it's not locked up better than this." Then the humor left him, and he stiffened at the noise coming from the first floor.

Either Roger was as stupid as Frank said he was, or he just didn't give a damn about details. Probably both, with a splash of arrogance and bravado hooked to it.

A passing security guard on his rounds flashed his light on the delivery door in a routine move that he had been doing for years. His motions had become so automatic he almost missed the open hasp on the door. Getting a closer look, he stepped on the broken lock, and it scared the daylights out of him, yelping, "Holy shit. Now what?"

His gray uniform, which attempted to cover the beer gut, was a sign of authority, making it unnecessary to carry a weapon. So, with the grace of a walrus, armed with his flashlight, he tiptoed through the door into the dark building.

Radios to call for help cost a lot, and the Surefire Security Company could get along without them since there were never any problems to warrant the expense.

Covering the first floor and rattling each door, he went to the stairway and looked up the dark opening to the second-floor landing. "I really don't want to go up there. No way, not up there." Squinting into the darkness, he made a move that made him feel very foolish, but at the same time, very safe. "Hello. Is anyone up there? Hello." Waiting and not getting an answer, he moved as fast as his bulk would allow, to find a pay phone "Let the cops figure it out. I'm not getting into that shit for six-fifty an hour."

Hidden in the darkness at the top of the staircase, Roger stood holding the closest thing he could find for a weapon, the sharpened and deadly screwdriver. When he heard the shuffle of the guard and the slamming of the dock door, he went back into the office to look around quickly for something with a name he would recognize. He pulled papers out of the fax machine but only looked at the cover page and dropped them on the floor, leaving empty handed.

On his way out he stepped on the fax papers he had discarded, wrinkling the heading, *Emily Parkhurst, Case File #1374495,* his shoe print emblazoned over the wording.

Done with the 911 call at the pay phone, Fat Guy did the dumbest thing possible; he went back to the delivery door to wait for the police. Nervously, he paced around the loading dock when he realized he had wet his pants. "Oh, God no, they're gonna see this." With his hands over the wet fly of his uniform, in the middle of deciding what to do next, he was jarred by the searing pain of the screwdriver plunged through his neck. He sensed the gush of warm blood flow down his chest and before his heavy body hit the cement, the blackness of death was upon him. Calmly, without ceremony, Roger stepped over the guard and got into his Oldsmobile, to find Highway 61 for the drive north to Grand Marais.

The crime scene investigators had so much evidence they thought it was a set up.

Leonard was called into the office and tried to find what the object of the break in was. The fax copies on the floor were from DeAnna Wishoult, signaling the danger to Emily and Rosalie. The fingerprints in the office and on the murder weapon were a glaring announcement of whom they were looking for. The police saw the purpose of the whole thing as an attempt to find Emily Parkhurst and the child. The murder of the guard was senseless, but nobody realized at the time that it was an indication how unstable Roger really was.

● ● ● ● ● ● ● ● ● ● ● ● ● ● ● ● ●

Back at Buzz's house, Jim got the first call from Leonard. "Jesus, Jim, the blood was all over the place. That bastard didn't care who knew, or was just too stupid."

Jim reiterated the capabilities of Roger, "He's remorseless, Len. Tell the police up there they need to be careful."

Leonard's second call was to DeAnna. "Dee, Len here, from Duluth."

DeAnna sleepily answered, "It's nice to hear from you Len, but it's four in the morning. You're too serious to play games at this hour. What's up?"

The attorney laid out what happened and that the files she sent were on the floor, "So, he has to know Emily and the girl are around. They have to be protected. Is there anyone down there who can lift the charges on her so she can find some safety?"

"I'll call Judge Bacon right away. Len, this is horrible.. Those two have to get put into protective custody."

Len anxiously said, "Let me know as soon as the charges are dropped and send me a fax of the order so Emily will know I'm telling the truth. She's awfully nervous about the law being involved, and I can't blame her."

Jim called Wally and woke him up at home. "Yeah Jim, they're both asleep in the other room. There's no way anyone will find them here, and there are no listings for the address or telephone, anywhere. While I've got you on the phone, we need a picture of him so we know who were looking for."

"We'll get the file faxed to you first thing tomorrow, Wally. Make sure they stay right there, I'm coming back as soon as I get done here." Sincerely concerned, he added, "Wally, don't let him get to them."

Wally slowly set the phone back onto the stand and stood looking at it, full of dread that something horrible was about to happen. He just didn't know how close he was to reality.

● ● ● ● ● ● ● ● ● ● ● ● ● ● ● ●

Jim and Buzz met DeAnna in her office at the Minneapolis Government Center. She told them, "Here's the file I faxed to Leonard yesterday. It doesn't have any more than the history of what happened between Emily and Roger. Rosalie's testimony isn't in it, so I know it's been tampered with."

Buzz, being a cop again, asked, "What about a file on Roger Parkhurst? We need to know who we're looking for."

"Well, Mr. Peterson, that's an excellent idea, but according to the records section, there *is* no Roger Parkhurst."

Jim frowned, "That can't be. Emily said he was a cop. Dee, you have more influence here than we do, can you find out what happened to Roger?"

Frustrated, DeAnna lashed out, "Jim, you don't have *any* influence here. If you start poking your nose into official corners, you're going to screw everything up. Leave the legal work to me. I'm going over to the courthouse to see Captain Dawson. I might get stonewalled because I held back the file he was asking for, but he's the only logical one connected to this."

Nervously, Jim told her, "Me and Buzz have something to do here, then I have to get back to Grand Marais."

Firmly, DeAnna told him, "Jim, I know you too well, and I'll tell you again, don't go outside the system and screw everything up."

Jim knew she was right and tried to cover his meddling with a smile. "I knew there was a gentle side to you. I should have never let you get away. Here's my cell number. If you can't get me, call Sheriff Stearns or Buzz here."

Rolling her eyes, she told him what he already knew, "Jim you're an asshole. You'd chase yourself out of town just for the thrill of it. Yes, I'll call as soon as I get something. Go back home, and don't do anything stupid."

Back in the Impala, the starter motor had hardly quit spinning before Jim had the big machine in gear, leaving black tire marks in the parking lot. Buzz held onto the door handle, trying to push his feet through the floor boards. "Let me know when you land this thing so I can open my eyes, Jim."

Bouncing off the curb in front of the Ellsworths, Jim ran to the house and opened the door at the same time he rang the bell. George Ellsworth was almost knocked over. "Mr. Cooper, I was just going to call you. Roger left a little while ago, and had a suitcase with him." Beaming at his amateur-detective status, George added, "That was just before they towed away the murder car."

"That's a good observation, George. What time did you say he left?"

"About eight this morning, like I said, just before the tow truck got here. He went that way," and George pointed up the street.

Jim asked, "You said he had a suitcase?"

George answered, "Well, more a bag of some kind. It wasn't very big."

"What was he driving?"

"A rusty Oldsmobile; kind of maroon, a four-door, and the right front side is damaged."

Frantically, Jim quickly announced, "So, he's gone now. We need to break into that house. We'll do it in the back so the neighbors won't get aroused. I imagine people are still shaky here."

George was proud to be helping. "Wait, I have a key that Emily gave us long ago." Scurrying into the kitchen, he asked his wife, "Helen, Sheriff Cooper is here. Where is Emily's house key?"

Wiping her hands with a dishtowel, Mrs. Ellsworth handed Jim the key. "Are Emily and the child all right?"

"Yes, they're doing very well. I'm not going to tell you anymore because I don't want you involved. I hope you understand."

With a comforting smile, she added, "Of course we do. Please don't underestimate how we can help."

A patrol car was cruising the street with nothing more to do than let the citizens know they were working. They paid little attention to the two men running through Roger's yard.

As Jim and Buzz raced through the yard to Roger's house, Jim noted that he had parked on the same spot where Gary O'Meara was brutally murdered. Jim felt a pang of sorrow for the fallen officer, but there was no time for compunction right now. If a cruising patrol car were to stop and question them, too much time would be lost.

At the front door, he handed Buzz his cell phone. "Can you call the Grand Marais office with a description of the Olds? Then have Wally check with DMV for the license number. Even Parkhurst has to have a registration." They both entered the house, hoping George was right that Roger had left. Just in case, and partly out of habit, he reached behind his jacket and drew out a snub-nosed Smith and Wesson .32 revolver. The well-worn weapon fit in Jim's big hand as if it had grown there, and guided him cautiously through the house.

The small rambler was quiet and surprisingly neat. Jim heard Buzz talking on the phone while he slowly made his way from room to room.

In the bedroom he looked at the unmade bed, carefully opened a few drawers and moved to the closet door. Inside, there was nothing more than the normal things a man would keep in a closet: shoes, shirts and whatever. However, Jim's interest was drawn to a clump of dust clinging to hangers on top of the rod. Looking up, he studied the trapdoor that led to the small attic space above.

Jim had to go all the way back to the kitchen to find a chair to stand on in the closet. Being careful to avoid making a mess that would show his entry, he lifted the panel and reached through the opening.

Taking a shoebox down, he stepped into the light of the bedroom window. Buzz was at his elbow now, and they both peered into Roger's collection of child pornography with explicit photos of Rosalie, with different men in disgusting arrangements. What stood out in Jim's mind was the pleading and almost tearful look on Rosalie's face. "Buzz, this man is going to die. I promise." Also in the box were several cassette tapes and an address book with names, a coding of some type, and dates. The most frequent entry was *FD*.

Jim put the box back, the cover in place, and the marks from the chair legs were brushed out of the carpet. Jim, on the phone, "DeAnna, can you get a search warrant for the Parkhurst house, specifically, the access hole in the bedroom closet? Also, you need to be here for the search to confiscate what they find so it doesn't get lost."

"Jim, you clod. Are you in that house?"

"Never mind where I am. Can you do it?"

"Yes. Judge Bacon is working on the file now. Soon Emily will be free from being arrested, and we need to put her into protective custody."

"I hope it's not too late for that. I'm going up there now. Keep in touch, please."

On their way out the door, Jim grabbed a framed picture from a tabletop showing the once-happy Parkhurst family sitting together and smiling, with Roger beaming at the camera.

CHAPTER 13
ROGER'S GAME

● ●

ON A NORMAL ROUTINE DAY, WALLY was in the office at six in the morning. Today he had guests that needed taking care of. However, Emily was not the type who took to being controlled and, in her irascible manner, let Wally know just where he stood. "Oh, for Christ sake, Sheriff, we can't be any more protected than this. Go to work and leave us alone. We'll do just fine, and tonight, after a hard day shuffling paper at the office, you get to come home to your little family."

Emily's offhanded remark was designed to be a simple smart-ass poke, but Wally took it literally. He didn't realize his smile gave him away. "Emily, I'll leave, but don't go away, please. I'm serious about this, and I need to know you won't do something stupid."

Wally led both her and Rosalie to the kitchen and showed them a red push button sitting on the countertop. Two small wires snaked their way into the back of the telephone. "It's connected to the telephone but works on a battery back up, just in case. Here's the alarm for the house, and this is the setting to arm it. Just punch in the code and it's set. Okay?"

He jotted the four number code on a pad to be sure they didn't forget. "It's armed now, so all you have to do is punch it. If the wires get cut for some reason, the alarm will get activated." He stood back thinking of anything he could have missed. Satisfied, he added, "Well, that's it."

Emily, in an infrequent moment of appreciation and tenderness, "Thank you, Wally. I know what your concern is, and I'm aware of the danger." She put her hand on his shoulder and stood on her tiptoes to plant a soft kiss on his cheek. "See you later," pushing him out the door.

Turning to her daughter, she playfully said, "And that's how you control men, Rosie. Wanna have some fun today? Come on outside, I want to teach you something." Emily went into the bedroom and came out with the flannel package she snuck out of Jim's house, and unwrapped the .38 revolver and a box of shells.

Standing in the yard, she instructed Rosalie, "Honey, take these tacks and put this paper on the side of the old shed." Stepping back about twenty feet, she put the weapon in the child's hands. "Baby, you don't have to be afraid of it. It's only a piece of metal, but if you know what to do with it, you can use it for protection. It's not evil, but it can keep the evil away from you. If you think you need to point it at something that is going to hurt you, you need to use it. You need to stop the evil."

Rosalie grimaced and started to tear up at the thought of shooting a gun at someone. "Mommy, this is wrong. Sister Alysia said we …" and Emily cut her off.

"Honey, Sister Alysia isn't being chased. She didn't go through what you did, and she doesn't have the evil after her. God is not going to stop Daddy from hurting us. We need to do that ourselves, and then ask God to help us deal with it." In a stronger and firmer voice, she said, "Get mad, honey. Get totally pissed and tell yourself that you aren't going to be hurt again. You are going to stop it from happening."

Rosalie smiled at her mother's moxie, "Okay, Mommy, lets shoot the bastard."

Emily smiled and put a huge hug on her daughter. Together, they rolled on the ground laughing hysterically, throwing leaves and grass at each other in a frenzy of seldom-seen happiness.

However, the gloom still loomed over them, and it was time for Rosalie to learn how to kill somebody. Emily showed her how to hold the gun, how to cock the hammer, take aim and squeeze the trigger. Then she learned how to open the cylinder and put the bullets in.

Taking the loaded weapon from her, Emily said, "Babe, find a rock."

Rosalie asked, "A rock?"

"Yeah, find a rock and throw it at the paper on the shed."

So she did. The little hand grasped her rock and launched it, bouncing off the paper target, settling back on the ground.

Handing the gun back to Rosalie, Emily said, "Now, aim the gun at the paper and squeeze the trigger."

Looking from her mom to the gun and then the paper, she raised her arms, pointing the gun, and it exploded as she commanded. Almost breathless, her eyes wide, Rosalie gaped at the hole in the center of the paper.

"So, little girl, now you know why so many cave men died throwing rocks. Do it some more. Empty it."

After about an hour of shooting, Emily felt her daughter had enough confidence—and had overcome her fear of the gun.

"Killing a piece of paper is different than taking a human life, honey. That piece of paper is just hanging there waiting to get full of holes. If you need to point the gun at a human who is going to hurt you, don't ever hesitate. Get it over with before you talk yourself out of it. Just remember that you will never point it at anyone who is not going to hurt you. Got it?"

"Sister Alysia is going to shit when she hears about this."

Startled, Emily said, "Is that the language they taught you there?"

"From the kids it is. The younger ones would say, *Thee will shit.*"

"Well, let's see what we can cook for our sheriff when he comes home." Hugging each other, the gun dangling from Rosalie's little hand, they went into Wally's house to cook dinner.

● ● ● ● ● ● ● ● ● ● ● ● ● ● ● ● ● ●

Poor Wally was in a fog most of the day, until Jim showed up with a picture of Roger Parkhurst. Wally called in Ted, the dispatcher. "Take this over to the printer and get it enlarged and about a hundred copies made, and put this message on it. Then fax it to Ryden's store at the border, and to the Canadian guard post. Also, get a copy to the highway patrol and the sheriff's station at Two Harbors and Little Marais."

Ted Marks was eager to let his boss know he was good at his job. "I've called in Bill Pierce from the senior center to sit on the phones for a while, boss. He's at the desk now."

"Thank you Ted, I'm totally impressed. Now, burn heels and get it done." The young deputy almost left a trail of smoke as he ran out the door. "I've got an APB out for the Oldsmobile, Jim. The girls are at my place, and I showed them how to use the alarm."

"Good. Good, Wally. Now we just have to find this asshole. I don't want the girls to know I'm here yet. They need to stay in one place as long as possible. I'll be out at my house, and tomorrow we'll see what comes from DeAnna and Leonard." Jim stopped to cover a few details with the replacement at the dispatcher's desk before going outside to the Impala.

When Deputy Marks came back from the print shop, he settled into working the fax

machine, alerting every law enforcement agency between Minneapolis and the Canadian border. Wally praised him some more, thanked Bill Pierce at the desk, and went home to the girls.

Wally's job was to be observant and analyze. Getting out of his Cherokee in the driveway, he smelled the cordite hanging in the heavy summer air. Walking up to his small house, he did a double take at the shredded side of his wood shed. Opening the door to the odor of Hamburger Helper, warm biscuits from the Doughboy, and seeing two happy faces smiling at him, was something totally new to him. They could have cooked ragweed, and he wouldn't have been more pleased and dumbfounded.

"Wow, this is wonderful. You two did this?"

Rosalie, as much of a smart-ass as her mother, chirped, "No, the maid just left." All three were in stitches, and Wally's little house rolled with laughter.

Emily handed him a can of beer, "Sit down and tell us about your day of saving lives."

Wally confronted them, "I know what you guys did outside, and I don't know if I'm upset or what. Where did you get the gun?"

"It's Jim's. My daughter needs to know that prayer isn't going to stop a maniac who wants to hurt her. I taught her to hurt first. Let's eat, and we'll give you a demonstration."

The meal was delicious. The small chatter while they passed dishes back and forth gave Wally a taste of "happy family" that he didn't want to go away. He tried to concentrate on his plate, but couldn't suppress an urge to keep peeking at Emily. She saw what he was doing, but ignored it.

Emily helped him wash the dishes while Rosalie played solitaire at the kitchen table. When they touched each other in the cleaning-up process, they would lock eyes and unspoken messages passed between them. It was an awkward silence, but a warm one.

Just before twilight dropped in, they went outside where Rosalie went through the target routine for him. She was as professional and cautious as she could be, impressing Wally very much. All the cartridges were picked up, the target taken down, and her handling of the weapon was perfect.

Inside, he sat Rosalie down at the table with a cleaning kit, showing her how to disassemble the piece. The somewhat pleasant odor of Hoppe's cleaning fluid filled the room. A couple hours of small talk, and Rosalie got up and kissed her mom goodnight. Kneeling on the sofa next to Wally, she kissed his cheek and said, "Good night Wally. Thank you."

They watched Rosalie disappear into the spare bedroom and Emily softly said, "That's very good, you know. She's got a shyness towards men, and won't let many get near her. Besides you, Jim is the only one she will allow to get anywhere close."

"This is all new to me, Emily. I haven't had anything like this for a lot of years, and then it was with my folks. I've been too involved with school and the job to make any room for this in my life. Having you two here is as close to having a family of my own that I've ever had. I don't know where this is going or what is going to happen next, and I'm kind of scared."

Boring a hard look into him, she said, "I'm grateful for what you're doing for us, Wally, but in a way that's also your job. To be honest, for now it's not going anywhere. You are the nicest guy I've ever known, but my life is a piece of shit right now, and I can't have any complications until my daughter is safe and happy. I'm fully aware that I may not live through this. Nobody knows Roger's capabilities nor really understands how resourceful and dangerous he is. If anything does happen to me, I need to know Rosie will be taken care of by Sister Alysia. If I'm lucky enough to get out of this alive, and don't go to jail, I would love nothing more than to start a life with you. After you get to know me, you probably won't want anything to do with me. I've been around the block a lot, Wally, and I've had to make some hard choices to survive. Can we just put us into neutral until it's over?"

Squeezing her hand, he added, "I can wait. Goodnight Emily." He went to bed alone, and enjoyed a delightful sleep filled with a fantasy of love and lust.

Emily sat alone for a while, tearing her mind into little pieces, with a premonition of something terrible happening. Just the idea of teaching her daughter how to kill somebody had pulled her into a hole that had no bottom.

● ● ● ● ● ● ● ● ● ● ● ● ● ● ● ●

Roger stopped at a Holiday gas station in the little town of Beaver Bay, settled on both sides of Highway 61, south of Grand Marais. He gassed up and bought a Mounds bar and a cup of coffee for the road. Before heading out, he stopped in the restroom to take a leak.

Standing in place, he blankly looked around at the grime and came face to face with a picture of himself taped to the wall over the urinal. To the left of his face was the tip of a small ear, and to the right was the edge of his wife's head. "Jesus Christ, that came from my house. What the hell ..." He ripped it down and ran to his car, spinning out onto the highway, speeding north.

A few miles out of town he pulled over to look at the picture again. "Son of a bitch, they've been in the house. It's over now." He punched the number on his cell phone to get Frank–but only heard a mechanical voice "The number you are calling is no longer in service. Please ..." Roger smashed the phone on the dashboard, pieces flying around the in the car. Livid, he swore, "Okay Asshole, I'll get them–and then it's you. It's payback time, you jerk."

The wording on the photo had a description of him and the Oldsmobile as well as the license plate number. "I've gotta ditch this car, now." Slowly he drove a few miles when a driveway appeared on the Lake Superior side of the road. The mailbox was a replica of a barn, all painted red with white trim. *Immelman, Box 174* was painted on the side.

He followed the driveway that wound its way down away from the road through thick clusters of pine trees. He couldn't see the house from the road, which was perfect for him. Slowly coasting down, the driveway became steeper as he got closer to the lake. Finally, a small cabin that resembled the mailbox came into view.

The front was covered by dead vines and screen porch, but most important, an older Ford F150 pickup was parked in front. He pulled alongside the truck, keeping it between him and the cabin, obstructing a view of him. He checked the Glock, making sure there was a round in the chamber, and clicked off the safety, putting it in his jacket pocket.

Stepping out he was greeted by a stiff, cold wind from the lake. The screen door creaked open and he reached for the bell. In a few moments, a small shadow moved behind the curtained window and opened the door.

A tiny gravely voice asked, "Yes? Can I help you?" It could have been Grandma Moses standing there. A small, frail woman in a faded pink apron who seemed to force her voice out of her mouth, stood in the doorway. The gray hair was piled on top of her head in a tight bun, emphasizing the scrawny, turkey-skinned neck. Two skinny legs poked out the bottom of her gingham dress, her feet covered by big fuzzy slippers.

With a smile and syrupy politeness, Roger said, "I'm sorry to bother you ma'am. My car broke down, and I need to call for help. I managed to get it down your driveway, but I had to coast to get this far." He fingered the stock of the gun in his pocket.

She looked around him and saw the back end of the Oldsmobile behind the truck. She frowned and eyed him closely, then managed to croak out, "Where you from. Have I ever seen you before?"

"My name is Roger, ma'am. Like I said if I could just use the phone to call."

"Oh, come in; the winds blowin' up good today, real chill in the air." She turned around to lead him into the kitchen when he brought the pistol from his pocket and plunged the butt into the top of her head. The thudding force crushed her fragile skull, sending her body to the floor like a rag doll. She lay splayed across the old linoleum, the head resting at a right angle to the torso in a grotesque display of disrespect. Her eyes were wide open and her tongue hung limply out of her lips, blood draining onto the just-washed floor.

In the kitchen, he rinsed Mrs. Immelman's remnants off the butt of his Glock. A fresh pot of coffee sat on the stovetop, so he took a clean cup from the cupboard and poured one out. Looking around the kitchen, he found a large wooden key mounted to the wall near the door with little cup hooks screwed into it. The unmistakable shape of a Ford truck key, connected to a plastic tag advertising the local bank, was what he wanted. "Man, this couldn't get easier."

Stepping over her body, Roger's foot left its track in the pool of blood. Leaving the front door open, he slid into the pickup, still holding the coffee cup. As he turned the key, it ground into life. In just ten minutes, he had taken an innocent life and was back on Highway 61 going north again.

The cover he had enjoyed was blown and now, the chaser was being chased. This had become a suicide mission, and if he was successful, two more people, minimum, would die. The third would be Frank, then himself. He tossed the empty coffee cup onto the highway and held his forehead tightly to keep the pain at bay.

Bill Immelman had gone into town to get his mother some groceries. His dad couldn't get out anymore so it was up to him. He had been wrestling with the nursing home idea for a long time, but just couldn't move her out. His dad wouldn't be a problem as he would probably not outlive his mom anyway. That was her home and she deserved to live out her life where she was happy. The cancer had wrapped around her throat, and she was having trouble talking. His dad was unable to converse these days, so she didn't talk that much anyway.

Pulling his Saturn up to the house, the difference wasn't apparent at first. Then it hit him. The old truck was gone and a strange maroon car sat in its place. He gave the Oldsmobile a cursory glance and noticed the house's front door was open. His first thought was that somehow she had taken his dad to the hospital, but what was the maroon car all about? Stepping inside, he saw his mom's body on the floor. Dying on her feet and just falling down would have been expected, but this was not right. When his eyes caught the pool of congealing blood, a chill went up his spine. Looking up from the shoe's pattern in the blood, his glazed stare went straight into the bedroom at his father, propped up on one elbow shaking violently, pointing his finger toward the door.

A few minutes after the frantic 911 call, the wheels of investigation and forensic science were well in motion. Detectives from Two Harbors and Duluth were on the scene and put the obvious story together. Sheriff Stearns in Grand Marais had been given the details and a group of off-duty police was on the way to volunteer in a manhunt for Roger Parkhurst.

Where the Cascade River crosses the highway, just south of Grand Marais, a highway patrol car met Roger going the other direction. He kept an eye on it as the distance between them grew—and then he saw the brake lights come on. Quickly he pulled into a gravel approach with a rustic sign: Grand Goose Road. The old pickup plunged down the winding lane toward the lake until it crashed into a cluster of poplar and birch trees. He rolled out of the door with the Glock in his hand, watching for the patrol car, but heard only the sound of the cold waves of Lake Superior washing up on the shoreline.

Crouched down, Roger ran toward the sound of the lake, stumbling over a birch log set down as a border for a flower garden. Ahead of him was a two-story log house with a cozy, warm appearance, with wooden shake shingles covering the roof. A brass plate set in the wall told him the house was protected by an alarm system, so he could just turn around and take his trouble with him.

At the door, he was met by a slim, balding middle-aged man who took too long to say *hello*. Roger put the Glock to the guy's chest and blew a hole through him, covering his shirt with powder burn, and spraying blood over the wall behind. There was a slight *thud* as the body toppled straight back onto the polished wooden floor.

The sound of footsteps rushing into the room were followed by a middle-aged woman yelling, "Chuck! What was that?" Seeing her husband lying on his back in a pool of blood brought a scream from deep, deep in her throat. Roger swung the pistol across her face, knocking her to the floor. He sat on her chest to expel her remaining breath, and put his hand over her bleeding mouth. Then he listened for any sounds within the house. Except for the muted throbs of Vivaldi coming from a distant stereo, the house seemed to be empty.

A book lay open on a stool, with a glass of wine sitting near it, Roger joked, "It looks like I've interrupted contemplation time."

Standing up, he grasped the woman's hair, pulling her to her feet. "Chuck is dead. If you want to die, I can help with that. If you want to live to see your kids or whoever, then do as you're told." The woman was sobbing hysterically as he dragged her through the house by the shock of hair clenched in his fist. When she stumbled, she cried out in pain as he yanked her up again.

"Nice place, Emily would like this. Maybe I'll bring her back here."

Now, his game was to control her with fear and humiliation. As long as she wanted to live, and he kept the string of life hanging before her, he could make her do anything he wanted. Roger often thought that the most important lesson he ever learned was in that hole in the ground in Cambodia so many years ago: Survival.

He guessed she had a family someplace, and with the need to survive for them, she would cherish the promise of being kept alive. They came to a downstairs bedroom where he thought he would keep her during the ordeal he had in mind.

Pushing her onto the bed, she tearfully stammered, "What do you want? There are a few dollars you can have, and there is a car in the garage." She shakily pointed to the dresser, "The keys are there. Please take what you want, and let me go to my husband."

Roger growled, "First things first. Take your clothes off, I want you naked."

She didn't think the horror could get any worse. Her lips quivering, she muttered, "You murdered my husband, now you're going to rape me? I won't fight you. I just want you to leave." She stood and took her blouse and jeans off, followed by her bra and panties. Standing exposed in front of him stricken with fear, she wailed, "Do what you want. Get it over with and leave." Her face was contorted with grief and wet from tears, yesterday's mascara streaking her cheeks.

Looking at her, knowing he was in complete control, he assessed her as a sexual object. Average height, brown hair to her shoulders with a streak or two of infringing gray, and although a bit overweight, she was quite attractive. Stepping close enough to feel her breath on his face, he ran his hand over her stomach, and then caressed her breast.

The sexual assault took no more than a couple of minutes and was made special to him by the forceful strains of Vivaldi in the background. Satisfied, he stood up and teetered, holding his head together with both hands. He was seeing sparks in his eyes from the headache, and swayed as he stood, waiting for it to pass. He barked, "Into the kitchen. I need to eat something."

Stumbling out of the bedroom she looked down the hallway at the heap on the floor that used to be her husband. "Oh, God, no. Chuckie, oh, no." She started towards him but was pulled back.

"There's nothing to be done for him now. Were you people religious?"

Looking at him with utter contempt mixed with a chilling fear, "What? Yes, we are. We believe in God and the goodness and love he shares with us. We always …"

Cutting off her sermon, he snarled, "Well, you can bury him with some prayers when I leave." Pushing her into the kitchen, he barked, "I want a sandwich. Peanut butter, and put some mayo on it. And some milk. You got any aspirin?"

Shaking, and all of a sudden embarrassed at being nude in front of him, she took a bottle out of the cupboard. His hands were trembling as he managed to get five tablets into his mouth with the rest of the aspirin falling onto the slate countertop and the floor.

Reeling over his intrusion between her legs, she felt filthy and violated. Ashamed of her nudity, and her mind in turmoil over her husband lying helpless, she pleaded, "May I please go to my husband? Maybe he's still alive and I can help him." Her arms wrapped around her breasts she leaned forward in a futile attempt to hide.

His vision was blurred from the pain in his head, and she was beginning to irritate him. Squeezing his eyes tightly, he snapped, "Shut the fuck up. He's dead."

She flinched at the outburst. What he said was obvious, and at that point she lost hope and just gave up. Self-respect was to no avail now, helplessly dropping her arms, she moaned, "You're sick, aren't you?" Let him look at her. Let him ravage her all he wanted. Nothing mattered anymore.

Submissively, he admitted, "I get some bad headaches, that's all. Where's the milk?"

As she shakily poured it for him, splashing most of it, she had fleeting thoughts about trying to harm him in some way. There must be something someplace she could plunge into him. But she was neither aggressive nor clever enough, and certainly not brave.

He caught her eyes darting around and was entertained by her need to survive. "Don't think about it. You'll just piss me off and get yourself hurt."

At that point, she just gave up and leaned against the counter and cried, holding her hands to her face. Her nakedness was open to him as she was beyond embarrassment, pitifully telling him, her sobbing voice wavering, "Please, please leave. Do what you want to me and leave. I'm not going to say or do anything to make you angry. Please eat your food, take anything and leave me tied up. The phone wires are outside, you can rip them out. There's money in the top drawer of the dresser. We have no drugs or liquor. Just some wine."

Her voice distracted him and there was a lull in the pain lodged in his forehead. Time for another assault, he commanded, "Get over here."

She obeyed, standing in front of him thinking that no matter what he asked, she would do her best to satisfy him. It was the only route to survival she could think of.

As he dropped his pants, he made a motion with his hand, telling her, "Get on your knees; get closer." He grabbed her hair again and pulled her face to him, and she did the best she could.

It only took a moment for him to finish; pushing her away he pulled up his pants. She slowly lowered her head to the floor, as she buried her mind in prayer. She wrapped her arms over her head to hide, wailing in agony, crouched in front of the monster.

Pulling her up to her feet by her hair, she groaned at the pain, "*Uhhnn*," her face grimaced in fear. Showing a false compassion, he draped his arm over her shoulder, pulling her close to him. Softly speaking into her ear, "It's going to be all right. Let's go back into the bedroom, then I'll leave." He guided her as she stumbled, trying to wipe the filth from her lips.

Pushing her to the bed again, he ordered, "Lie down." Looking into the closet, he took out two of Chuck's neckties, using them to tie her hands to the headboard. Her body stretched open on the bed, he made a game of caressing her, when the eerie silence in the house was shattered by the telephone ringing. He sat on the bed next to her listening to the voice as it was sent to the answering machine.

"Hi, Mom, Shelley here. Just checking in, give me a call. Love you both, bye."

"Where is Shelley?"

She whispered, "In Duluth."

Slowly stroking her body, he asked, "What's your name?"

Quavering in defeat, she muttered, "Jeanine. Jeanine Brooks."

"Hi Jeanine Brooks. I'm Roger Parkhurst."

"I heard about you on the radio. They said you were dangerous." The tears were rolling down her cheeks onto the duck decorations on the pillow.

"Yes, Jeanine, I am dangerous. I came up here to kill my wife and daughter. How does that sound?"

Horrified that any human could do such a thing, she rolled her head and whimpered something he didn't understand–nor did he care. He took the keys from the dresser top and opened the drawer to find two hundred dollars inside. "I killed a man for two hundred dollars once."

Jeanine sobbed out the only prayer she could think of. "Oh, dear Jesus, please save me." Her lips quivered while she mumbled all the words she could think of that the Almighty would listen to. "Oh, Heavenly Father, now at our time of…"

"I'll leave you and your God alone now. I'm going to check out your house." In the living room he looked out at Lake Superior and the spray from the waves washing up on the tall windows. Vivaldi had taken a rest, and the blood under Chuck was congealing. His thoughts went back to the patrol car on the highway– and he knew he had to leave, now. Jeanine Brooks' agonizing moans floated from the bedroom, irritating him just a little bit.

Wiping a bit of mayo off his cheek, he detoured into the kitchen to rummage through the drawers. Finding what he needed, he went back to the bedroom and raped her one more time. During the assault she forced her body to ride with his motion, hoping he would be satisfied and not hurt her. His action slowed, and relieved, she thought it was over. However, when she saw him bring the large butcher knife into view, her body lurched and stiffened. In spasmodic falsetto shrieks, her terrified noises filled the room as she futilely tried to bury herself into the mattress, writhing to escape. "*No, no, no, no.*"

His work in the Brooks' home was done now. It was time to leave. As he walked to the front door, the silence was stifling. The only sound he heard was his own breathing, and the deep ticking of an antique clock somewhere in the house.

Killing the woman brought temporary relief to his throbbing head, giving him enough strength to leave. He still had an arousal in his groin, and stopped when he came to Chuck's lifeless hulk in the entryway. Turning, he went back into the bedroom to ravage her one more time. Staring at the naked woman, her eyes open wide from fear, he followed the blood down to her breasts, but the life-less body had lost its appeal to him–so he left her alone.

The garage was separate from the house and the side door was open. To his delight, the gleaming black Mercedes had a full tank of gas. Leaving the carnage behind, he put a Mozart CD into the car's player.

The mellow and relaxing strains of Mozart, with the floating sensation of the luxury car, the tremor in his groin was getting active again, and he was sorry he killed the woman so soon. The memory of Jeanine Brooks, helplessly spread on the bed, sent a surge of blood to his groin. He realized that it wasn't the naked woman or the sex that drove him–it was the killing. It was the easy motion of slic-ing flesh and watching the horror and disbelief in the eyes as he followed the vic-tim into death, and heard the final sigh of giving up. For Roger, this was the ultimate form of control.

Interrupting his euphoric dream, he remembered that he had left his stuff in the Olds. His clothing, the information in the envelope, the stash of pot, every-thing was all sitting in the Immelman's driveway. "Man, I'm stupid. No wonder they have a tag on me."

If the law knew who he was, it really didn't matter. Sooner or later, he would have to die anyway. He always knew it would end this way, and accepted it. His mission was to kill Rosalie and his ex-wife, and he was going to do it. Taking his daughter's life would be a problem because deep down he had a fondness for the child. However, as much as he still loved Emily, she had to die before he did. The thought of watching the horror in her face as she knew she was going to die, painfully, was the driving force that pushed him ahead.

"Maybe I'll give Emily a poke or two before I do her, for old times." Euphoria swept over him, fueled by the gentle strings of Mozart, and the image of Emily satisfying his needs before he killed her.

"The kid will squirm and cry too much so I'll just douse her quick. Yeah, do her quick so I don't have to think about it." Rogers' demented logic wouldn't allow him to linger on his daughter's fate. His feelings for the child were buried so deeply he was denied their existence, betrayed only by the new moistness in his eyes.

CHAPTER 14
DeAnna's Mistake

D EANNA WISHOULT TOOK THE search warrant to the desk sergeant and requested a squad car for back up. The officer on duty took the paper from her, "I'll be right back, Ma'am. Have a seat." He nodded to a wooden bench near the door, and disappeared into the sanctum of the police station.

Knocking on the glass-walled office of the captain on duty, "Captain Freeman, sorry to bust in, but you should see this." He handed the warrant to the captain. "Isn't Roger Parkhurst the one they're looking for up north? I think Lieutenant Dawson was working with him, or someone with a similar name."

"Yeah, I think so. Wait outside." The glass door rattled shut behind him.

Punching a button on his desk phone, "Frank, Captain Freeman here. You connected to this Parkhurst guy? I've got a search warrant for his home. You want me to send a squad out? If it isn't acted on, there may be some fallout."

Frank, on the other end, "Who brought it over?"

Looking at the signature, he said, "Let's see, it's being served by someone from Child Services, uhmm, a D. Wishoult signed it."

Frank Dawson gritted his teeth, knowing he couldn't interrupt the warrant without a lot of questions. "Give it back to her and tell her the squad will meet her out there. I'll send the unit from here."

The desk officer gave her the instructions and then busied himself with something so he would be too occupied to answer any questions.

When she got to Roger's house in the Minneapolis suburb of Brooklyn Park, the squad car with two officers was waiting for her. She followed them to the front door and was surprised when they opened the door and walked right in. No announcement, no guarded entrance, and the door was unlocked. She had expected a reasonable search, but the two officers only followed her through the empty house.

Remembering what Jim had said, she went directly to the bedroom and looked up at the ceiling in the closet. Turning to the nearest officer, she said, "Would one of you get a chair for me, please?"

The box was where Jim said she should look, and she cursed him for meddling, and also thanked him for being a good cop. As she thumbed through the pictures of Rosalie, a wave of nausea swept over her. Thumbing through the plastic tape cases, she came across the notebook. Setting the box on the dresser top, she was about to look into the book when one of the officers pushed her aside, grabbing the box away.

Almost being knocked off her feet, he took the box lid also, "Sorry Ma'am but this is evidence and will be turned over to the proper channels at the station house." She slid the book behind her so the officer couldn't see it, and confronted him, "What? I'm the one with the search warrant. I want that box back."

The officer was adamant, "We were told to bring all evidence back with us. If you have any questions, you're supposed to see Lieutenant Dawson. That's the way it is. Sorry." The two officers left her standing alone in Roger's bedroom, totally dumfounded and angry. However, she had secreted the mysterious book behind her.

Racing back to the station house, she slammed her car into a no parking zone and launched her anger on the hapless desk sergeant. Leaning forward over the startled man, she snarled, "I want to see Lieutenant Dawson, and it better happen *now*."

Holding his hand up in defense, "Holy shit, lady. Back off. I'll see if he's in."

After a moment on the phone, he led her to Frank Dawson's office. Pushing him aside, she stormed through the opaque glass door.

Inside, she was greeted with, "Aha, Ms. Wishoult. Good to see you. How are you today? Sit down. Tell me what's on your mind." Frank's sarcasm was as irritating as his smug smile.

Grabbing a generic oak chair, her hand teetered on the back for support. Angrily, feet spread defiantly, she spouted, "I got a search warrant in connection to a child molestation case from Child Services. A box of evidence was taken from that search—and you have it."

Setting back in his chair, he mocked, "How's that case going for you?"

Almost to the point of yelling, "Don't placate me. I want my evidence."

Leaning forward, his elbows on the desk, he snidely said, "I recall this same scene in your office not long ago. What's different now?"

"The difference is that I have legal right to that evidence."

"The case concerning Roger Parkhurst is a police matter. It seems we have a conflict, Ms. Wishoult. You should go back and take care of welfare cheaters and wife beaters."

Standing with her fists supporting her on the edge of his desk, their faces just inches apart, she menacingly told him, "The only conflict is you. I want that box, and if I don't have it in twenty-four hours, I'll get a subpoena. I know what is in it, and it had all better be there." Like a gulf-coast hurricane, she turned and left.

His eyes narrowed to her confrontation, squeezing his fists to ease the shaking. Fuming, he stepped to the door, quietly closing it, aware that the disturbance had caught the attention of those in the squad room.

The shoebox was sitting on the floor between his feet when she had barged into his office. He sat with it on his lap now, looking through the photos and tapes. He slid one of the tapes into a player and discovered what Roger had been doing. "You son of a bitch. You were going to blackmail me, you asshole. Well, I've got your stash now, buddy. Do your job up there, and I'll have your ass down here."

Dawson tried to think of a way to use parts of the box to nail Roger and get rid of what information pointed to him. The whole collection was poison to him, so he decided to destroy it all without leaving a trace, and find a way of circumventing Child Services.

There was no clean way out of this, and he hoped Roger would take care of the two people up north. He would just have to get rid of Roger for good when it was over.

Frank's only fear was exposure. If there were any inquiries from other agencies, it would all fall on him. The connection to Roger had been severed, and now the angry and meddling social worker needed to be dealt with.

He looked longingly at a couple of pictures of Rosalie, and put them into his pocket. Gathering the contents, he wrapped his coat around the box as he left for the rest of the day.

● ● ● ● ● ● ● ● ● ● ● ● ● ● ● ● ● ●

DEANNA TOLD HER SUPERVISOR ABOUT the incident. "Sure, DeAnna, we have first right to the seizure, but at the same time we can't impede a police matter. We need to stay political on this. Don't make any waves until we hear what happens with this Parkhurst thing. I understand there's a search on for him up north."

Dejected at losing to a slime ball like Dawson, she gave in to her supervisor, "Fine, I can buy that, but I want a safe house set up for Emily and the child. If Parkhurst is looking for them, we have to act."

With those wheels set in motion, DeAnna decided to take a breather from the tension. She picked up a bottle of wine and went home to let the pressure out. Her condo was on the edge of the downtown area. An old, yet attractive neighborhood had been renovated to provide over-priced living for upper-scale professionals. She punched the buttons on her alarm system and noticed the little light behind the panel was out. Tapping it a few times didn't get it to come on, so she would have to tell maintenance to look at it.

Taking care of business first, she tried calling Jim, but with no response, her second choice was to Wallace Stearns. "Oh, Wally, I'm glad you're in. Listen, I found a box of pictures in Parkhurst's house. They were explicit photos of Rosalie, but I didn't have time to scan them to ID the men in them. The police took the box, and now that Lieutenant Dawson has it. It's obvious that he's involved somehow. So, when the Parkhurst thing is over, there are still some unanswered questions. We definitely have a child exploitation case here. The mother and daughter need to be protected."

"Thanks for the update, Dee. We've got a net strung out for Parkhurst, and the girls are safe where they are. This should end soon, and then we'll get together with you. This may involve the attorney general's office."

"Oh, Wally, there was a book the police didn't get. It's coded, and was with the photos so it has to be connected. I'm going to have forensics take a look at it."

"I wish you were working up here Dee. We could sure use your analytical know-how. When we build a case against Parkhurst, we're going to need to work closely with you. Thanks again."

They exchanged a few words about how each other was doing, and that they should really stay in contact more often. The niceties put aside, she hung up and looked forward to a relaxing evening.

The wine was warm and comforting, and feeling satisfied, she glided through her condo and finally settled into the bathtub for some steamy relief.

Mumbling to herself, "Oh, I don't know if it's all worth it." She was getting an ulcer from the worries and problems, and had become very irritable. Thinking about Emily and Rosalie, she realized that their problems were worse than hers.

"When this one is over I'm going to Florida for a couple weeks. I have to get out. Maybe I'll spend some time with old friends, and I might even look into going back home, maybe become a teacher. Screaming kids has to be better than this." She took another sip of wine, rolling the delicate glass between her fingers.

● ● ● ● ● ● ● ● ● ● ● ● ● ● ● ●

MOST PEOPLE HAVE AN INSTINCT THAT tickles the subconscious and is supposed to flag an alert to intrusion. She vaguely felt uneasy, and she had sensed that something was wrong, but put it aside as being fallout from her confrontation with Dawson, and the pressures from the job.

The relaxing hot water lulled her into a fog, shutting down the edge of her mind that screamed out the warning. In the void that clouded her mind, she felt a weight of on top of her head. For a fleeting instant she thought she was getting a massage and was so thankful, until the hot water covered her face so she couldn't breathe. Panic took over as she clawed against the slippery sides of the tub to pull herself up. The pressure on her head was hurting, and as she gasped for air, she sucked water in. The wine glass broke and cut her hand while she pushed her foot against the faucet for leverage.

She felt a surge of strength and almost overcame the force on her head, but it was over-powering. Thrashing at the water, her arms flailing, she grabbed at the intrusion pushing her down—an unmistakable hand. Screaming into the denseness of the water, her claustrophobic fear sent panic through her. At the same moment that death took her, she knew for certain it was Frank Dawson—and the mysterious book became more important.

The very last thought that went through her mind, "*He is seeing me naked. I am so embarrassed.*" A searing white pain went through her collapsing lungs, up her spine and out the top of her head, and her body sank down into the water—into the darkened depths of death where nothing else mattered.

Frank had heard her make the phone call, but from where he was hiding, the conversation was just muffled sounds. He picked up her cell phone and saw the name and number of the Grand Marais Sheriff's office, which told him what his next move would be.

Drying his hands on the thick towel DeAnna had set out for herself, he looked over his victim. "I never realized she was so good looking. Too bad her attitude got in the way."

CHAPTER 15
STOP

● ● ● ● ● ● ● ● ● ● ● ● ● ● ● ● ● ● ●

ALMOST MOTIONLESS, THE BIG, comfortable Mercedes floated, rather than drove. Sound from the stereo system engulfed Roger in exotic tones as he glided into the small town of Grand Marais, Minnesota. Decorations along the street reminded tourists they were in walleye and moose country. Side-by-side gift shops were filled with charms resembling cozy cabins and lofty pine trees, made by artisans in the area, and some had *made in China* on the bottom.

As he passed the Cobblestone Garage, he missed seeing Clovis wave, amazed at seeing Chuck's Mercedes on the road.

So he was here, now what? All Roger knew was that the inquiry for Emily's file had come from this town, requested by a Sheriff Stearns. The sheriff's station was easy to find, and when he slowly drove past, he was amazed to see, right there, sitting in front was the old Chevy Impala that had belonged to his neighbors. Likely not a coincidence, he thought he had made the first connection.

Near the center of town, the sheriff's station sat at the bottom of a hill that towered over it. A rustic brown sign invited people to drive up to the overlook to see more of the town and the endless stretches of Lake Superior. Roger cruised up and parked next to the guardrail where he could keep surveillance on the old blue Impala parked in plain sight. "Something's got to happen, that car's there for a reason. That bitch has to be around here, someplace. Last time I saw it, she was driving the damn thing."

A slight fog rolled off the lake, clouding some of the boat traffic floating in the bay. Sailboats were moored, and larger yachts sat idle, farther out. Small outboard motors could be heard as local fishermen went out for a day of lake trout and walleye fishing.

Pedestrian traffic along the shoreline swarmed in and out of the restaurants and gift shops. The tourists were easy to spot with kids in tow; Dad wearing a Grand Marais tee shirt, and Mom with sandals and straw hat. Roger gazed longingly at them, confused by the appeal.

Settling back, he tried to imagine what he would do next. Planning was not his strong point, and Frank was not here to guide him. He had created too much of a mess getting this far, and had to finish it. It didn't matter that Frank was pulling his strings–he was fully prepared to die for it. However, if he did survive, he knew he would definitely murder Frank Dawson.

He had his mission, and he was going to go as far as he could with it. His head was throbbing again; his vision blurring. The cushion of the leather seats almost put him to sleep, which would be a blessing to him, but he needed to stay awake. So, he opened the door and stepped out to stretch when a large man came out of the building below and squeezed himself into the Impala. Bingo, he had a new target. The Chevy pulled onto the highway and went north, with Roger trailing a mile behind.

Mostly out of habit, and now for a precaution, Jim was watching the passing traffic and the cars behind him. "Damn if that doesn't look like Chuck's Mercedes. He hardly ever takes it out now." Of course, Jim was watching for the Ford pickup, and ignored the car behind him. Jim slowed down at Hovland, crossed the Flute Reed River, and swung north up Arrowhead Trail, disappearing in front of the dust from the gravel road. A cut at Tower Road, then Tom Lake Road, and the long driveway to home was near.

Roger had slowed down to keep from overtaking his prey. The settling dust off to the left had to be from the Impala, so he carefully kept the cloudy trail as a guide. Having to backtrack at the Tower Road junction, he finally brought himself to Jim's driveway. He went about a half mile farther until he came to a deserted shack where he parked in the tall weeds behind it. Sitting with his hands squeezing his head, he waited until the daylight started to dim before walking the gravel road back to Jim's mailbox.

The Glock in his pocket, he crouched in the ditch across the road for a few minutes, just watching. "Why in any part of hell would anyone want to live out here?" Creeping across the road, up the driveway, staying off to the side, he wondered, "Where'd he go? This is the longest goddamn driveway."

His mind went back to the trek through the Cambodian and Viet Nam jungles when he had Frank leading him. Alone now, he had to use his own wits and cunning to stay ahead of everyone else.

"Yeah Frank, you're next. First I'll murder my family, and then I'll kill the only friend I have. Man, am I ever screwed up." Roger knew he was bad and what he was doing was wrong, but he also knew he was going to do it no matter what.

Finally, seeing the light from the cabin, he moved deeper into the woods and crouched next to a poplar tree to watch. Around eleven that night, the door opened and a big yellow dog came out, running in circles. Roger's plan, if the dog discovered him, was to let it attack and bury the muzzle of the gun in its gut to muffle the sound, or use the knife.

The chipmunks and squirrels were tucked away for the night so Bella followed a new scent to look for some action. Roger had become nothing more than a shadow, as still as the tree trunk he was resting against. The two couldn't see each other but each knew exactly where the other was. Bella, growling, gave herself away as she crept closer; then froze. Aside from the cacophony of the nocturnal life in the woods, the only sound from the strange scent was the solid click of the slide on Roger's pistol, moving a round into the chamber.

The dog moved closer as a soft tongue clucking sound came from the scent. Curiosity was her master now, and she wagged her tail. A moment later she was being caressed. The muzzle of the Glock was imbedded into her belly, and Roger's finger was closing on the trigger. Then he froze. His mind was screaming, *"Squeeze, squeeze another life. Kill again,"* but he couldn't do it. Gary O'Meara, Mrs. Immelman, and Jeanine Brooks, and all the others he put through hell, didn't deserve a moment of compassion or concern. He was going to brutally take the life of his own flesh and blood, but somehow this animal had captured the compassion of this blood-thirsty and remorseless killer.

Roger sat with the dog for another hour, stroking its rich hide and nuzzling his face into her fur. He had forgotten how many human lives he had taken without a flinch, thinking all the way back to the other prisoners and guards at the hole in Cambodia. Frank had paid him to slaughter many hapless people, but he just could not take the life of this beast. The dog's life meant more to him than little Anna Swanson—or even his own daughter.

Shielding the beam of his small flashlight to read the name on her collar, he said, "Hi Bella, it's my pleasure to meet you. I bet Emily and Rosie would like you. Would you like a new home? Come on, girl. Let's take care of you before someone starts looking for you."

The Golden Retriever followed her new friend back down the long driveway to the Mercedes. "In you go, girl. Good girl. Yeah, they're going to really like you." The insulating qualities of the auto were excellent. The barking was muffled as Roger's instincts took him through the pitch black of the night, back to his post at the base of the poplar tree. Off in the distance a wolf was calling, and he suspected that there could be a bear wandering around. The only thing that would give him away would be his scent. Roger crouched absolutely still against his tree, watching the cabin.

Certain the girls weren't inside, this man was his key to finding them. He knew he shouldn't give in to sleep, but he needed to let the pain in his head go some place else for awhile, and slid into a light slumber. He was exhausted from the day's activities, and eventually a deeper sleep took over. So deep that he was dreaming. He saw himself with Emily and Rosalie on a beach, running with Bella. Rosalie was laughing and rolling in the sand. In the background was the large log home with strains of Vivaldi coming from it. Dr. Goodhue was there, kissing Rosalie, and then Frank was kissing her. He didn't like that because it spoiled the picnic. And they shouldn't be kissing his daughter anyway. He was having sex with Emily, but it confused him. It wasn't sex this time, he was making love to her, and for the first time, she enjoyed it and made love back to him. It was soft and gentle, and they did it because they were a family. Anna Swanson was there, and he tried to warn her to leave before Frank also kissed her.

He had to stop making love to Emily and push the men away, but when he looked back at his wife she was gone—and Jeanine Brooks was there instead. He turned to look at Rosalie but was blinded by a bright light and a different kind of pain to his head. Through the bright light and pain, he saw Rosalie, but it didn't look like her. He couldn't tell if it was Jeanine Brooks, Mrs. Immelman or Rosalie looking at him, and it frightened him. He thought Emily was dead, and that made him sad. Then he saw Rosalie, but she was laughing but an evil look covered her face. "No Rosalie, be nice. I'm your father."

EMILY RECALLED THE LAST TALK SHE HAD with Sister Alysia, who explained, "Rosalie has adjusted to the regimen of life on the farm. There is never any doubt as to what was to happen during her day. She has duties to keep her busy, and it keeps her from thinking." The most disturbing thing that Sister Alysia told her, "Her talks have been becoming more candid. I think we're getting to the core of her subconscious. A week ago she screamed it out to me in more detail. She felt a little better after that." Sister Alysia went on with some good news for Emily, "When you started visiting more often she became sociable, and now can even worm out a smile, sometimes."

After hearing the details of Rosalie's abuses, Sister Alysia took a hiatus to talk to a counselor herself, just to keep her mind focused on helping Rosalie and not diverting into hatred for the men who did this to her. Her faith had taken a serious tumble when she learned what this child had gone through. While Rosalie was on this visit with her mother, Alysia went into a treatment center to cleanse her mind and soul from the filth and tragedy Rosalie had confessed to her. "If God created man, how could he have allowed this flaw to be?"

Sister Alysia's counselor tried to straighten it out for her. "God created us in his image and gave us the power to guide ourselves. What we do with that power is our own decision, and has nothing to do with God or whatever plan he may or may not have."

It made sense—but didn't make her feel any better.

Emily slowly came out of a restless sleep and laid looking at her daughter's soft face nestled in her arms. She was such a child and showed the wonderment of youth as if she didn't have a care in her world. But Emily could look beneath and see the strain and destruction of her innocence. Her little round cheeks would prompt a kiss from a proud grandparent, if she had one, but the twitch was there like a big ugly scar. The child's thrashing in her sleep kept Emily awake most of the night, and she woke up exhausted. Emily reached out to stroke Rosalie's blonde hair that draped over her shoulder. Whispering, "Such a beautiful child; she doesn't deserve to go through this."

Before going to sleep at night, Rosalie and her mom would talk quietly to each other, and sometimes they would get the giggles and just be silly. It was difficult for Emily to see the strain on her daughter who was desperately trying to be a kid.

Last night, Rosie confessed to her mom that there was a boy on the farm she liked. "The coolest boy I've ever seen. He's awesome, Mom. His name is even cool, Skylar Colee Clay. He knows why I was on the farm, and we even talked about it. It was easier than talking to Sister Alysia. Can he come here, Mom? Just for a visit?"

"Of course, Honey, if he can. Wait until we get back at Jim's place, then we can go get him for a few days."

Emily dragged herself out of bed with the idea of making a family breakfast for her daughter. With the inclusion of Wally, it would be perfect. She made scrambled eggs, hash browns, and venison sausage, discovering she loved to do it, in spite of being a terrible cook.

She had no way of knowing at the moment, but Wally had fallen in love with her. It made his head swim to walk into his kitchen and having this beautiful woman, dressed in an old flannel shirt, with the blonde hair framing the cutest face he'd ever seen, handing him a cup of coffee, and announce, "Good morning, Wally." He wanted to kiss her so badly, he couldn't think straight.

And to complete his confusion, Rosalie ran up to him and gave him a big hug. "Hi Wally. You look nice today."

"Good morning Rosalie. Thank you, but I know I'm just a plug with a clean shirt. Thanks to your mom for that. The shirt, I mean. Uh, you know."

"Oh, for Christ sake, sit down and eat. What's on the schedule today, Sheriff?"

Emily's caustic demeanor and directness had an effect on Wally that crawled into his mind. It was the influence she had on men, and Wally was no exception. Acting on an impulse, he reached out with his hand behind her neck and pulled her gently into his arms, kissing her softly on the lips. Too late, the reality of what he did hit him. "Oh, God, no. I'm sorry, Honey. I mean Emily. Oh, God. What have I done? Please, don't get mad, I'm so sorry." He danced around the kitchen like a little boy caught doing something bad.

Emily answered him by returning the kiss with a little more passion, softly telling him, "Just eat your breakfast Sheriff–and don't apologize.

Rosalie filled the small kitchen with a shrill giggle that came from a strange, yet deep and happy place in her, lyrically chirping, "Mommy's got a boyfriend."

"Shush, Rosie. So, Sheriff Stearns, all I asked was what was on the schedule for today. I can only imagine what would have happened if I had said more."

Rolling his head in his hands, "Oh, man, I really screwed up."

Emily couldn't let this go and extended his agony, winking at Rosalie. "Kissing me is screwing up? Now that's how to impress a girl."

"Oh, come on, now, you're making this worse. I'm really embarrassed."

Rosalie was just as mischievous as her mother. "Am I supposed to call you Dad now?"

"Come on you two. Leave me alone."

They finished the meal with a lot of giggles and more ribbing. Emily made the most of it at Wally's expense because she saw the light in the little girl's face when they played the family game. She put her hand on top of his and squeezed it, sending Wally to the moon.

"This is nice Wally. Thank you." She leaned over and kissed his cheek, putting a finality on the flirting, firmly asking, "Now, what in hell are we doing today?"

"Well, if I manage to live through the most embarrassing moment of my life, I need to talk to Jim, and I think the two of you should go along."

Excited to see Jim again, she said, "He's back? Oh, good. When do we go?"

"The sooner the better, I guess. Now?"

"Let me clean up the mess I've made, and we'll be ready," said Emily as she started clearing the dishes from the table. Rosalie disappeared into the bedroom.

Wally helped, and when Rosie was out of sight, he said, "Emily, I've really wanted to kiss you for a long time, and I'm afraid I made a mess of it this morning." He held her arm while she stood at the sink with a dirty plate in her hand.

With a surprising softness, Emily said, "I told you before that nothing is going to happen until this is cleared up and my daughter is safe. Please be patient Wally. We can be very good friends and hope for more, later. I want you to try to understand. Please."

Wally looked toward the bedroom to be sure Rosalie was out of earshot. "There are some law enforcement volunteers coming from Duluth and Two Harbors. Some of them are at the station now, and we're going to get a manhunt started after I leave the two of you with Jim. Roger's on his way here, and already has done some very, very bad things."

Emily glanced at the bedroom. "Don't underestimate him, Wally. What makes him the most dangerous is he doesn't give a shit about what or who he hurts. Please be careful."

He could see her eyes water and the trembling roll up her body. This hard, abusive, straight-talking bundle of soft woman was scared beyond belief. He held her softly and whispered into her ear, not aware of saying it out loud, "Oh, God, I love you Emily."

Startled at what she heard, she pushed away and looked into his eyes. With her hand on his cheek, she pleaded, "Please wait, please."

And they kissed again, long and soft.

Rosalie saw them, but waited before interrupting. She had her backpack and kept it close to her. Emily knew why, and if it made her comfortable, she let it go.

When Wally went out to the patrol car he used for his own, Emily held Rosalie by the shoulder, "Is it loaded?"

The child, in all her grownup savvy, defiantly nodded yes. Emily warned her again, "Be careful, and don't forget anything I've taught you." She held her daughter close, adding, "Let's go, you little shit."

Emily sat in front, with Rosalie in the back seat, listening to their small talk. She liked Wally and best of all, she trusted him. The family fantasy was making her smile, and she wondered what it would be like to have Wally as a dad.

Pulling into the familiar long driveway going to Jim's house, they expected Bella to greet them.

● ● ● ● ● ● ● ● ● ● ● ● ● ● ● ● ● ●

Roger snorted and woke himself up. He was disoriented from the dream and was looking for his family and their dog on the beach. Everyone was gone, there was no beach, and he couldn't move. Crouching against the tree all night, his legs had cramped into a folded position. He struggled up to stretch his muscles and shake off the sleep, stepping around the tree to pee on the other side, when he heard the crunching of car tires on the gravel driveway.

"Oh, shit, man, I'm open," when he realized he had exposed himself. As the police cruiser slowly drove past his position, he kept behind the tree, startled at how ominous and large the vehicle appeared. On the backside of the poplar tree, he stood in the wet spot he had just made, straining to look through the thick foliage at the unfolding scene in front of the house.

A man got out of the driver's door, but he was dressed as a civilian. When he saw the side arm, he knew Wally was a law man. The large man who drove the Impala came out of the house and shook hands with the driver.

Then, Roger's world opened up, and what happened next almost made him shout. First Rosalie stepped out, and then Emily. Everyone was hugging and talking at once. They all went into the house except the large man who was calling, "Bella. Here girl. Bella."

Concerned, Jim said, "I'm worried about Bella. She stays out sometimes, but not usually overnight."

Wally, anxious to get back to the station to get the volunteers moving, "Emily, can you and Rosalie go out to look for Bella? Stay next to the house though."

Emily understood and took Rosalie, and her backpack, outside. They both sat on the ground leaning against the house. Squinting up at the sunshine, Emily kept a steady stream of talk going to keep Rosie busy. "We can go back to the farm and maybe Skylar will be able to come back with us. How old is he, Honey?"

Teasing, Rosalie said, "Thirty-seven."

Playing the game, Emily went with it. "If he's cute, I might take him."

"You've got Wally."

"You get Wally, or I'll get them both." They giggled again, but a cold chill ran through Emily.

Crouching in the woods, Roger watched his ex-wife and daughter, and got set to make his move.

Inside, Wally said, "Jim, I've got to get back for the manhunt volunteers. We'll start at Grand Marais and sweep north. It's going to be difficult if he's moved inland. They found Chuck and Jeanine Brooks, murdered in their house. Their Mercedes is missing and the Immelmans' truck was dumped in their driveway. He ditched it and took the Mercedes."

"Oh, no, Wally, not the Brooks. What is he after? What in goddamn hell is his game?" Then it hit him with a king-size load of anxiety, "Oh, my God, I saw Chuck's car yesterday. It was behind me on Hwy. 61. Start that sweep right here in Hovland from 61, north up to here. Get the state patrol to put up two choppers, one on each side of Arrowhead, then come this way." Jim put his hand on Wally's shoulder, and said coldly, "He's close, Wally. Bella disappearing is a bad sign."

Wally tried to appear calm as he left, but Emily could see his apprehension. She pulled Rosalie closer and told him, "Please be careful. He's not like anyone you've ever chased."

Wally squeezed her shoulder and said, "I'm peaked now, I'll keep watch. A lot of people will be coming this way. Jim, your GMC is at my place. I'm going to use it for a transport."

Jim gave him a thumbs-up.

Wally had the cruiser started and was backing up when Emily ran to the open window. Leaning in, she kissed him and said, "I love you too, Sheriff."

All he could do is smile and nod.

Wally drove quickly out of sight while radioing Ted Marks to take a volunteer and go get the GMC. He then called up the highway patrol dispatcher who told him it would be about an hour and a half before they could get the pilots into service. Frustrated, Wally yelled into the microphone, "That's not good enough. I need those choppers up there, *now.*"

The dispatcher responded, "OK, buddy, its *code king*. If I have to, I'll fly the damn thing myself."

Jim, trying to be calm, "Come on girls. Let's go inside. There's just too much nice weather out here," escorting them out of the yard. The last thought Jim had was to grab his gun.

Inside, Emily busied Rosalie with a game of King's Corners when Jim announced he was going out to call for Bella again. Rosie got up, expecting to help him but was met with a stone-hard look from Mom that told her to stay where she was.

Roger was still leaning against the tree when Jim came outside calling, "Bella. Here girl. Bella." The big man was walking across the yard, closer to the tree line that hid Roger, so he knew it was going to be show time.

Jim slowly walked along the edge of the driveway looking into the dense growth on both sides. Roger was moving closer to the gravel, hoping he could get behind him to shoot him in the back, but Jim stopped. His senses were on red alert, and he knew something was wrong, but he didn't know how bad it actually was.

Roger, filled with blind faith in his superiority and the chances of striking first, stepped out of the brush directly in front of Jim. "Hey, Mister. What's going on?"

Jim wasn't startled because he had been so tense. "Hello Roger. Do you have my dog?"

"No, but I have my dog. I named her Bella. I'm going to give it to my wife and kid."

Jim, talking softly, "You know you're never going to get out of this. Why don't you quit hurting people and put the gun down. We can settle this and the girls, and even you, can get away alive. There's no need to hurt any more, Roger." Jim felt the emptiness in the back of his belt where the .32 should have been—now realizing his fatal error.

Roger said, "You're wasting your time if you think you're going to analyze me into giving up. There's no reason to do that. If you step aside and let me at them, I can let you live. What could be better than that? I heard them call you Jim. Is that your name? Jim?"

Backing up to lead Roger into the yard's clearing, "Yeah, I'm Jim. Where's the dog, Roger?"

"The dog is no longer your concern, Jim. She's mine now—for my family. My daughter will really like her, my wife, too." Roger walked faster toward him and raised the Glock to chest height. Jim didn't have time to get frightened or think of a way out. He had survived for so many years in law enforcement by always having a way to unscrew himself when he was in a jam. Well, this was a jam—and he knew he was screwed.

The handgun hardly made any noise in the dense surroundings. The nine mm slug slammed into Jim's massive chest, lodging deep inside. It didn't hurt anymore than his heart attack had. The next two hit him in the face, and Jim Cooper fell backwards, thudding to the earth. No time for a last thought or any chance to ask for forgiveness. His life had simply ended in one swift motion from a madman. This morning he was alive to have his coffee and enjoy the coming home of the young woman he loved so much. If there was anything left he needed to do, it would be to put the crooked wreath back up in the window.

Emily heard the last two shots and came running out of the cabin screaming. Paying no attention to the man with the gun, she pushed past him and threw herself on top of her beloved friend. "*No. No, no, Jim. No.*" Hugging the large hulk, she felt herself being hauled up to her feet and clung to Jim's shirt, absolutely certain this wasn't happening. Her grip was torn loose as Roger pushed her against the side of the Impala, put the gun to her forehead, and squeezed the trigger. Click, click, click. Three times … and Roger realized he had made an unforgivable mistake. The pistol was empty, and with the slide pulled back, useless.

"Son of a bitch." He dropped the gun and groped for his knife. Emily, pinned against the car, struggled and tore at him with super-human anger and strength. She wasn't trying to get away, she was trying to kill him. She knew she was all that stood between him and Rosalie—and if she died, the girl would be his. She was not going to let that happen. She had made a promise.

Roger's fist hit her in the face with a crushing blow that sent her reeling. He went after her, and was startled when she lurched up from the dirt and thudded against him with a shuddering head butt to his chest. She didn't stop or lose a step. She followed him down and dug at him with animal ferocity, clawing, chewing, biting, and screaming.

Getting his leg under her, he pushed her up and away. She hit the Impala again and the wind came rushing out of her. She wasn't breathing, and couldn't see him, but she lunged forward swinging out at air, and swung again. The second blow to her head put her into a fog. She was in a heap at the side of the old large Chevy, getting her legs under her to charge again. She can die, that's okay, but she has to know he is dead first. That's the only way this can end.

Blood running down his face blinded him, and with a piercing pain in his chest from a broken rib, he grabbed a full hand of hair and yanked her upright. She screamed in pain and lashed out again, trying to dig her nails into anything, groping for his eyes.

He had his knife out and pressed the point against her throat with her hands wrapped around his fist, pushing it away. She was being pressed into the Impala, and used it as leverage. Shaking from the strain, the knife point drew blood, and he felt victory was near.

She tried to bring her knee into his crotch, but he was far too battle hardened for that, and wedged his knees between hers.

A terrifying blast rolled out of her gut and charged up through her throat as she screamed through clenched teeth, "*AHHHHRRRRRR.*" The outburst, fired by her fear and anger, gave her the last surge of strength, and the knife was pushed away a bare fraction–not much, but enough to get the point out of her flesh.

Surprised at losing his grip, he knew she needed to be taken down. He swung his free arm back and sunk his fist into her stomach. She grunted and doubled into the blow when he brought his knee up into her face. He pushed her crumpled body down to the ground, grabbing her by the hair for leverage with his foot on her chest. He was about to plunge the blade into her when a new sound caught him off guard.

Standing behind him, as he held Emily's fading life, Rosalie was screeching, "*Stop. Stop Daddy, stop.*"

Almost amused, Roger let loose of Emily and turned around to face a little girl. With both arms stretched out in front of her, she held a large heavy piece of blue gray steel. "*Get away. Leave her alone.*"

"Hey there, Sweetie; what have we got here? Let me have that Rosie, before you hurt yourself." The vision of his daughter in the dream came back, and he knew what was going to happen. If this was the way it would be, it was the best way.

Rosalie's next act should have told him she was dead serious. Her knees and her body were shaking with fear, tears were streaming down her cheeks and her lips were trembling, but her arms and hands were even and steady. She put both thumbs on the hammer and pulled it back to lock it into position. *Click.*

Her fierce eyes were looking straight into his, but she peripherally saw her mother collapsed on the ground, struggling to get up. She sighted along her arms and saw the barrel of the .38 cover his face. Her mother's words screamed into her head, "Never point it unless you're going to use it. Kill the evil. Kill the evil. *KILL!*"

Her dad was slowly moving toward her when the flash of gunpowder and fire followed the heavy slug into Roger's face, mushrooming in his skull. His head snapped back, and he fell backwards. In the finite split of time that held his last infinitesimal moment of life, Roger understood what his dream was all about.

The evil was dead and lay in a bloody heap on the ground.

Emily, on hands and knees, dragged herself over his body to be sure he wouldn't get up again. She rasped out to her daughter, "Rosalie. Rosie Honey."

The girl sat on the ground next to her mother, stroking the back of her head and whispering, "It's gone Mommy. The evil is dead. *Shhh*, it's okay now Mommy." The warm and smoking weapon laid in her lap, and she kept one hand on it, just to be sure.

While her mother was getting thrashed in the yard, Rosalie had called 911. The beating of Emily lasted as long as the phone call took, and as long as it took to tear open the backpack.

The thumping sound of a helicopter slowly invaded the silence of death in the yard, followed by sirens–and then chaos. Wally's cruiser was first into the yard, followed by another. Later, Jim's GMC came in with seven armed deputies. All but Wally and a highway patrolman fanned out to be sure the area was secured. The Mercedes and its prisoner were discovered and Bella ran home to a new way of life.

After the confusion settled down, everyone knew that things would never be the same again.

Nobody could tell what damage Emily's body had sustained, and they couldn't wait for an ambulance. Both girls were carefully put into the police cruiser, and it was *code three* lights and siren to the intersection of North Road and Arrowhead, where the chopper had clearing to land. Carrying Wally and Rosalie with the battered Emily, the helicopter thumped its way skyward to the landing pad at St. Luke's Hospital in Duluth. Wally carried Rosalie in while the EMTs rushed Emily into the ER. Alerted earlier, they were in action immediately.

Bella stayed behind, guarding her old friend, whining, with one paw and her nose resting on him, waiting for the ambulance.

Emily had a broken cheekbone, a ruptured bladder, a concussion, and lacerations on her arms, neck, and face that required stitches. Her eyes swollen nearly shut and her cut lips gave her the appearance of a prize fighter. The bruises were too numerous to count as they ran together into one ugly splotch.

Wally saw to it that she had a private room with an extra bed for Rosalie. He made it absolutely clear that the child would not be asked to leave her mother for any reason. He could only imagine what Rosalie would be going through after this. She was lying on the bed, cuddled up to her mom, staring blankly.

Emily had a tube feeding her, with wires connecting her to a beeping monitor. Wally's stomach twisted tightly with pity when he looked at her, marveling at how much he loved her. "Emmy, you're going to be here for awhile, and then we can go home together. Rosalie is all right, and she's going to stay here with you."

Looking at him through puffy eyes, she whispering hoarsely, "Roger?"

"He's dead."

Emily nodded slightly.

Talking softly to the girl, Wally said, "Rosalie, you're staying here with your mom. It's over now, and you don't have to be afraid. When your mom is better, we can get Bella and go home. I want you to think about the happy time we had at home and wait for more. It'll be there for all of us. Honey, if you ever needed to be strong and help your mom, now is the time."

Rosalie looked up, expressionless, and then snuggled in closer to her mom.

He bent over and kissed Emily on the forehead and whispered, "I love you."

She blinked, her lips quivering, "Yeah, me too."

In the hallway he talked to an officer from the Minnesota Highway Patrol, "It's not over yet, they're still in trouble. The lieutenant from Minneapolis, a Frank Dawson, is involved, and I don't know where he is. Do you have the manpower to post a guard here?"

"We can't do it, but I think we can get some MPs from the National Guard to stand in."

"As soon as possible. Thank you for everything."

The volunteers weren't getting paid, and they all had jobs and families to tend to, so he showed his appreciation released them. Stopping at the nurse's station, he warned that there may be another attempt on Emily, and the girl was to be watched at all times.

Standing at the door to Emily's room, he looked in at the shell that was left of Rosalie, and the shattered remains of Emily. Fighting back the emotion, with a lump in his throat, he thought, *My God, she has gone through so much, and I love her even more.*

He made Jim's funeral arrangements, which left him with a huge hole in his heart. Jim was like a father to him, and was his main guide in being a decent sheriff. That was all gone now—and the danger was still out there.

The trouble was not over, he was certain of that. This time, he was on his own.

CHAPTER 16
FRANK'S GAME

● ●

WALLY CALLED LEONARD WALBURN and unfolded what had happened to Jim. "Oh, no. He didn't deserve that. Listen, Wallace, there's a lot of stuff I don't understand. I'll give you some time to sort this out, then I need to speak to you and Emily."

"Okay Leonard, but there's still some problems. I don't know all of it yet, but I think there's another person involved here. The name I heard from Jim was a Lieutenant Dawson from the Twin Cities."

"DeAnna has all the details, but I can't seem to find her. I'm going to check with her office. I'll keep in touch." After Wally's call, Len Walburn let the phone drop to his desk and put his head in his hands as his mind fell into a deep, dark hole.

Leonard's call to Child Services prompted an inquiry into DeAnna's whereabouts. The request for an investigation was intercepted by Frank, who then hand picked a detective named Harold Bruntz, to send to DeAnna's condo. Detective Bruntz was a miserable excuse for a detective, and a human being. He reeked of cigars, bad whiskey, and cheap women. He was a lazy drunk who had been an outcast for years, and only showed up a few days a week just to log time for his pension.

Detective Bruntz was one of the people Frank kept in his stable just like he kept Roger. Frank knew what each was capable of, and expertly used their individual talents for his own purpose. In Harold's case, it was his bumbling and ineptness that were going to be put into play.

● ● ● ● ● ● ● ● ● ● ● ● ● ● ● ● ●

WALLY KNEW THERE WAS AN OPEN connection hanging loose with Frank Dawson at the end of it. He wanted to set some bait to see if the man could be brought out—he just didn't know how. He needed a longer reach and called Jim's old partner, Buzz Peterson.

"Mr. Peterson, I've got some bad news, and I need your help." He told of Jim being shot, but left out the details. As far as Wally is concerned, there is still a problem and he wants to stay in control of what happens. The tragedy of the killing can come out later.

Buzz's response, "I don't know what to say, Sheriff. He was my partner and friend. What do I do now? He's gone. I can't believe it."

Wally was caught between being a sheriff investigating a case and losing a friend who was as close as his own father. He wasn't allowed the luxury of expressing his grief to people who would influence the garbage he had yet to sort out. With his eyes shut tightly, he tried consoling Art, "It's the flaw of the business we're in Mr. Peterson. People like Jim Cooper are what make it all worthwhile. Will you do something for me?"

"Just ask, I'll do anything."

"Thank you, Sir. Can you get into DeAnna's department at Child Services and find out what she had? I need to find out who else we're dealing with. Talk to her boss and see if the name of Lieutenant Dawson means anything. Just don't tell her why you're asking."

Digesting the shock of his friend's death, Buzz vowed to help as much as he could. He found his way into the Child Services department and sat down with DeAnna's supervisor.

"Yes, the last time I talked to her she said Lieutenant Dawson was holding some evidence. She was really steamed over it."

"And you don't know what it was or who has it now?"

"Mr. Peterson, I've told you everything I know. Lieutenant Dawson is heading the investigation into her death, and according to her, he did have items taken from the Parkhurst house. But, there's nothing odd about that, seeing who he is."

Offering a small condolence, Buzz said, "Thanks for talking to me. I've briefly met Ms. Wishoult, and I thought she was very nice."

After they exchanged nods of sympathy, he had one more thing to check on. Then he went home to grieve over an emptiness Jim's death left in him. The young sheriff from up north was right on both counts. There was a flaw in what they had tried to do to keep society safe, and it was definitely people like Jim Cooper who made it all worth doing.

At home, Buzz opened a bottle of Grain Belt and toasted his friend, "Good-bye, old buddy. I'll see you some day, and we'll have a beer and call up the girls again. I hope they let us do that up there." Then he reached for the telephone.

"Sheriff Stearns, Art Peterson here. This Dawson guy has the box Jim and I found in Parkhurst's closet. I saw things in it I didn't like, and I'm sure if it's missing, it's not an accident. That kind of stuff will burn a lot of people."

"What kind of stuff?"

"Pictures of the little girl. Sad, sick pictures about men doing stuff to her. Child porn crap. No wonder the mother took off with her. Also, the records at the precinct show DeAnna went to see Dawson the same day she died. If that box doesn't turn up, the only connection died with that poor woman."

"I can't thank you enough, Art. I'll let you know about the arrangements for Jim. It's going to be a sad day for everyone."

Sheriff Wallace Stearns had his connection. He needed to run it by someone for an opinion, and the only other person was the dispatcher, Deputy Marks. "Ted, if you're going to be effective in this office, I need to know you're on top of things."

"Sheriff, I'm not really the bozo you think I am. I want to be a good deputy, and I want to help."

"Good. Here's what we have." Ted knew all that had happened, but Wally needed to put it in some kind of order. "This cop from Minneapolis is going to show up, and I want to be ready. He might want the girls the same way Parkhurst did."

Ted added, "That can only mean he was involved in the abuse and needs to get rid of them. Destroy any link."

"Nice going, Ted, you're right. That's why we do this Deputy Marks—we brainstorm and come up with answers. My friend, you are now officially a good law man."

"I always was, Sheriff. We need to get the mom and the girl out of here now, don't we?"

Wally couldn't allow the girls to go back to Jim's place, not yet. He firmly believed his house with the alarm set up was safest, and it would keep them closer. He thanked the National Guard troops stationed outside the hospital room, and asked if they could stay for two more days, even though the room was empty. A weak diversion, but an easy one to set up. The head nurse said she would see that Emily's name stayed on the admissions register as long as the guards were there.

Visiting their hospital room, Wally discovered the guards had provided them Emily and Rosalie with clothing, food they weren't supposed to have, a TV/VCR with movies, and friendly chatter.

Emily was looking better every day, and Rosalie was talking again. Not as cheerful as before, but it looked good.

Emily remarked, "Those guys are awesome, Wally. They kept Rosalie busy and really loosened her up. At first she was a basket case, but they kept being nice. How can we ever thank them?"

"I think they'll just like seeing you two healthy. They're doing this on their own time for free. Just like the volunteers. It's what us small-town bumpkins call friendship and compassion."

Wally couldn't be certain that they weren't being watched. Getting them out of the Duluth hospital and back to his house turned out to be overkill, but Wally felt safer. After dark, they left by the basement garage door used by maintenance. He drove around in circles for a while and then parked, just watching everything. Any strange cars or people would be pulled over by Deputy Ted, in the marked sheriff's cruiser.

Sitting in the back seat of Wally's Cherokee, waiting, Rosalie asked, "Mom, what are we doing? We're just sitting here."

"Well, Wally wants to be sure there's no more trouble, and it gives Deputy Marks some training."

"Are we still being chased, Mom?"

Wally broke in hoping he could soothe her fears. "It's all just police procedure, Rosie. We do a lot of things that don't make sense if you aren't used to them."

Leaning over the seat, she asked, "Do you like being a sheriff?"

"Yeah, I like it a lot. Sometimes more than others, but it's a good way to spend the day."

"Jim was a sheriff, and now he's dead. Did you ever shoot anyone?"

This was going in a dangerous direction, and touched a sensitive nerve in him, but he diverted it by asking, "Did you like the soldiers at the hospital?"

"They were so nice, and I knew we were safe with them."

"Well, they are like police, but for the Army. They keep people safe."

Keeping up the chatter, she said, "How'd you ever get a name like Wallace?"

"I wasn't asked when they chose names. My middle name is worse."

"My middle name is Marie, after my mom's mom. It's my mom's middle name, too. Tell me yours."

He had gotten her on a normal kid track and wanted her to feel comfortable talking to him, so he pressed on knowing it was going to embarrass him. "If I do, you'll never stop teasing me."

She giggled, and it was the most beautiful sound. "No I won't." Winking, she showed her mother her crossed fingers.

Wally knew and went along, hoping she would laugh some more. "All right, it's Marvin. You happy now?"

And indeed, she did laugh. A chortle that filled the car with a happy sound he never wanted to go away. He laughed with her, welcoming anything that would allow her to be cheerful and silly.

Emily sat quietly in the back seat with Rosalie, smiling through it all. She just now, at this precise moment, knew that she indeed did love this man. It wasn't just lip service to fill an obligation. It wasn't a gut-wrenching sickness. It wasn't a lofty vision of a fantasy. It was something that Wally had worked for and earned. Sitting in the front seat—making her terribly disturbed child laugh in the shadow of disaster—was the man who would become the new father of her daughter, and her new husband. If she could just get through this without screwing it all up, or dying.

He picked up the microphone and talked to Ted in the cruiser. "It's all right Ted, we're going now."

Ted responded, "Yeah, it looks good, but I'll follow."

The trip from Duluth to Grand Marais was slow and cautious, and a surprise waited for them at the house, in the form of a large yellow dog.

"Mommy, it's Bella." Rosalie sprang out the door, not waiting to shut it, and embraced the dog, rolling on the ground with her.

Emily gently squeezed Wally's hand and said, "Go inside, Honey. I'm going to let this happen for awhile. She's happy, and I don't want to end it."

Smiling, and sensing there was another message in there someplace, he left them alone to romp and be happy. Mumbling to himself through a wide grin, "Honey?"

Emily sat on the ground with the two jumping and rolling over her. Bella settled down, giving mother and daughter a moment of calm. "Rosie, do you like Wally?"

"Marvin?" The giggling trailed off and Rosalie added, "You like him, huh?"

"I know how I feel about him, but before I decide to let it go further, I need to know it's okay with you. He's going to belong to you also, you know, and you have to like him as much as I do."

"Yeah, Mom. I like him, and I'd like to have him around as a father. He wouldn't, you know, do stuff to me."

Emily hugged her so tightly she squeezed out a protest, "Mom, I can't breathe."

"Baby, that's not going to happen again, you know you need to talk to us and Sister Alysia about it. It all has to come out, and some day we can look back and just be glad we stopped it."

Staying serious, Rosalie said, "Sure, Mom. I like him a lot."

Holding her daughter closely, Emily asked, "Should we keep him?"

"Can we keep Bella, too?"

"She's part of the family."

Pausing a moment to weigh the next thought, Emily tested the water some more. "Could you let Bella sleep with you tonight?"

Rosalie got solemn for a moment. "Mom, don't let this go so far you can't get out if you need to."

Totally amazed at her daughter's wisdom, "Making love is a part of being in love, Honey. And I really think I'm in love with him. God, where did you get so smart?"

⬤ ⬤ ⬤ ⬤ ⬤ ⬤ ⬤ ⬤ ⬤ ⬤ ⬤ ⬤ ⬤ ⬤ ⬤ ⬤ ⬤

LATER THAT EVENING, ROSALIE KISSED THEM both goodnight and took Bella to bed with her. She was worried about her mother's attachment, and how it would affect herself. She knew she had to share, but why now? She went to sleep hugging Bella and dreaming of Sister Alysia and the cute boy named Skylar.

Sitting on the sofa with a glass of wine, Emily had to let Wally in on something. "I've changed, Wally. Since Jim was killed, and seeing Rosalie shoot her father, I feel like a spark is missing. I feel like I'm falling into a hole, and I'm worried."

"Depression takes many forms and affects us in different ways. It's important to confront it and get help. The hospital gave me the number of a doctor in Duluth. They thought this might happen to you."

Comforted by his caring, she said, "Why hasn't some girl snapped you up before this?"

Pulling her closer to him, he smiled, "I was waiting for you."

He was working on something in his mind but didn't know how to make it sound right.

She saw it happening and said, "The best way to say something is to just say it. Spit it out, Wally."

Kissing her forehead softly, he said, "When I told you I loved you, I was serious. From, the first time I saw you, I couldn't get you out of my mind. Then I needed to separate physical attraction from love, and settled on love. You're drop-dead gorgeous and any man would be attracted to you. I just don't know if I'm good enough. How could I ever compete with other guys?"

"Maybe you don't have to. Maybe I'm in love with you as much as you are with me. Maybe we're both taking a chance, and maybe there are more maybes to wrestle with. I always thought you were a nice guy, and I even fantasized about being with you. I couldn't allow any feelings to interfere with the most important thing to me–Rosalie. You have to accept the fact that I come with a package. My daughter is going to need some serious work on her mind, and I will not get involved unless you are going to accept that as a part of accepting me. You get us both, and whatever we bring with us is just a part of it. Yes, Honey, I am deeply in love with you, and I want to be with you forever."

Letting that sink in for a moment, she added, "I want you to answer one question, and only you will know if you are honest. If Rosalie was crippled for life and needed constant care, would you be there for no other reason than just loving her enough? If for some reason I wasn't here any more, would you still do it?"

Without hesitation, he answered, "My mother was in a wheelchair, and I watched my father take care of her every day. He never complained or asked for help. He did it because he loved her. If I could be half the man my father was, I'd consider myself lucky. Yes, loving you is loving Rosalie."

They snuggled for awhile, and then she stood up and stretched. "Well, I guess we're in love with each other. I'm tired." She took his hand and led him into his bedroom.

As the door closed behind them she couldn't help but taunt him with, "Marvin?"

● ● ● ● ● ● ● ● ● ● ● ● ● ● ● ● ● ● ●

JUST BEFORE DAWN'S MORNING LIGHT WOULD peek through the window, Wally woke up to find Emily propped on her elbow, staring at him. Shaking the fuzz out of his head, he asked, "Emmy, what's wrong?"

"Nothing's wrong, Honey. It couldn't be more right."

Confused, he said, "How long have you been awake?"

"Most of the night. I've been watching you. I'm in love with you, and I wanted to watch you."

Sitting up, he started to say something, but she put her fingers to his lips to silence him. "Don't talk, let me say this first."

"Uh, yeah, sure."

In a quiet sincere voice, Emily asked, "Will you marry me? Now?"

Stunned, Wally leaned towards her, "I thought you wanted to wait.

"No, I want to marry you, now. Today."

● ● ● ● ● ● ● ● ● ● ● ● ● ● ● ● ● ● ●

WITH HIS CONNECTIONS TO THE CITY GOVERNMENT, Wally was able to get a marriage license in less than twenty minutes. Before a judge, with Ted Marks as witness, and Rosalie as bridesmaid, Emily Parkhurst became Mrs. Emily Stearns. As a wedding present, Wally made arrangements with the judge to start adoption proceedings for Rosalie.

Emily loved Wally with all her heart. However, her true deep love and bonding lay with her daughter. She fully understood that there was a good chance that before this mess was over, she might very well die. If that was going to happen, at least she knew Rosalie would be loved, safe, and with a decent father.

According to Emily, that's what a good mother should do.

● ● ● ● ● ● ● ● ● ● ● ● ● ● ● ● ● ● ●

FRANK DAWSON SAT AT HIS DESK WITH instructions to not be disturbed by anyone. The fallout hadn't reached him yet, but he knew it would. The only thing left from the box were the two pictures of Rosalie he had kept aside. The tapes and the rest of the pictures were destroyed and spread so they could never be put together. He covered his tracks, and the only thing left to get rid of was up north.

He read the report on Roger being brought down and was thankful the fanatical killer was gone. "I would have had to kill him myself anyway." He thought back to the hole in Cambodia, and wrote Roger off as a necessary tool to further his own cause.

The official statement from the Grand Marais Sheriff indicated a team of volunteer law officers caught him and, as it stated, *shot him.* He was dead, that's all. It included a list of victims he *killed on his rampage.* The report made it look like he was a crazed killer just bent on taking lives. Frank thought: "No surprise there."

One thing that was missing, and although not there, it stood out like a flashing red alert. The ex-wife and daughter were never mentioned, and they were the reason he was even up there.

So, the problem still existed. "If they escaped Roger, they had to have had protection."

The inquiry from the lawyer in Duluth, and the report from the Grand Marais sheriff were the keys, and that's where he needed to find them. "They have to be in one of those places."

The little girl he held the fascination for was a witness to his sickness, and her mother would be as much of a problem as the girl. No telling how much her daughter told her, so the sooner they are gone, the better his chances are of skating out of this.

Holding the pictures of Rosalie, the old sensation came back to his groin and set his mind into a spin, his legs getting weak, and his breath affected. He was in love with the child, just like he loved Anna Swanson. Before he put the pictures safely back into his pocket, he told himself, "I have to have her, just one more time."

A warning flashed and he muttered, "If I'm ever caught with this, I'm going to be torn to shreds." Roger's warning about cops and child molesters in prison chilled him. "What if it got into the papers and the news? With the mayor's crime campaign, he'd crucify me."

If it came to that, it would be better to put a bullet into his head. But, oh, God how could he do it. That's what he had Roger for, and he was sure Roger would have killed him easily.

Frank knew for certain he didn't have enough guts to kill himself, and eased his mind by saying, "No, I'll get away with this. It'll be okay."

He knew it was despicable but, like Dr. Goodhue said, "It's a sickness." The image of Martin Goodhue giving him advice on child molestation made him laugh. "Like a priest giving advise on child raising. The doctor is as bad as I am." Frank actually thought that as soon as he got the girl and her mother out of the way, he could reform himself. Keep it a secret, and don't do it any more. There was always a chance.

Looking at Detective Bruntz's report, he worked his way through the bad grammar and poor spelling. On any other report he would have sent it back to be retyped, possibly dictated to a secretary. But, this was perfect and exactly what he expected; the work of an inefficient police officer that needed to be fired.

DeAnna Wishoult had two many wines, combined with tha warm water in the bath, sukumbed to ineberation and drownt while pissed out. Awtopsy is not considerd nesasary.

"Bruntz, you idiot. Thank you." DeAnna body was shipped to her family in Wisconsin. Case closed. If there were any questions, it would fall on Harold Bruntz. Frank could handle any criticism on not having it redone.

The inept and incompetent Detective Harold Bruntz made a phone call to his old friend. "Hi Buzz, Hal Bruntz here. How's retirement treating you?"

"Oh, for Christ sake, you old boozer, good to hear from you. Say, Hal, you heard about Jim, didn't you?"

"That's why I'm calling Buzz. I read it in the report, and I knew the two of you were close, so maybe there's something I can do for you. Keep your eye on the mailbox in a couple of days. I'm not going to last much longer here, so I'm going to retire and join my brother on a fishing boat in Tarpon Springs."

As promised, in two days, the code book from Roger's stash came in the mail. The attached note, fashioned in the typical Harold Bruntz style. *Found this in the social werkers apt. Im to close to the Lt. and he wold bury it. So, if you want to fuck him up, do it.*

It was signed simply, *H.*

On the phone with Sheriff Stearns in Grand Marais, Buzz related the news. "The initials FD show up, and there are a lot of notes with dates. Some sick shit about stuff I can't even talk about, Sheriff. This is the asshole's own daughter, for Christ sake. What do you want me to do with it?"

"I don't know how deep in the department this sickness goes, so I can't rely on help there. Make copies of all of it. Do you know anyone you can send it to at the *Star Tribune?*"

"Yeah. Julie Krum is one of the editors. I'm going to make more copies and send them to IAD, the Attorney General, and Child Services also. I'll hide the book until it's needed as evidence."

"Thanks Mr. Peterson. You're still thinking like a cop."

Art responded, "A pissed-off cop!"

● ● ● ● ● ● ● ● ● ● ● ● ● ● ● ● ● ●

F<small>RA</small> NK NEVER REALIZED HOW SERIOUS others took this case, and had no idea of the interest it was taking on. At the same time that Harold Bruntz was digging through DeAnna's apartment, Frank had a visitor.

"Lieutenant Dawson, I hope I'm not interrupting anything."

Surprised, Frank stood up and extended his greeting, "Officer Slocum. I've always got time for you. Please, sit down. How is life on the streets going for you?"

Slocum answered, "A lot better than undercover. My wife is still nervous, but at least I go home every day."

"Well, I'm glad of that. What can I do for you?"

Hesitating a moment, he finally said, "Parkhurst was working for you, I know. I was kind of suspicious when I talked to him at the scene of Gary's tragedy. I felt he was into something connected, and I'm positive he had a hand in what happened."

Frank hid his fear by squeezing his leg, and then methodically asked, "Have you mentioned this to anyone else?"

"No, I know what the chain of command is, and I'd never go over your head."

"Thanks, I appreciate that. He was dealing in a very sensitive case, and it won't be ready to be let out until a couple of loose ends are tied up. So, please keep mum on any suspicions you have until the right moment. I'll ask for a statement then."

Officer Slocum stood up, "Yes sir, I'll keep it under wraps until you say so."

Relieved, Frank said, "Good, I always thought you were one of the better operatives. Say hello to your wife."

"Yes sir, I will. She's going to have a baby in a few weeks; our first. We bought a new house also."

Two days later, a quiet Minneapolis suburb was rocked by an explosion. Both occupants were killed. The newscast mourned the passing of the Officer Harry Slocum family, calling for safer conditions in all homes. Frank attended the double funeral, expressing his sadness.

● ● ● ● ● ● ● ● ● ● ● ● ● ● ● ● ● ● ●

FRANK HAD RESOURCES AT HIS DISPOSAL that became useful when someone had to go undercover. One was a file of false identities. He picked out an identification package that had his picture and the name Sergeant John Thayer of the Minneapolis Internal Affairs Department. It was not unusual for high-ranking police officials to add names to the rosters of various departments for safety in undercover work. John Thayer just became a member of the elite group that investigated its own.

Then Dawson took a two-week vacation, up north, to catch a couple of fish.

The trail of disaster Roger left all started with the lawyer in Duluth. His best bet would be to just walk in under the guise of IAD putting together Roger's crime spree.

The next day, in Leonard Walburn's office, he approached the secretary and announced, "Sergeant John Thayer, Minneapolis IAD, to see Mr. Walburn. I'm kind of in a hurry so maybe I can get in right away."

The receptionist took his card and dismissed the brusque attempt at intimidation. Carla was a salty old gal who didn't take crap from anyone. She was short, heavyset, and had a raspy voice that could drive a nail into concrete.

Sounding unconcerned, she said, "There's a meeting room down the hall, I'll see if I can get hold of him. There's some magazines and coffee while you wait." She pointed to her left, and sat waiting for him to leave.

"Look, I came all the way from …"

She had enough, and was following her boss's instructions. "I don't care if you came from the frigging moon. If you want to see Mr. Walburn, you will wait, or make an appointment and come back when he's here." She wasn't about to get pushed into a corner by the city boy, and she set out to let him know who was in charge.

Frustrated, he asked, "Well, when can I get an appointment?"

She flipped open a ledger book, running her finger down several pages. "The soonest is Tuesday, in two weeks, at nine in the morning, I can slot you in for a ten-minute session. If this is going to involve legal advise, I'll need a hundred dollar retainer first."

"Holy shit, I just want to talk to him." His agitation was just what she wanted.

"Holy shit yourself. You in or out?"

"Aw fuck it." He left a trail of disgust and frustration behind as he bumped into the door trying to open it. Feeling like a buffoon, the redness climbed up his face, and he knew she was laughing at him. Which of course, she was.

Looking down from the upper lobby window, she saw him exit onto the street and climb into a black Buick. Walking into Leonard's office she handed him the card, "Boy, is he a prick."

"Carla, you're a marvel. Thank you, and let me know if I can ever repay you."

She drolly replied, "You got you're choice of a BMW or a raise."

Len, fencing with her, said, "Your charm is overwhelming."

"I'd rather have the Beamer." She went back to her desk and took out the fingernail file to finish making herself feminine.

The name of John Thayer meant nothing to Leonard but coming from the Minneapolis Police, at this particular time, he turned on the alarm and called the Grand Marais Sheriff's office.

"Sheriff Stearns, Len Walburn here. Listen, somebody was here, supposedly from the Minneapolis IAD office. He gave his name as John Thayer. I didn't talk to him, and he left in a black Buick. If he's the connection you're looking for, he is more than likely coming to see you next. Is there anything you want me to do?"

"Thanks, Len, but we don't know for sure how deep he is in this yet. I don't think he's going back to Minneapolis, so maybe we can net him here. If we get more police, or the Minnesota Highway Patrol into this, it's just going to tie every-thing into knots. And, I don't want to tip him off."

At the Grand Marais Sheriff's office, Ted's desk sat at the front window so he had a view of anything that happened outside. Calling out to his boss, "Sheriff, the Buick pulled into the parking lot and is just sitting there. Why can't we just go arrest him?"

Wally came to the window to peek out, "Arrest him for what? We need to wait and see what he's going to do. We need some evidence we know will stick. If he slips out on a technicality, we're just going to make him even more dangerous. I can't risk putting Emily and the girl into that position. Can you see the license plate?"

Ted answered, "I've already got the number."

Smiling at the rookie's abilities, Wally said, "Good job, Buddy. Pull up the DMV and get a make on it. If he comes in, stall him for a few minutes."

Frank sat in the Buick for a long time trying to pretend he was John Thayer. He checked to be sure he had the phony cards and ID. The parking lot in front of the small brick building had two cruisers labeled Cook County Sheriff. The other cars were a white Cherokee, an old Chevrolet Impala, and a Plymouth Reliant. He picked up his mobile phone and made the call to the Minneapolis DMV. "Lieutenant Dawson here, I need the makes on three vehicles; code 11-28." The request for a special rush on the information brought the response quickly. It showed the owners to be, respectively, Wallace Stearns, James Cooper, and Theodore Marks. He asked for, and got, the addresses of all of them.

At the same time, Ted brought Wally the name of the Buick's owner, Franklin Dawson, with a Minneapolis address.

The cats and mice were now circling in a very serious game.

Entering the sheriff's office, Frank put on his best John Thayer demeanor, "I'd like to see the sheriff?" then flashed his ID and badge.

Ted, overly polite, told him, "Have a seat. I'll see if Sheriff Stearns is busy."

Frank had learned his lesson in Duluth and decided to play the *Mayberry* game, taking a seat.

Ted took a stack of papers into Wally's office. In a clandestine whisper, he asked, "He's sitting out there Wally, what do I do with him?"

"I don't know, Ted. Give him a blow job, or cook his dinner. Just keep him busy. I asked the Minneapolis records section to fax the ID of Frank Dawson. When it comes in I want to see it, right away."

The desperation on Ted's face told Wally he needed to take control. "Okay, spare the male bonding and the dinner and send him in. But keep a watch for that fax."

Sitting in the office of Sheriff Stearns, John Thayer laid out the reason for his visit. "We've been looking at Parkhurst for some time. He became a rogue and uncontrollable. Now that he's dead, we need to put the report together and make sure nobody goes this far again. I do expect your cooperation, Sheriff."

Sergeant Thayer's attempt at sounding official and important made Wally chuckle to himself.

Wally leaned back in his chair, hoping the casters wouldn't send him scooting across the room, or worse, tip him over. "What do you want from us? The report has been sent down to you people." Aware of Frank Dawson's involvement, and assuming this man was Frank Dawson, Wally was treading water to see where this went.

Thayer said, "I need to talk to any witnesses and people involved."

"Hmm. Well, Sergeant Thayer, we'll do what we can for you. Read the report and you'll get as much of the story as we have." Sitting upright, the chair made a bang when the casters hit the floor.

The phony sergeant felt like he was talking to Mayberry's police chief, Andy Taylor and expected Deputy Barney Fife to walk in. He raised his voice a notch in an attempt to intimidate, "A number of officers were involved in the manhunt for Parkhurst. Do they know anything?"

Getting agitated now, he blew his cover by loudly asking, "What about his wife and daughter? They were the ones he was after, so they must have been around here for him to come to this stupid town in the first place."

The bell went off in Wally's head like an explosion. Emily and Rosalie had never been mentioned in any report. Wally stood up and said, "Excuse me a moment Sergeant, I'll be right back."

In the outer office Wally was frantic. "Ted, where's that fax?"

Ted's excited response was, "I can't crawl into the machine and pull it out. You have to wait."

Wally learned a lot from Jim, and one thing was to always be suspicious. This man in his office just didn't sit right, and was obviously a phony. Hedging for time and more to go on, Wally stonewalled him as much as he could.

Back in his office, Wally said, "All the people in the manhunt were volunteers, and my understanding is that the mother and her daughter are runaways. Maybe the FBI can help."

Knocking softly, Ted brought the fax in just as John Thayer was getting ready to leave. The front and side identification photos of Frank Dawson were fuzzy, but unmistakable.

At the door, Wally told Thayer what the limits to his involvement would be. Also, he needed to let Sergeant Thayer know he wasn't going to roll over for him.

"Sergeant Thayer, if you stick around, I want you to know this is my town and you are out of your jurisdiction. Don't go around questioning a lot of people. It's going to make a big stink if the town's folk get riled up. If there's anything you need, you have to start here. It's still an open case, and I want it kept clean. Okay?"

Sergeant Thayer paused, digesting what he heard, and scoffed at the hick.

Wally threw out something else out to test the reaction. "When we checked with the Minneapolis Records Section we couldn't find a reference to Roger Parkhurst as a police officer. Why would IAD be interested in him?"

Caught off guard by the small-town sheriff, "He was undercover. No Federal crimes were committed so we try to keep it in our own house."

Wally kept pressing, "Even if he was undercover, wouldn't his ID be on file?"

"Don't worry about it, Sheriff. I'll take care of anything to do with Parkhurst."

The confrontation got warmer with Wally saying, "As long as you are in this town, I don't want you to do anything unless you check with me first. Have a nice day, Sergeant."

There was a definite conflict between the two. Frank thought he was above these Looney-Toon amateurs, and wasn't about to let them interfere. How could they possibly get ahead of Lieutenant Frank Dawson–the accomplished senior officer of a large city law enforcement agency.

Sitting in his Buick, Frank fumed, "All right you clowns, let's see who the real cop is here."

Standing at the station window, Wally calmly talked to his dispatcher. "He took the bait, Ted. We got a live one on the hook." Heading back to his office, he added, "Get a part-time replacement from Two Harbors, or even that guy from the senior center, to sit on the desk. You're about to become a real deputy."

Returning, his side arm strapped to his waist, Wally said, "I'm going to see what Sergeant Thayer is up to. I'll be in the Cherokee, so keep in touch."

CHAPTER 17
SHOWDOWN

● ●

F RANK PULLED INTO THE GRAND MARAIS Holiday service station to fill up the Buick, taking a casual look around to see if Barney Fife or the abrasive sheriff were watching him. If he were in their shoes, he'd be glued to the suspect. Rural law enforcement seemed to be a loosely held, almost part-time and matter-of-fact arrangement. He tried to think of this whole mess as comical and definitely below his status as a cop. Still, he surveyed the area, just to be sure. He wouldn't admit, even to himself, that he was nervous.

As professional as Frank deemed himself to be, he still didn't notice Wally's Cherokee parked on a side street, down from the Holiday station.

Waiting for the tank to fill, he watched the passing traffic and could easily pick out the locals from the tourists. The slower-moving, flannel-clad, baseball-capped and smiling people were obvious. They all said *Hello* to each other as if the whole town slept in the same bed. He held contempt for them because he wasn't one of them. They had friends and family and would sit and have a beer and laugh at jokes from the past. All Frank could ever consider as a friend was a dead homicidal lunatic. One that saved his life many years ago, but still a lunatic.

Roger was dead now, at the hands of these bumpkins and amateurs, so it was up to Frank to clean it all up. If he didn't …, well, that was not something he'd even think about.

● ● ● ● ● ● ● ● ● ● ● ● ● ● ● ● ● ● ●

W HILE FRANK STOOD AT THE GAS PUMP, his mind wandered from the local traffic to reminisce about his past. He contemplated how he got so deep into this situation to start with. His wife, Carolyn, saw it happening long ago. Her suspicion peaked when her niece, Anna, was murdered. Carolyn had come across a black and white photo of the girl, and demanded answers. He deftly explained the photo was crime scene evidence and belonged in the case file. He never explained why the girl was nude. Carolyn had suspicions but didn't have enough nerve to make an issue with her sinister husband.

By no coincidence, Frank was in charge of Anna's case, but according to the cold case file, there wasn't enough evidence to point to anyone. Way back when the sophistication of forensic science was minimal, the child just passed into the memory of her family, and the case died.

The dissension between Frank and Carolyn grew through affairs and alcohol, finally divorcing. His wife's devout Catholic family disowned her for the divorce, and she just faded away. Frank was now free to wander in his perverse lifestyle without the fear of discovery from a nosey wife.

Things were never the same though. Politicians were following the protests of parents, and thus laws were passed to protect children. The favorite topic on talk shows became abuse of women and children. When a child molester was caught, Frank would rally with the rest of the outraged, calling for the head of that slime ball.

Frank was able to float in his abhorrent world at will. However, with his ex-wife being aware of the perversion, he needed to cut the loose end she left behind. He put a trace on her and found she had settled near the West Coast. He met with Roger a few days later and asked him, "How would you like to take a trip to Seattle?" A week later, Carolyn became another cold case for the Seattle police department. Certain of protected anonymity, Frank confined his perversion to Roger's basement enterprise.

● ● ● ● ● ● ● ● ● ● ● ● ● ● ● ●

Now, HERE HE WAS, IN A SMALL RURAL TOWN, finishing what Roger had started— and failed. He picked up a map of the region showing all the interesting sights, and fishing locations. It had a detailed road map, which was all he needed. He drove to Hovland to find Arrowhead Trail and James Cooper. Frank hadn't spent enough time on the streets to become savvy on the instincts and gut feelings most investigators work with. His cunning in the jungles happened a lifetime ago, and he didn't have Roger to clear the way for him. The name James Cooper was in the official report as a victim, but there was no mention of who he was. Any rookie would have seen the flag waving, but Frank operated with blind arrogance.

At the end of Jim's driveway, with the yellow crime scene tape stretched across, he asked out loud, "What the hell is that for?" Getting out, he stood dumbly in front of it, staring down the long tree-lined gravel lane. His confusion was interrupted when he heard the Cherokee slowly crunching the gravel as it rolled to a stop next to him. Surprised to see the sheriff, the thought crossed his mind that maybe he wasn't too dumb after all. Frank had been followed and wasn't aware of it, so this sheriff needed to be dealt with.

Stepping out of the Cherokee, Wally asked, "Sergeant Thayer, are you looking for anything special here?"

Frank answered, "Oh, hello Sheriff. No, just sort of looking around."

Getting irritated at the charade, Wally confronted the imposter. "I asked you a direct question, Sergeant Thayer, and I expect a direct answer. This is a crime scene, and you have no reason to be here." Deciding to play his trump card, Wally's next move was probably a huge mistake. "I know who you are, Dawson. Now I want to know what you're doing here."

"All right, you know who I am. I was Parkhurst's commander, and I want to find out what went on here."

"Don't you think you could have gotten more information by letting us know who you were?"

Frank, groping for something believable, said, "I made a mistake. Okay? What has this Cooper got to do with it? Can we go in there?" He motioned down the driveway.

"I don't trust you. Why are you interested in the mother and the girl? Their names were never…"

The gun shot stopped Wally from going further. If he saw Frank reach back to pull out the weapon, he didn't react soon enough. The 9mm slug tore across the side of his head, ripping flesh, and part of his ear on its way. Wally's hand went to his holster to draw, but the second shot hit him in the chest, and he collapsed on the road.

Cautiously stepping towards the grounded sheriff, his gun stretched in front of him, Frank nudged him with his shoe. Certain his prey was dead, Frank dragged him into the back seat of the Cherokee and drove it far enough down the driveway to get it out of sight, the yellow tape festooned across the grille. He checked the motionless sheriff before trotting back to his Buick.

"Brainless hick. He deserved it." The almighty and invincible Frank Dawson was running smoothly, and nothing was going to stand in his way. He knew for certain he would come out of this without anyone knowing of his sickness. Sitting in the Buick, he took out his list and the map to see where his next stop would be.

Frank cruised south on Highway 61 back to Grand Marais. Parking a mile out of town to wait for nightfall, he mumbled to himself, "Stupid guy thought he was Matt Dillon. If he hadn't reached for his gun, I could have let him be. Well, maybe he won't be discovered until I get done here. The girls must be with that idiot deputy, or squirreled away with the sheriff. Ex-sheriff." Frank's grin was evil, yet twitched nervously.

Following his map, he found the house listed as the residence of Theodore Marks; an old two-story frame structure with a cat walk and turret on the roof. Set back on a hill overlooking Lake Superior, it reminded Frank of the house featured in the film, *Psycho.* Ted's mother and aunt kept the house and jointly raised the boy. Now, just Ted and his aged aunt, keep the place alive.

Large, old and gray with decay, the place looked like it could hide someone very well. Making sure the deputy was still in the office, he went up to the door and rang a bell that sounded like a fire alarm. Several minutes later, an old woman with a walker came to the door. Pulling the curtains aside, she yelled through the glass panel, "What do you want?"

Cupping his hand to his mouth, he returned the yell, "May I please see Mrs. Parkhurst?"

"Who? Who's Parkhurst?"

"Is Mrs. Parkhurst and the little girl here?"

"No. Go away." That conversation was over and she disappeared into the house.

He carefully tried turning the knob, but it held fast. A plaque next to the door proclaimed:

Victoria Security Service. Hoping there weren't cameras watching him, he slunk back to the Buick and waited.

Around nine that night, Deputy Marks parked in front and joined the old lady inside. A few lights went on, but there was no sign of anyone else. He had one more place to check, and the darkness of night was the best time to do it.

● ● ● ● ● ● ● ● ● ● ● ● ● ● ● ● ● ●

WHEN WALLY DIDN'T COME HOME, Emily worried about him. There was still something out there that was after them, but she didn't know what it was. Roger's contacts went deep, and now she had dragged Wally into it. Before, she at least knew about Roger, and now, not knowing was even more frightening. Frequently, she would go out to the road to look and listen, but there was no sign of the Cherokee.

Bella had run off into the woods to follow the coyote howls, so just she and Rosalie were home. As she thought about the last time Bella disappeared, she didn't welcome more to worry about. Every time she thought about Jim, her stomach would twist into a knot, and she knew she would never get over it.

After they put some leftovers in the microwave, the two played rummy and "Go Fish." Emily tried to hide her apprehension, but Rosalie had been hardened to see things that other kids didn't. Being perceptive, she said, "You're worried about Wally, aren't you, Mom?"

Looking at her daughter for a moment, she met her question with a smile. "Yeah, I'm worried, Honey. But, he's a sheriff, and who knows what domestic squabble he had to break up. What do you want to play now?"

"I want to play truth, Mom. Are we still in trouble?"

Rosalie had an edge of awareness around her, and was concerned about anything she couldn't see, hear or touch. Her mom has been trying to get her to be a kid and worry about her hair, or the color of her socks. Not a man ravaging her body. On the outside she was just another little girl, but inside there was a hurricane rushing through her mind, sending her into dark hiding places.

Emily sighed and didn't know how long she could keep up the happy mom-and-daughter scene. She was getting worn down by not sleeping and by constant worry. Wally coming into her life had brought her more comfort than she has felt in years, with his calm reassurance; however, he was now another person to worry about. Her body still ached and showed signs from Roger's beating, making her motions difficult.

Now, she had the loss of Jim to deal with, and couldn't imagine how that void could ever be filled. Emily's face was still swollen and bruised, but she managed to smile, "Wally hasn't mentioned anything else we need to worry about."

Rosalie became animated, talking louder and faster, rhythmically beating on the table top with her clenched fists. "There were others, Mom. One guy was there a lot. Daddy took pictures, and they would give him money." Her agitation escalated to anger, her face becoming hard, her eyes fierce and burning.

"Sweetie, please. We're safe here, and nobody's going to hurt you."

Rosalie, her face smearing with tears, yelled, "Then why can't we go home?"

Emily, hugging her distraught daughter, was racing for an answer which would make sense when the phone rang. "Oh, good, that has to be Wally."

Jumping up and grabbing the phone, she hoarsely answered, "Hi Honey."

Ted Marks, on the other end, "No, Emily, It's Ted. Wally must not be there either."

Concerned, she said, "No, we haven't heard from him. Is anything wrong?"

"I don't know. I can't raise him on the radio. Some guy was in here today pretending to be from the police in Minneapolis. Wally said he was a phony. It doesn't add up. I'm going to keep looking for him. If he shows up, have him call me right away." Ted kept the news to himself about the stranger who came to his home.

Scared to death, Emily slowly replaced the handset. She thought she heard Bella and went outside to call her home, but no dog appeared. She sensed a disturbance near the road, but didn't dare go out in the dark to check on it.

Outside of the small house, Frank was crouching in the bushes, watching the shadows in the window, Bella's lifeless body lay a few feet away in the roadside ditch, blood oozing from the bullet hole in her chest. He couldn't see much in the dark, and although it was a good cover, he didn't know where he was and what obstacles were in the way. The sheriff was gone, the dog couldn't warn anyone, and so he might as well wait for daylight. The surrounding area was desolate, eliminating discovery by a neighbor.

He got an immense surge of satisfaction when Emily came out of the door calling for what must have been the dog. Bingo, he had done what Roger couldn't do. Walking back to the Buick to wait for morning, he didn't have the faintest idea that this same scene had been played out earlier when Roger found them at Jim's house. And, Emily was definitely not ready for it to happen again.

When Emily came in from calling for the dog, Rosalie saw the strain on her mother's face and read it perfectly. She demanded, "Tell me, Mommy." She had a fierce determination, yet her body was trembling.

In a clam, worn-out voice, Emily answered, "It may be nothing, Honey. We've just got some worries with Wally not here, and Bella seems to have run off again. The doors are locked, and we're safe. That was Ted. He's got something for Wally and can't find him. C'mon, let's go curl up on the sofa and wait for Wally."

Rosalie had another restless night with Emily holding her close, stroking her hair, humming into her ear. Although the child slept, it was a nervous, light sleep. Emily's arms were busy with hugging so she had to let her own tears just flow onto the cushion.

The thought of Jim's revolver in the sheriff's evidence room made her aware that they didn't have the same advantage as last time. She couldn't bear to see her daughter do that again, and if something were to come up, it would have to be different. Something was still out there trying to hurt them, but she didn't know what.

Emily was drained with hardly enough strength left to move, but she was the shield, and if she had to, she would protect this child, at any cost. Her head started to throb, and the puffiness in her face bothered her.

When her thoughts floated back to the man in the church, she murmured, "Please dear God, give me strength to finish this. Let it end."

The memory of Jim and what he had sacrificed for them tore her to pieces. No one could ever fix the hole in her heart. As long as it hurt, she will always be reminded of the deep, sincere love she held for him, and she worried that she didn't tell him often enough.

Dawn was just breaking when Emily worked her way off the sofa to see about Wally and make some much-needed coffee. He wasn't home yet, and no one answered at the sheriff's office. Turning around, Rosalie was standing in the doorway.

Solemnly, the child asked, "Did Bella come home?"

"No Honey, neither did Wally. Maybe they're together. Do you think so?"

With no response, the child glumly turned and left Emily alone in the kitchen. All she could do now was sigh and wait. Sigh and wait for the man she just fell in love with—her new husband. Sigh and wait for some unknown evil to say good-bye, so there would be no more trouble. Cradling a cup of coffee, she settled on the sofa waiting for the phone to ring, or the Cherokee to pull in.

Sip, sigh and wait.

She dozed on and off last night, never really finding sleep. She was exhausted and wanted to lie down, letting the world and all the problems slip away. But, she knew that couldn't happen.

Emily wasn't aware that Rosalie had gone outside to look for Bella. Rosalie didn't call or whistle, or anything. If she had called for the dog, her mom would have known she was out there and brought her back in. She quietly went outside not only to look, but to get away from her mom's gloomy mood. She wasn't sure if she was upset with Mom's attention to Wally, or missing the farm, or Skylar. The evil was dead and they should all be happy, so why was everyone so sad? She wanted to go home, but didn't know which home she belonged to, or who was going to be happy and laugh.

She walked towards the shed, aimlessly kicking a stone, absently looking for the dog, when she was grabbed from behind. She screamed, but her mouth was covered by a large hand, pressing tight against her face, and the noise went nowhere. A leg was wrapped around her, keeping her pinned while a piece of heavy gray tape, smelling like medicine, was pressed across her face. It partially covered her nose, and she panicked at the suffocation.

Thrown against the side of the shed, the hard thud jolted her. In fear of what was happening, she didn't realize her arms were being forced above her head, and held to a loose board by more smelly tape.

Her legs were kicked out from under her so she was hanging by her up-stretched arms. The force that was controlling her knelt in front of her so she could see what it was. Her eyes were saucer big, looking at the face of the man who had done so many terrible things to her–the smiling face of another evil. Instinctively, she tightened her legs together to deny him what he did to her before. Screaming into the tape across her mouth, she became nauseous sick, with millions of nee-dles jabbing inside. She tried to struggle, but was helpless.

Frank was on his knees in the dirt with his hand on her trembling leg that she tightened to resist him. "I'm not going to hurt you, Rosalie. I want to make you feel good."

He knew, he just knew, he should have killed the child when he first grabbed her. He could have, he had the chance. It would have been so easy, but he could not, simply could not take this thing of obsessive pleasure out of his life. He fin-gered the photos, still in his pocket, and couldn't throw the child away any more than he could discard the photos.

The force of the blow to his back sent a jarring pain through him, knocking him over. The second blow to his head was so fierce it caused the shovel handle to break in two. Emily held the broken handle in both hands and beat him, and beat him, and beat him, until it went flying out of her hands from the force of the last beating to Frank's back.

Catching her breath, Emily aimed her foot into his side and ferociously con-nected as hard as she could. As he rolled over from the blow, his hand landed on the broken shovel handle, except this one had the steel spade attached to it. From his knees, he swung the shovel blade and buried it into Emily's left leg.

A deep, throttled scream came from Emily. She went down on her side, rais-ing her left arm to ward off the next attack. It cut deep into her forearm, and she felt the crunch to the bone, leaving her breathless.

She struggled up on her right knee as he raised the broken shovel over his head and swung down. Up on her knee, she lunged with her one good arm at his crotch and grabbed the bulk in his pants, the shovel glancing off her back, leaving two ribs in shreds, torn flesh showing red through her shirt.

His testes firmly in her grip, she squeezed with all her might and twisted, pulled, and tried to dismember him. Her grip on him was as strong as the jaws of a vise as she savagely tore at him, but he came down again on the top of her head, both fists clasped together, with a blow that crushed her. Added to her concussion from Roger's beating, her head felt like it was split open.

Frank doubled over with a sick feeling that paralyzed him. He wheezed out, "Oh, you bitch, I'm going to love killing you." His voice was a harsh whisper, and he couldn't move from the sickening destruction in his groin.

Emily dragged herself across the dirt to Rosalie, hoisting herself up with her right hand against the shed. Tearing at the duct tape on Rosalie's wrists, the girl dropped down, free.

"*Run, Rosie. Run. Run.*" The screech from Emily's throat was deep and terrifying, and Rosalie ran. She ran into the house and slammed her hand down on the big red button on the countertop. Still running, she flew into the kitchen and tore open a large drawer, sending it to the floor.

Leaning against the shed, Emily reached around the corner and grabbed something to use as a cane, and hobbled back to finish what had been started. The world was spinning wildly around her, and she only knew where he was because she *had* to know.

⬤ ⬤ ⬤ ⬤ ⬤ ⬤ ⬤ ⬤ ⬤ ⬤ ⬤ ⬤ ⬤ ⬤ ⬤ ⬤ ⬤

THE DEPUTY'S CRUISER WAS PARKED behind the Wally's Cherokee in Jim's driveway. While Ted was putting a pad on the hole in Wally's chest, he saw the blinking light. "Hang tight, Wally, the alarm light is on in the unit."

"Oh, God, Ted, go. Leave me and get to the house, now." His voice was a rasp and hardly audible.

Ted left him lying on the seat of the Cherokee and launched the patrol car towards Grand Marais. On the radio, he yelled his 11-99, "Send an ambulance to

Jim Cooper's house on Tom Lake Road, and all patrol units available to Sheriff Stearn's house in Grand Marais." In a code 3 situation with the siren screaming, flying over Highway 61, Ted had the big engine absolutely wide open, pulling him as fast as it could.

Frank saw Emily struggling towards him and tried to straighten up, knowing he had to kill her. Now.

Emily, using an old axe for support, stopped in front of him, with all the hate and ferocity of a mother grizzly protecting her cub. Her chest was heaving, screaming for air, with a thousand volts running through her nervous system. The sharp pain searing through her back only made her more ferocious.

Frank reached behind him and withdrew his pistol from the holster. The gun came slowly around to point at her, and she stared at the tiny hole that held death behind it. Still hunched over from the devastation that took place in his crotch, he had trouble getting his gun to point where he needed it to; his arm weak from the sickness in his groin.

The entire left side of her body was useless and hung limp on her frame. Emily fingered her cane with the weight of her body on it. She wrapped her hand tightly around the knob at the end of the handle, feeling the deadly iron weight below. With snarling determination, she flexed her arm, her tiny muscles reacted and reassured her grip. With a small sway to get it in motion, on the back swing she sent it in a full arc over her head. Through twisted tight lips, a guttural scream guided her strength and launched the dull rusty axe head from the ground, in full circle and down with all the force and might she had, her feet literally lifting from the ground.

Rosalie, still running, had a large butcher knife clutched in both hands, with the duct tape dangling from her wrist. Using her head to butt the door open, she charged her target, running as fast as she could, the knife held out in front of her.

Frank saw it coming, but was mystified and all sound was muted. He was just watching it happening–hoping it wouldn't hurt too much. He hoped it would hurt less than a bullet in his head. It was all quiet and in surreal motion. The axe and the child with the knife–his child that made his sickness feel so good.

"The knife will hurt. Oh, no, not a knife, plea …"

Frank's frantic effort to save himself and kill Emily was rewarded. As the axe was swinging down onto his head, his finger flinched on the trigger of his weapon, sending a 9mm slug ripping into Emily's stomach.

The force of Rosalie running into his side with the large knife, piercing his belt and splitting soft flabby flesh, pushed him aside just enough to divert the bullet meant for Emily's heart.

The dirty, rusted edge of the axe blade, Emily's cane, came down with the terrible force and might of a small woman with a red glare in her eyes and fire streaming from her nostrils, smoke rolling from clenched teeth. Glancing off the side of Frank's head, it tore through flesh, ripping the ear away to bury itself deep into his shoulder. The axe, imbedded into his torso, made him look like a grotesque tripod from a Hollywood horror movie. The remnants of Frank Dawson slowly toppled to the side, blood spurting from his neck.

Emily still balancing on one leg, with her left arm dangling and bleeding at her side, looked at Rosalie through the blood and haze. She gasped out, "Here, Rosie. Come here." Blood was coming from the corners of her mouth and spreading over her stomach. She collapsed to her knee and rolled over onto her side.

The faint welcome sound of a siren came from far away, but the mother and daughter wouldn't need it. They had each other.

Ted landed the cruiser in Wally's driveway and was out the door with his revolver drawn before it came to a stop. The bleeding mess that used to be Sergeant John Thayer was just a hulk laying on the grass with an oddity protruding from the top of his torso. He holstered his weapon and cautiously approached the gruesome scene in Wally's yard.

Emily was laying on her right side with Rosalie sitting on the ground next to her. The small child, cross legged with her arms in front of her, was pointing the large knife at the hideous tripod. Ted noticed the dangling piece of duct tape, and looked at the drip of blood hanging on the tip of the blade. She was shaking and mumbling incoherently, "Mommy, Mommy, Mommy."

Slowly he went to see if Emily was alive, and the red tip of the knife followed him. He stepped back and knelt on the ground in front of the knife. "Rosalie. It's me, Ted, from the sheriff's office. You're safe now. It's all okay." His voice was soft and soothing, but to Rosalie it was a scream from a demon who was going to hurt them. More evil–and it will hurt them. He saw Emily make a motion and knew she was at least alive, for now.

Emily couldn't move. Her entire left side was dead, and she couldn't hold or stroke her daughter to comfort her. Cracking open her eyes, everything was blurred. Hearing a male voice, she twitched at the panic of another attack. Then she ciphered out the easy sound of Ted Marks.

"Emily, can you hear me? It's Ted Marks. Emily?"

She moved her lips and moaned. That was all she had. She wanted to ask about Wally, but couldn't. She saw the heap on the ground, just feet away, and wondered what she could do if it came after them again.

In a few minutes the yard was filled with paramedics, police, reporters, and gawkers. Vehicles were parked everywhere, and most of them had flashing lights and sirens. Emily tried yelling at them, "*Get out of here. Go away and leave us alone.*" But the best she could do was to lie there, silent, with her daughter snuggled up to her.

Everyone was horrified at the scene in the yard, and people were yelling to get the knife away from the child. Ted stood up, shouting, "Shut up. Everyone shut up. If you aren't with the ambulance or the police, get away." He got some help from a few highway patrolmen who cleared most of the spectators out of the yard. "Go home. There's nothing here for you to see. Leave them alone."

There was plenty to see, but the locals understood, and in a wonderful show of respect they cordoned off the area with a human chain of friends. Local, home-town people taking care of their own. Reporters, gawkers, and the morbid curiosity seekers were kept far away.

The medics needed to get to Emily, but she was guarded by Rosalie and her butcher knife, so Ted took over again. He took off his gun belt and knelt down in front of the knife point. Gently speaking directly to her, "We need to get your mom to the hospital, Honey. She's hurt, and I need you to help me take care of her. Please let me have the knife, and we can make you both safe. Please, Rosalie may I have the knife?"

The child was relenting and the stiffness in her arms softened, lowering the weapon slightly. She was sobbing and her little body was shaking.

A soft voice from behind her whispered, "Rosie, give Ted the knife. Give Ted the knife."

Looking around, she saw a gentle smile on her mom's reassuring face. "Go ahead, Honey. Give Ted the knife." It was all right then. Mom spoke and she is all right. It's safe now because Mom spoke. Emily's blonde hair was matted with blood and dirt, her face was swollen and covered with blood, yet she smiled pleasantly at her daughter to tell her it was safe now—and she was loved.

Rosalie allowed Ted to carry her to the ambulance and sat on the stretcher with her mom while the investigators filled the yard, trying to piece the story together and clean up the carnage.

Before being put into the ambulance, Rosalie her arms wrapped around his neck, looked over Ted's shoulder to see the evil lying silently in the yard. The evil was dead—again—but the image and fear had burned itself into her mind, to fester forever.

The scene inside the ambulance was frantic and efficient. They worked on saving Emily's life while Rosalie sat beside her. The only help Rosalie needed was far away at the time, in the form of Sister Alysia.

EPILOGUE

● ● ● ● ● ● ● ● ● ● ● ● ● ● ● ● ● ● ● ●

My innocence stripped
In your awful game
Now I walk
In the shadow of shame.

TED SAT WITH ROSALIE ON HIS LAP in the waiting room for seven hours. She declined offers of juice and food, just settling for the safety and comfort of Ted's shoulder. The doctor appeared, announcing that Emily would be in ICU for twelve hours until she stabilized, and yes, Rosalie could sit with her.

Slowly waking up and staring at the starkness and sterility of the hospital, Emily didn't know if she was dead or alive. The lights and ceiling were blurred, but she felt the warmth of a little hand on her arm. She smiled and moved her hand slowly to meet the touch of her daughter reaching through the guardrail on the bedside, and happily whispered, "Oh, thank God you're alive."

Nobody heard her except Rosalie. The two could talk to each other without saying anything. Their thoughts were blessed with a spiritual connection, and they loved each other just by touching.

Soon, Ted's face appeared and she welcomed the smile. Forcing her lips open, she quietly asked him, "Where's Wally?"

"He was shot, Emily, but he's going to be all right. He's here in the hospital and is asking to see you."

A calm feeling of contentment flowed through her, and as she squeezed Rosalie's hand, she fell into a deep slumber. She and Rosalie were safe now, so she could finally get some precious sleep.

Ted and Rosalie stayed next to her until morning when she was taken to a room. After everything was in place, and the details of hospital stays were taken care of, Ted left. He turned to look back at Rosalie, lying in bed with Mom, sound asleep. Emily looked back at him and mouthed the words, "*Thank you.*" He nodded and left.

This time no guards were at the door, but the same National Guard soldiers were constant visitors. The TV/VCR was back and pizza boxes were strewn about. Rosalie's presence made an impact on the staff, and they adopted her, bestowing the title, *Honorary Nurse,* on her.

Nobody told Emily, but at one point they thought Wally was dead. He came out of it, but never told anyone about the light, and seeing Jim or the euphoric sensation, and looking back at Emily and Rosalie laying on the lawn of his yard. He could have given up and succumbed to the wonderful floating trip, but he loved her too much to leave. He loved Emily and Rosalie, and they were his family. He said good-bye to Jim and Bella, and then came back. He would share that experience with Emily, but not for many, many years.

His visits to their room, in a wheel chair, were happy and welcome. They managed to pass a kiss back and forth, but the bed and wheelchair were not made for romance. Rosalie would sit on his lap, and they would speed down the hallway doing wheelies and shitties. They visited some other patients and spent more time in the children's ward.

Rosalie read to the little kids and helped them make presents for the kids that had parents. The others were led on expeditions up to Emily's room where Rosie announced that her mom could be their mom also. The presents from those kids adorned Emily's room and made it look like a daycare class. Rosalie also discovered the lost-and-found closet, and from there selected an assortment of caps for the bald-headed kids undergoing cancer treatments.

Detectives from Minneapolis visited and wanted more details from Rosalie, but Emily stopped them. Leonard Walburn intervened and informed everyone that if they had anything to ask of the two, they would have to see him first. He met with Wally and Emily, informing them that Jim had willed his entire estate over to Emily. There was a sizeable bank account, the sixty-acre property on Tom Lake and yes, even the old Case tractor. Also, Jim had bought the adjoining acres on either side of him to ensure his privacy.

Wally told Emily that through Roger's record book that was given to the media by Buzz Peterson, more men were in jail, including Dr. Martin Goodhue.

Sister Alysia came from Wisconsin, and was given a room with Ted and his aunt in the old gray mansion. She stayed for many months working with Rosalie, and even Emily and Wally.

Emmy, as Wally called her, changed. The old fire and rebellion were stuffed away and only brought out when she really got pissed, which wasn't very often. She wouldn't let anyone call her Missy. That was a special name reserved for a special memory. Some understood, and if you didn't, it didn't matter. If you didn't know Jim Cooper, you weren't very high on her list of important people.

Rosalie will never be the same. She will laugh and giggle if it's all right to do that, but she bypassed the little-girl part of her life, and was never given the chance to be spoiled and throw tantrums about ridiculous things. Emily knows that some-day, hopefully in the far future, she is going to have to leave her daughter. She spends every day teaching the child to be able to cling to hope, remember the good and fun things, and learn to love without reservation. Emily isn't so sure she will ever get that far.

Sister Alysia home schooled her for a few years, working toward weaning Rosalie into joining other kids. The day came for her to go to junior high school with all the preparations for a queen's coronation. She had been prompted all summer, and when that September day came, her mom and dad watched her disappear through the huge front doors into a new and wonderful life. She made a few friends, but wore a label as "that girl." The idiots who called themselves human beings would tease her with pictures of bloody knives and say stupid things to her. It all set her back more than it should have. When enrolled in a private school, she finally did very well.

Once in awhile she would visit Skylar Colee Clay on the farm, but she was too much of a problem for him. He didn't know how to react to her mood swings and sudden bursts of anger. Medication and counseling helped her level out, but unless you knew the happy giggling side of her, she would scare you away.

Emily and Wally lived happily in Jim's cabin. Emily still liked to make out and thought she needed to in order to keep Wally coming home every day. It wasn't the case at all for Wally, but it was what Emily had been forced to do her entire life. He worked at convincing his wife that it wasn't sex. Making love was a part of loving. Wally was kind and patient and handled his wife and daughter with love, care, kindness, and respect. He did that not only because they needed it, but that was how he was raised.

He tried going back to work as the Cook County Sheriff, but was miserable. His girls at home worried about him constantly, and it became, as Wally put it, "Not really worth it." He finished his degree and graduated as an Electronic Engineer. His Masters degree was a breeze, and then he needed to find a way to earn a living playing with electrons, protons and neutrons.

His first idea was a remote home detection device that would sound an alarm in any number of different places by many means of activation. He sold the idea to a security company and went on to start a consulting firm. He was happy, his family was happy, and he didn't have to chase idiots on the highway anymore. Or, look for killers.

Emily walked with a limp and never regained all the feeling in her left arm. She could move it and get around just fine, but it was always there, and always a reminder of the horrible thing that happened. She simply accepted it as the price that needed to be paid to be where she is now. If things were different she would have never met Wally, and those perverts would still be alive and preying on other children.

Wally set up a computer in the small cabin and both Emily and Rosalie took to it immediately. Emily started surfing the Internet looking for others who had similar things happen, and found out it was a growing and serious problem. Women and children all over the country were desperate to get help, or find help for others who were trapped in the darkness of abuse.

Child Services in Minneapolis gave her a good list of resources, and Emily started a web site naming it after Anna Swanson, who lost her life when it was just beginning. She published the phone numbers to child protection services and psychiatric help lines for every state in the union.

DeAnna's supervisor connected her with a group in Minneapolis that was trying to push the death penalty issue. They ran a bunch of shelters for battered women and children. She would visit them once in awhile, but that wasn't enough.

More had to be done that would stop it from happening. She got involved with some Minnesota State Legislators who started working on protection bills. To publicize the cause, she started giving lectures to groups, and became quite busy.

Eventually, Rosalie got her high school diploma and decided to make her frequent visits to the children's ward in the hospital her avocation. She managed to conjure up a warm and friendly connection for the kids who didn't stand much of a chance living much longer. Cancer and any number of debilitating illnesses that racked the little guys was turned into a way of life for them. They saw hope in looking for tomorrow, and peace in accepting their fate.

She always lived at home because she still had a problem, and would always have a problem. She allowed Wally and her mom the space they needed to be happily married, but would never leave them. Nobody could guess if she would ever get married, and if she did, how disastrous it might be.

All of the damage that continued through all of their lives and followed them everywhere was caused by the selfish greed of a few sick sons of bitches that were not good enough to rot in hell.

One day, when they were all sitting outside watching the sun slowly crawl across the sky, a cryptic conversation started.

Rosalie said, "Mom?"

"Yeah, Babe?"

"Remember when we were practicing shooting the gun against the shed?"

Emily paused for a moment, not because she forgot about it, but she needed to be ready for why this came up. "Yeah, I remember. Why?"

"I don't know. 'Shoot the bastard' just came back to me." After another pause, Rosalie said again, "Mom?"

"What Honey?"

"I wish we could."

"Could what, Rosie?"

"Shoot all the bastards."

"Yeah, I know, me too."

"Mom?"

Amused now, with Wally grinning at the exchange, Emily answered, "What Babe?"

"I love you."

Emily paused, a slight satisfied smile lit up her face, "Yeah, I know. Me too."

They reached out to each other and sat in the lawn chairs holding hands, bonded forever.

● ● ● ● ● ● ● ● ● ● ● ● ● ● ● ● ●

It WAS ANOTHER WARM JUNE DAY, and the most important thing to do was to do nothing. Wally was working on the computer, and Rosalie was playing with the new puppy. They couldn't agree on a name so he was just called Dog. The name *Bella* belonged to another dog, and off limits to be used again. On purpose, it was a Golden Retriever. Emily walked around the yard checking on this and that, holding her favorite coffee cup. The warmth from the fresh brew felt good on her left hand, and also when she held it against the scar on her forearm. She stopped and gazed at the spot near the driveway that had been turned into a memorial for Jim. Wildflowers took over the place where he had died.

The old wooden chair that had been abandoned in the yard for so many years now sat next to the special spot. Emily slowly lowered herself onto it and gazed at the little blossoms. She talked to him often, but today was different. "It never ends, does it you old fart. I miss you Jim, I really do. The scars never heal, and time moves on leaving the shit in its wake. You and Bella got off, and I wonder who got on in your place. I love you Jim. I love Wally because he's my husband, and I love Rosalie because she's my daughter. But, Old Man, I love you because I love you. I'd do the same for you. You know I would. And I know you would miss me like I miss you."

She blotted the wet from her cheek and walked over to the old Case tractor. They had to have the starter rebuilt, and she set about bolting it back into place. She heard the car on the gravel driveway, but ignored it. She knew who it was, and wanted to ignore them also. When the call came yesterday, she agreed to meet them. They hadn't earned the right to be here, and she didn't welcome the intrusion. Nothing about anything was said on the phone, except that they could come out if they wanted to.

A green Subaru slowly crawled up behind the Case and stopped. Nobody got out for a while, and finally, both front doors opened. A teen-age boy was on the passenger side and the woman stood by the other open door, squinting at the brightness of today. She was dressed in a silly pant suit with silly shoes that matched. Emily had been trained to hate her, but she promised Wally she would be civil.

The woman closed the Subaru's door and walked towards Emily with her hand held out in front of her. The boy followed, but never closed his door. "Hi, I called yesterday, I'm Mary Beth, and this is Jim's grandson, Jason." She turned to point to him to be sure Emily knew who she was talking about. "Jerry, the other son is with his father today. He wanted to come, but, um, couldn't. With his father." Her hesitation had a sadness attached to it.

Wiping the grease from her hands, Emily thought to herself, *Fuck You.* She remembered Wally's warning and simply said, "Hi." No smile or handshake had been mentioned, so Mary Beth didn't get one.

Clasping the unwelcome hands in front of her, Mary Beth looked around the yard. "This is just as I remember it. Oh, and that old tractor. Does it still run? Dad used to fix that thing constantly."

Turning to Emily, Mary Beth said, "I'm sorry, I didn't get your name."

"You didn't ask."

"Oh, I'm sorry. And you are, who?"

"Emily. That's my daughter, Rosalie." Rosie had joined them, standing behind her mom.

Jason grinned at Rosalie, getting a blank rejection in return.

The tension level was getting higher, and Mary Beth tried to save herself. "I'm sorry if we caught you at a bad time, I just wanted Jason to meet his grandfather."

Emily had extended her politeness as long as she could. Unable to let this charade go any further, she issued her confrontation. "Why did it take so long?"

Startled, Mary Beth questioned, "What?"

Emily couldn't hold it back any longer. She exploded, "Why did it take you over twenty years to decide to be a daughter again? Why didn't you at least call to tell him you were safe?" Emily's arms were waving wildly. "Why do you think you can just fucking waltz in here and say 'Hi Dad, I'm home'? Why do you even give a goddamn about him?"

Mary Beth and Jason were stunned by the verbal attack. "I don't understand. Who are you and why are you so angry at me? I just want to see my dad."

Her tirade getting louder, Emily launched the attack. "Bullshit. You've had over twenty years to see your dad. He did everything he could to find you. He left the light on for fifteen years so you could find your way home. He hung a wreath in the window to make you feel welcome when you showed up. You just fucking walked out, and now you want to just fucking walk back in?"

Rosalie cringed at her mother's language, but understood what the force was that drove her. For now, the old spirited Emily was back, and going for the jugular.

Jason had backed up to the car, ready to hide inside.

Confused, Mary Beth answered, "Who are you to get so angry at me? I don't even know you."

Fiercely yelling, Emily answered, "I was Jim's friend, his lover, his buddy, his companion, his cook, his bed mate and his person he could love in return. I woke up with him and went to bed with him. I laughed with him, and I cried with him."

Emily's voice trailed off and choked as she wiped a tear from her cheek. "He saved my life, and I saved his life, and it was my fault he lost his."

Her anger escalated again, "We said good night and good morning. We said hello and we said good-bye. We said we need milk. We said it's a nice day. We said maybe Mary Beth will come home today, but that never happened."

Deflated and confused, Mary Beth asked, "What do you mean, he lost his life? Is he here? May I see him?"

"Yeah, he's here. He's always here, but you can't see him. You can't see him unless you loved him so much his face is everywhere."

The tears were guiding her now, and she was going to get this out of her system at any cost. Years of holding this in opened the gate, and it flowed out. "He's fucking dead, you moron. He died saving my life and my daughter's. He died on this spot. Shot three times and just fell over dead."

Looking over the patch of wildflowers she sniffled the tears and went on, not nearly done yet. "Three bullets that were supposed to kill me and my daughter. The three bullets went into his chest and his face–and not into mine. Not into my daughter. We're alive and he's not because he loved us enough to do that, and I would have done it for him."

Hearing the tirade, Wally stood at the door watching.

Emily went on because she couldn't stop. It didn't matter that Mary Beth was standing there, she had been trying to get these words out for years, and now they flowed. "He dragged me out of the cold and made me warm. He took my shattered child and put her back together. He told me to love without reservation, and put hate into my pocket. He told me he loved me, and I told him I loved him. He told me he loved you, and you told him to die."

Emily turned to Rosalie, and they hugged each other. Rosie wiped the tears from her mom's cheek and ran her hand through the blonde mop. "Easy, Mom."

Emily smiled, nodded, and turned back for more. "I don't know, and don't give a damn why you are here. There are too many broken pieces to be put together again. If you want to see where he's buried I can show you, but why do you even care? You've had a life someplace, obviously got married and had some kids. You did what you wanted and walked away from your father because you were a spoiled snot who wasn't getting waited on. Now, you want to feel good and show your son who his grandfather is. There's nothing here to see."

Emily had more, but it wasn't going to come out. She was drained. Softening, she asked, "What do you really want here?"

Mary Beth, shaking from what she knew was the truth, wanted to apologize but didn't know how. She looked at Emily with a pleading for forgiveness and saw the locket, pointing to it.

"That . . . that's my mothers. That's my mother's locket. What . . . where?"

"Jim had wrapped it up to give to you the night you ran. Every Christmas he'd take it out and wait for you to come and get it. For fifteen Christmases, he put the package on the mantle for you. He gave it to me after he saved my life, and I saved him from committing suicide. He was going to get drunk and walk into the woods and give up. When I came along, he didn't do it. He gave it to me and said it was mine because he wanted me to have it. I gave him something that he would always have also. Myself. Myself along with my heart, my soul, and my gratitude."

Calming down, Emily said, "I asked what you wanted here."

Mary Beth pleaded, "May I have my mother's locket? Please?"

"No! Put your pieces together and find out what makes you happy. When you find your peace, things like the locket won't matter to you. I'll tell you where the cemetery is, and there is something I can give you."

She walked back to the cabin, brushed past Wally in the doorway, and came back with a box, taped shut. She didn't hand the box to Mary Beth, but put it in the back seat of the Subaru.

This visit was over with Emily announcing with finality, "Take a right at the DNR shack, go a few miles on North Road. He's next to Margaret."

Wally and Rosalie watched the Subaru drive away, but Emily had her back turned. She looked back to the patch of wild flowers, and chocked out, "I'm sorry, Jim."

Rosalie went back to teaching Dog to do tricks, Emily finished the tractor's starter, and Wally sat and watched them do it. Done with the tractor, she wiped her hands clean, took Wally's hand and led him into the cabin. "Rosie, dinner will be a few minutes late."

Rosalie rolled back with Dog on top of her, wailing, "Oh, no, not again."

● ● ● ● ● ● ● ● ● ● ● ● ● ● ● ● ●

MARY BETH KNEW WHERE THE CEMETERY was and drove right to it. Sitting on the ground, looking at the headstones of her parents, she felt lost and alone. She knew the angry woman was right about everything, and wanted to go back and talk with her more. Maybe some other time–after she puts her pieces together and finds her peace. Maybe she can start by trying to salvage her marriage, and getting her sons to love her. Or at least like her.

Jason asked, "Mom, can we go now?"

"Yes. We'll go" She knew she would be back some day. Some pieces back at the cabin, and pieces in her own life, needed to be put together–and things weren't going to be right until that happened.

Driving through Duluth to Highway 35 going south, she was listening to the mild sounds of Miles Davis on the CD player. Jason was in the back seat jumping to the beat of something harder. Almost to the Twin Cities, Jason bored of the noise and watched the passing traffic. He smiled at a pretty girl as they passed a camper, and glanced at the box next to him.

"Mom, what's this that lady gave you?" He held it up and shook it.

"I have no idea. I forgot about it. Open it."

She heard the rustling and cardboard noises and asked, "Well, what is it?"

"I don't know. Here." He tossed it onto the front seat near her.

She looked at the old dirty crooked wreath, and all of a sudden it all came together for her. She cut off a line of speeding cars, ignored the horns and fingers, and parked on the shoulder. Picking up the dusty ornament, she put her hand to her mouth and cried. "Oh, God, Dad. I am so sorry. Daddy, oh, no Daddy. Oh, no." She was shaking and sobbing uncontrollably over what she had done—and what she had not done.

The flashing lights of the patrol car and the officer at her window brought her out of the pain that was dancing through her mind. "You all right, Ma'am?"

"Yes, officer, I am. For the first time in twenty years, I am all right. Thank you."

She wiped her face off, smiled in the mirror at her confused son and said, "Honey, I love you. We're going home now."

The Subaru caught up to traffic and disappeared into the congestion. Someday later, she would return to put the pieces back where they belonged.

● ● ● ● ● ● ● ● ● ● ● ● ● ● ● ● ●

The lecture circuit, 2008

EMILY DIDN'T LIKE THE LECTURES, and certainly didn't like being looked at by strangers. However, others told her how valuable her words were, and that her talks were helping more people than she could realize. Skepticism and modesty led to a cynical tirade that only made Rosalie laugh at her.

She didn't have the old *Emily spark* anymore, her blonde hair was being crowded out by more and more gray. Sporting a more conservative shorter hair style, the ponytail was gone forever. What used to be up and perky, was aging as well as the rest of her, with a few well-placed wrinkles to complete her picture. The injuries that were beaten into her healed on the outside, give or take a scar or two; maybe more. The damage from Frank's pistol was going to kill her some day, but not yet. The scars that hurt the most were on the inside. Wally could see them, and Rosalie could even feel Emily' pain in her own body. That's how close they were. The pains that Rosalie carried were unbearable to her mom. The life Emily showed on the outside was to let people see that there is a life when you are healthy enough to know you are safe again. The pain inside that burned itself into Rosie's brain and came out as a nightmare, or a sudden jump at nothing, was something they all shared. The Stearns family lived with it, and they got through each day simply because they knew there was someone who cared, and loved them—and they were safe.

Standing behind the curtain with Rosalie, Emily put a few more of her parts back in place and straightened her skirt. Her glance pleaded to her daughter, but was instantly met with Rosalie saying, "No Mom, they came here to listen to you, and you *have* to do it."

Arguing was useless, so Emily sighed and said, "Okay you little shit, let's get it over with."

When Rosalie stepped onto the stage, the murmuring in the audience stopped. They knew who she was, and a round of applause showed her the respect and admiration she deserved. Taking it in stride, she made the same announcement she had been making to audiences for years, since these tours began. "Ladies and gentlemen, I take an immense amount of pride in presenting to you the bravest and most wonderful person I have, or ever will meet, my mother, Mrs. Emily Stearns." Emily's reputation preceded her, and she got a three-minute standing ovation. Following her interviews on then national news programs, "Oprah," "Good Morning America," the book signings, and the magazine articles, her message was known to everyone. Yet, they continued to gather just to hear this marvelous woman remind them again that the blight needed to stop.

Emily didn't try to hide her obvious limp anymore. If she could wear a sign that blared out her message, the limp did as well. Looking over the darkened audience, Emily realized that she was scared to death, and knew she would never get used to doing this. She swallowed hard and went into it, speaking clear with a driving force that let everyone know she was here to give her message. If she had to cram it down their throats or shove it up their butts, she was going to get her message to them.

"Thank you. I'm here because my daughter is the driving force in my life, and she told me I had to. I'm not much on speaking before groups, and I'm not sure just how much good I am doing, but you all came here to listen, so, I'll get on with it. She told me to keep the language clean, and that eliminates half my vocabulary. Giving credit where credit is due, my daughter, Rosalie Stearns is the real hero here. Don't ever let that get away from you. She is the one who suffered and endured. I'm the one who's too weak to say no to a speaking engagement."

The audience laughed and gave Rosalie a polite applause, while she blushed. It was as if Emily had a hammer and went through the audience and hit each person on the head–her words made a great impact. Her voice was loud and sharp, capturing everyone in the audience. "People meet, form relationships, fall in love, and look around for the storybook to open on a perfect and happy life. Sometimes that's exactly what happens. Sometimes it doesn't. We have expectations of what our partner is going to bring into the game to make the storybook a happy one. But, there are some sour notes. A lot of us spend time wondering what the hell went wrong– and then, how to escape.

"A woman marries Mr. Perfect, and he makes her life miserable.

"A man marries the most wonderful woman on earth, and she digs a hole for him.

"We crap on each other, fight, cheat, and kill. And sometimes we try to run away. When we don't run fast enough, or far enough, we get caught. And the dream dies with our spirit. Sickness and perversion chases us, and when we get tired of running, we either die or turn around, dig in and fight.

"Pain and misery follow the chase, and it's simply the price we are forced to pay. Pieces of us are torn off and thrown away. Pieces were torn from my daughter and thrown away. Pieces were lost, and the rest just wouldn't fit right. The price we have to pay is just too high." Emily glanced at her daughter with a small smile. Rosalie nodded, returning the smile with a silent *I love you* working its way off her lips.

Emily lowered her gaze, looking hard over the mesmerized audience, her voice booming through the hall. "Animals will kill for food, and man will kill for pleasure or sport. Which one of God's creations has evolved to the highest level? Who is more civilized, man or beast?"

As Emily stepped in front of the lectern, her words became stronger.

"The abuse of children and violence towards women is reprehensible and pulls mankind to a level far below that of the animal. There are no words strong enough to condemn this blight. The human animals that wallow in the slime of abuse of their own kind should not be allowed a place in any part of society. They are nothing more than cowardly terrorists.

"My story is my own story, and it's the reason I'm here. It happened, and it will happen again if we allow the disease to continue. I ran until I faced death, couldn't run any more, and laid down to die." Her voice softened, and she teared up at her vision of Jim lying in the driveway.

Choking up, she continued, "An unlikely friend came along that had the right key to the storybook, and helped me unlock it. My book opened to the story I knew was in there, but the price that was paid was just too high. I would have rather died myself than have it turn out the way it did.

"Some things never end. This story did in my book, but the same story is starting all over again somewhere else. Someplace, some despicable asshole is abusing a child or a spouse and ruining their life, if they manage to live through it. Pieces of a human's life fall because of abuse, and are sometimes put together, but they are never exactly where they used to be.

"Nobody knows for certain if the death penalty would deter abusers. If the sickness is driving them, they are going to satisfy it. At least killing them would bring a bit of closure. It would satisfy the outrage from people who hear about it, but wouldn't do much to heal the scars left on the victims.

"Take a karate class, learn self-defense, get pissed enough to stop it, if you can. The people who suffer the most can't stop it. The little children who look at adults to guide them into being grown-ups can't stop it. These are the victims who lose the look of wonderment and curiosity of life. They wait for birthdays and Christmas, hoping there is someone who loves them and will make them happy. They look at us and smile, waiting for something nice to happen.

"And some despicable bastard scars their little mind and throws the pieces so far away they never can get put back in the right places.

"The answer to stop it may be in the execution chamber, or it may be in a psychiatrist's office, or they can rot in prison forever.

"The answer to stopping it may be in educating the lucky ones who haven't been ravaged yet. The answer may be in the phone book under many different headings. If you are being torn apart by someone else, do something. Stop them so they can't move on to another victim. They are tearing you apart. Don't let them do that. Stop them. If you know of someone else who is being torn apart, help them. That person may be too tiny to know what is happening. They need you to help them before they are destroyed forever. If you are a person who is hurting others with a sickness you can't control, you're probably listening to me out of guilt or curiosity."

At this point, the audience stirred as a man stood up, struggling to reach the aisle. Holding his hat over his face, he hurried towards the exit. Emily's voice pierced the man in so many painful ways, as she pointed to him, calling out, "*If you don't have the guts to listen, get the hell out of here.*" As he stumbled through the door, her words clung to him, "Get out and get help! Stop, and leave us alone."

Turning back to the audience, she held her hand up commanding their silence, and continued, "If you know who that man is, turn him in. If you share his sickness, my message is simple. Get help and stop destroying. Seek a psychiatrist, or put a gun to your head. We don't care—all we want from you is to stop."

Emily and returned to the stand to take a drink of water. She wished it was a cold beer, but was satisfied. Glancing at Rosalie, she got a nod of acceptance and turned back to the audience, her voice rattling the rafters with her message.

"I've spent countless hours trying to convince myself that the poor people who were killed in the effort to get to me and my daughter are happy in heaven. Bull shit. They're dead. They don't want to be dead, but they were slaughtered because some sick, senseless bastard wouldn't stop.

"Polly Klass, Elizabeth Smart, Jessica Lundford—they and hundreds of other wonderful children have paid far too high a price. Yes, progress is being made, but as long as one child is torn apart and ravaged by some dirty son of a bitch, we need to do more. You all know what has to be done. Go out and do it. Make them stop."

Exhausted, Emily was done. Two more things to cover, and they could go home. She pointed to the man sitting next to Rosalie. "My husband is with us today. If I am anything at all, it is because he has held me up during the ordeal, and has never failed me. I want everyone here to know that he's a good man, and I love him."

She paused, looked at the exit where the man had disappeared minutes earlier, and then turned her attention to the back row. "There's someone special with you today. They might be sitting next to you or behind you. I'm not going to introduce them because they have to tell their own story in their own time. Maybe they will never share it; maybe they will never be ready. That's up to them."

Leaning on the lectern to ease the pain in her leg, she went on, "They ran away looking for something that wasn't there. They ran into the streets and became one of the victims. Their suffering was no less than the scores of others who have been raped and sodomized. They were too ashamed to go home again, and will pay for that forever. I want to tell then that I understand, and I welcome them into my life. They have their own horror to tell, and they need help, love, and understanding as much as the rest of us. It took me a long time to come to terms with them, but one of the pieces that is fitting right, is in place. I'm at peace with it, and I pray nightly that they have found their own peace.

"Good night and God bless you."

● ● ● ● ● ● ● ● ● ● ● ● ● ● ● ● ● ● ●

Amid the applause as Emily limped off the stage, Mary Beth sat in the back row, holding her husband's hand, her sons with her. Through a lot of counseling and learning to deal with the blight, a lot of fences were mended and most of her pieces were in place–the ones that mattered, anyway. Her mother's locket hung around her neck, mysteriously receiving it in the mail a short time ago.
Mary Beth, Jim's long-lost daughter, was finally home.

● ● ● ● ● ● ● ● ● ● ● ● ● ● ● ● ● ● ●

Outside, at the rear of the auditorium, as Wally held the car door for Emily, a stranger appeared from nowhere. Stunned, Emily stared at him, the muscles in her jaw becoming rigid. He shuffled his feet, tears streaming down his face, his arms held out pathetically. The man who had left the audience, his voice trembling in grief, babbled to Emily, "Please. Please help me. I am so bad."

She stepped forward, put her arms around him, and quietly said, "You need to stop what you are doing. Stop and we will help you." Emily looked deeply into the mans eyes seeing the pain he was carrying. A small smile crossed her lips, thinking, "*Maybe this is working.*"

The following is from the National Council on Child Abuse & Family Violence.
Their address is 1025 Connecticut Ave. NW, Washington, DC 20036.

~ TOLL FREE CRISIS HOTLINE NUMBERS ~

CRIME VICTIMS
National Center for Victims of Crime
800-394-2255

SPOUSE/PARTNER ABUSE (Domestic Violence)
National Domestic Violence Hotline
800-799-7233 and 800-787-3244 (TTY)

CHILD ABUSE
Childhelp USA
800-422-4453

CHILD SEXUAL ABUSE
Stop It Now
888-773-8368 or 800-799-7233

MISSING/ABDUCTED CHILDREN
Child Find of America
800-426-5678 or 800-292-9688

NATIONAL CENTER FOR MISSING & EXPLOITED CHILDREN
800-843-5678

RAPE and INCEST NATIONAL NETWORK
800-656-4673, ext 1

RUNAWAY YOUTH
800-786-2929

~

also
PEARL CRISIS CENTER
Domestic Abuse: 800-933-6914 / Sexual Violence: 1-800-522-2055

AUTHOR'S
NOTES

● ●

WRITING THIS STORY WAS DIFFICULT. Although it is fiction, it needs to be read and digested. The events that take place on these pages are born from seeds of creativity, but be assured, that these things happen. The subject of abuse to women and children is a disturbing one, and does not receive enough attention. Every day, there are countless cases of mistreatment to vulnerable people who just want to be left alone. Whatever the perpetrator's motivation, it is nothing more than an act of terrorism by a coward satisfying a sick depravity.

Adolescents and teens are prompted to run away, escaping an unbearable home life, only to fall into the hands of predators, pimps, and drug dealers. If running away isn't the answer, the alternative is suicide. What is in the home life of children to make them go to such extreme measures? What happened to the look of wonderment on their little faces when birthdays and Christmas came along? What happened to erase the silly chuckle that came from a feeling of excitement?

Think of this:

- Nearly 70 percent of child sex offenders have between 1 and 9 victims. At least 20 percent have 10 to 40 victims.
- An average child molester may have as many as 400 victims in his lifetime.
- 1 in 4 girls is sexually abused before the age of eighteen.
- The median age for reported abuse is 9 years old, and more than 20 percent are sexually abused before the age of 8.
- Most children don't tell, even if they are asked.
- Over 30 percent of victims never disclose the experience, to anyone.

· An estimated 39 million survivors of childhood sexual abuse exist in America today.

The book, *When a Child Kills*, by Paul Mones, lists cases of children driven to homicide to escape horrors in their home. I defy you to not be affected by the tragedies he lays out in the book.

In this story, Rosalie lives every day with how others have corrupted her mind. She will never be a normal, healthy woman able to love and share life with her family. That is fiction; however, way too many cases are real. I hope that the illustration of what Rosalie endured will lodge in your mind, making you give these people the respect and understanding they deserve.

All a child wants is to be loved-and know they are safe. If you know of anyone who is the victim, or perpetrator of abuse of any kind, I implore you to do something to stop it. Call one of the numbers listed here, scream and yell, call attention to it and get it to stop. If you are a victim yourself, please, *RUN*, call for help. It's always there for you.

As Emily said, *"The price that has to be paid is just too high."*

My deepest thanks to the wonderful people of Grand Marais, and Hovland, Minnesota. I apologize for rearranging some of the geography of the Arrowhead, the location of their police station, and a few details on Tom Lake, but as the story makes demands, I need to bend to them.

Thank you,
David P. Holmes.
www.davidpaulholmes.com

ACKNOWLEDGEMENTS

● ●

With deepest respect to Marc Klaas, founder of the non–profit KlaasKids Foundation started because his daughter Polly was kidnapped and abused. www.klaaskids.org

With sincere regard to John Walsh, who was recently able to put a closure into place by the discovery of their murdered son's remains.

And to Patty Wetterling and her family, *NEVER GIVE UP.* Jacob Wetterling was kidnapped on October 22, 1989 while playing with his brother and friend. He was 11 years old, and was never heard from again.

Finally, to Jaycee Lee Dugard, "Welcome home."